Above Reproach

By
Lynn Ames

ABOVE REPROACH
© 2012 BY LYNN AMES

ISBN: 978-1-936429-04-2

OTHER AVAILABLE FORMATS

E-BOOK EDITION
ISBN: 978-1-936429-05-9

PUBLISHED BY
PHOENIX RISING PRESS
PHOENIX, ARIZONA
www.phoenixrisingpress.com

This is a work of fiction. Names, characters, places, and incidents are the product of the author's imagination or are used fictitiously, and any resemblance to actual persons, living or dead, businesses, companies, events, or locales is entirely coincidental.

CREDITS
EXECUTIVE EDITOR: LINDA LORENZO
COVER PHOTOS: PAM LAMBROS
AUTHOR PHOTO: JUDY FRANCESCONI
COVER DESIGN: PAM LAMBROS, WWW.HANDSONGRAPHICDESIGN.COM

Dedication

To lightworkers everywhere—thank you for making the world a brighter place.

Acknowledgments

The seeds for *Above Reproach* were sown with the start of the Arab Spring. Watching the events of this transformative period unfold inspired me to look beyond the news headlines and to ask more questions. I knew I wanted to write about this extraordinary time in our history. The difficulty became writing a novel—which is a static document—about something that was on-going and ever-changing. Finally, I realized that to make this work, I would have to create a single event—a moment in time—and use the Arab Spring as a backdrop. And thus, the plot for *Above Reproach* was born.

As with any thriller, there are so many details that must be factually correct or at least plausible. To Mary Tracy, who provided mountains of essential background material about the Arab Spring and the countries of the Middle East and North Africa; to Clair Bee, who taught me everything I know about pyrotechnics and the world's least known and coolest technology toys; to my incredible sources in the US Marshal's Service, the CIA, and the Army's Military Police, for verifying facts and protocols—you all give my books the credibility that makes possible the suspension of disbelief.

I am blessed to have what I think is the finest team in the history of novel-writing. To my beta readers who read through my manuscripts chapter by chapter during the creation phase and give me critical feedback—you have my eternal gratitude.

To my primary editor, Linda Lorenzo, who looks forward with such relish to sinking her teeth into my manuscripts—may I never disappoint you.

To the readers who continue to clamor for the next book—you make it all worthwhile.

Happy reading!

CHAPTER ONE

29 June 2008 – Twelve Miles South of Baghdad

It just figured the flipping incompetent, idiot of a president would pick the run-up to the Fourth of July to move this shit. Seventeen years. That was how long the crap sat in the middle of the desert. That was how long damn green recruits who barely knew which end of the gun to shoot loitered around, pretending to guard 3,500 barrels of yellowcake—concentrated natural uranium—the raw material Saddam Hussein could have used to create lethal nuclear weapons. Now, all of a sudden, the powers that be were scrambling around, trying to transport the crap out of the Middle East and into North America. Canada, to be exact.

"Patriot Two, this is Patriot One. Do you read me?" The crackling of the radio brought Tony "Two Thumbs" Saldano out of his musings. He put down his binoculars and keyed the radio.

"Loud and clear. Keep it down, will ya?"

"The operation is a go. I repeat, the operation is a go."

"Roger that. In position and ready to rock 'n' roll." Tony took one last look down at the convoy of large, canvas-topped trucks on the dusty road below, stubbed out his cigarette, and clambered down the embankment to where a truck, identical to the ones he'd been watching, waited. He threw open the passenger door and climbed inside.

The driver, a scruffy-bearded, sturdily-built twenty-something in camouflage, looked at him expectantly.

"We'll wait here ten minutes to make sure everyone's gone, then follow at a distance. When we hit this spot, here"—Tony flipped open his laptop and pointed to an elevated section of roadway on a detailed satellite image—"a truck exactly like this one will be waiting. That's where I get off and you continue on your way. Make sure you step on it so you can catch up and slide into the convoy. If anybody asks why you were lagging behind, give 'em some bullshit about the gears sucking on this piece of shit."

The driver nodded.

"When you get to Baghdad and they start unloading the barrels, that's your cue to disappear. Got me?"

"Roger that."

"Good." Tony sat back to wait. If everything went according to plan, he would be back in this very spot by nightfall with a truckload of yellowcake, and the convoy's load, including thirty barrels of useless material made to look like yellowcake, would be on its way to Diego Garcia and, ultimately, to Canada.

≈≈≈

10 February 2011 – National Security Agency Headquarters, Fort Meade, Maryland

Sedona Ramos rubbed her tired eyes. It was ten o'clock Thursday night, and already she'd logged more than twenty-five hours of overtime that week. Not that that was anything unusual, nor did she mind. Sedona's work ethic was part of the reason the National Security Agency recruited her so many years ago—that and the fact that she was tri-lingual and could pass for Middle Eastern, Latina, or Native American.

All week she'd been plodding her way through hundreds of pages of top secret, intercepted, Arabic-language phone and Internet communications from Iraq. The last electronic file in the queue finished downloading.

"That's odd," Sedona said to the empty room. She scrolled through the document one more time. Unlike all the other files, this one identified by name neither the analyst who compiled the initial report, nor the individual who requested it. Instead, in the places where that information should have been, was a pair of numerical sequences. That was something Sedona had never seen before. "Huh. Well, let's just see what you are."

She clicked to open the document. A chill ran through her. "Never a good sign," she mumbled. When her eyes alighted on the three satellite images tucked in the middle of the pages of text, she understood why her blood ran cold. "What the hell? Activity at Tuwaitha? We were done with that place three years ago. Shit, I was there when we locked the gates for the last time."

Heeding her instincts, Sedona popped in a flash drive and copied the entire file, ejecting and pocketing the drive once the operation was complete. Then she hustled over to the series of file cabinets where a clerk would have logged and stored the corresponding physical documents as insurance against any electronic malfunctions. She thumbed through that week's files until she found the batch that pertained to Iraq. Although she paged through the series three times and searched adjacent batches of files, there was no matching physical file, a clear violation of protocol.

"Too weird. Looks like maybe someone's coloring outside the lines."

As if to confirm her suspicions, when Sedona returned to her computer, the screen was blank and there was no trace of the images or the surrounding pages of text. "What the fuck is going on? I know I left the file open." She sat down and stabbed at the keys, trying to find it on the server or on her hard drive. It simply had vanished. "Think, Sedona. Breathe and think, damn it."

The sound of the elevator opening down the hall and running footsteps startled her. "There shouldn't be anyone else in this part of the building at this hour." The pieces started to fall into place, and Sedona's heart pounded harder. She had logged into her computer with her regular username and password. Whoever this was, they would be looking specifically for her. "You can't stay here, sweetie. You're a sitting duck."

She grabbed several things off her desk and shoved them into her briefcase, then darted around a corner just as several figures dressed all in black appeared at the entrance to what Sedona and her co-workers affectionately called the bullpen. Somewhere, someone killed the lights. Sedona, who had spent most of her career in hot spots in the field, realized the implication—the intruders had night vision goggles. "Shit." Perspiration dotted her brow and her pulse hammered in her ears. She took stock of her surroundings.

As the appointed fire drill coordinator for the floor, Sedona knew every exit. She removed her shoes, tucked them into her briefcase, and quietly slipped into her boss's office, since it was farthest from the elevators. Once inside, Sedona felt along the wall until her fingers found a seam. She pushed in, and a section of the wall popped open to reveal a stairway. She sprinted down the stairs and, at the garage level, opened the door a crack to make sure no one was waiting for her. Satisfied she was alone, she dashed to her car, threw the briefcase in the passenger seat, and peeled out of the garage.

Sedona's hands were shaking on the wheel as she drove along the highway that would take her north. She didn't have a definitive plan; she just knew she needed to disappear. Whatever had happened back there, it wasn't good.

When she reached Baltimore a short time later, she pulled into a convenience store parking lot. She went inside and used the bathroom, splashed cold water on her face, and paid cash to purchase a pre-paid cell phone. Then she got back in her car and used the phone to dial a familiar number.

"Dex? It's me. I'm in trouble and I need your help."

"Anything, love. What do you need?"

"Can you keep an eye out for any unusual activity at my place?"

"Hold on a sec, love. I'll have a peek right now."

Sedona heard the scraping of a chair, Dex's footsteps, and the sound of him whistling. She imagined him peering through the living room blinds that faced her house. Several moments later, he was back.

"Holy shite, kiddo. What are you into?" He sounded shaken, which only made his Irish brogue thicker.

"Why, what's going on?"

"There are three black SUVs in front of your place and some guys outside who make the Hulk look like a midget. What's this all about, then?"

Sedona closed her eyes tightly as panic welled up in her chest. "Listen, Dex. If anybody asks you, tell them you haven't spoken to me all week and you have no idea where I am."

"Well, that would be the truth, now wouldn't it? So, where are you?"

"I can't tell you that."

"Can't, or won't?"

"Dex, please don't…"

"I'll accept that you can't tell me about what it is you do or who you work for, Sedona, but these men don't look like they're fooling around here. I can help you, but only if you level with me."

Sedona swallowed hard. Dex had been her best friend since she moved in across the street from him almost fifteen years ago. He was dashing and debonair, and as gay as she was, which took all the awkwardness out of their relationship. But this was a line she could not cross. It was her sworn oath. Beyond that, not knowing would keep him safe.

"Stay away from the windows, Dex. Don't answer your door. I'll call you when I can."

"Sedon—"

She didn't hear the rest, as she disconnected the call. The first thing she needed to do was get rid of her car and get herself somewhere safe so she could have time to think—time to regroup.

"What the hell did I get myself into?"

"She's in the wind." The man in black turned in a full circle in Sedona's living room as he spoke into a cell phone.

"Did you find anything?"

"There's nothing here to find."

"Well then, find her! Eliminate her and make it look like an accident."

Before the man in black could respond, the line went dead.

∽⑥⑦∾

The Marriott Marquis was bustling, which was exactly the reason Sedona chose it—a large, well-lit, well-respected hotel in the middle of Times Square in New York City, arguably the busiest city in the world.

"Hide in plain sight."

The bus ride from Baltimore had been long and tedious, but it gave her time to sleep and to regroup. Sedona hefted her briefcase and duffle bag on the bed. She'd removed the "go bag" from her trunk when she sold the car to the used car dealer in Maryland. "God, I hoped I'd never need this."

She sighed and unzipped the bag. In it, she kept hair dye, scissors, two pairs of fashionable jeans and tight sweaters, one pair of dress slacks and a silk blouse, a blazer, a pair of heels, a lightweight overcoat, sweats, a pair of sneakers and socks, bras, panties, a full toilet kit, a pair of eye-color-changing contact lenses, and ten thousand dollars cash. She nodded in satisfaction, glad that she'd listened to her mentor all those years ago.

Sedona still could hear Dominic's scratchy voice in her ear as he stood beside her at the firing range. "Listen, kiddo, there aren't many guarantees in this life, and certainly not in this line of work. But one thing you can always count on is that someday the shit's gonna hit the fan. When it does, you damn well better be ready to duck and run. A 'go bag' is part of your insurance policy. So, I want you to pack one when you get home tonight and put it in the trunk of your car. Always make sure it's on top of whatever other shit you've got in there so you can grab it without looking and skedaddle. Trust me, it could save your life one day."

"I wish it had saved yours, my friend." Sedona's eyes welled with tears as the agony of loss clutched at her heart. Sometimes, it crept up on her silently; other times, it hit her like a freight train. Today, it simply stared her in the face, daring her to flinch.

Instead, Sedona closed her eyes and took a deep breath. She pictured herself walking down a path lined on either side with beautiful flowers. Monarch butterflies opened their wings to the start of a new day. A pair of hummingbirds joyfully flitted around her, and a pair of hawks circled protectively overhead. She envisioned a white light surrounding her—enveloping her in its protective embrace. *Archangels, angels, ascended masters, guides... Thank you for your constant presence in my life. Archangel Michael, I ask for your help now. Please grant me the courage to face whatever is happening, and protect me as I battle the unknown.*

"Dominic, I know you're with me. I'm going to need your experience and insight. I have no idea what I stumbled into, but it sure stirred up a hornet's nest."

"No kidding. Watch your back, and don't trust anyone in the chain of command. You've got to go right to the top, kiddo. No middlemen. And since when do you use my full name?"

Sedona's eyes popped open. The president? Dom wanted her to go to the president of the United States? Was it possible she'd heard him correctly?

She strode into the bathroom and splashed water on her face. When she looked in the mirror above the sink, her mother's reflection stared back at her—the sleek, long black hair, the deep dark eyes, the olive complexion, the prominent, high cheekbones, and the dimple to the left of her mouth...there was no mistaking the resemblance. As a youngster, Sedona had endured the cruel taunts of the kids at her school.

"Your mother is a freak, and the apple doesn't fall far from the tree."

"She's a hippy who dropped too much acid."

"She's possessed, and so are you. We should do an exorcism, like in that movie."

And it wasn't just the kids—it was their parents too.

"She's a sorcerer. She even named her child after some New Age commune. No wonder the girl isn't normal."

"I don't want my kids near that house. That woman is mentally ill. She 'sees' the future? 'Talks' to dead people? She's crazy."

"Don't pay them any mind," her mother would say, when Sedona came home in tears. "They don't understand what they cannot see. Their vision is so limited. What you and I share, it's a gift."

"I don't want it. I don't want it." Sedona would put her hands over her ears, run to her room, and slam the door.

Eventually, her mother would come into her room, sit down on the edge of the bed, and rub her back. "Someday, sweetheart.

13

Someday you're going to embrace all of who you are and be grateful for having been chosen."

"Humph."

"I know it's tough, now. Growing up is hard work. Growing up different is harder. But I promise, there will come a time when your gift will help save the world. I have seen it. That's why it's so important for me to teach you everything I know."

Sedona shook her head and water droplets dotted the mirror. She looked to the Heavens. "I love you, Mama. I miss you, even though I know you're here with me, always. Are you watching now? You were right, Mama. Thank you for showing me the way."

⊰⊱

In the end, Sedona couldn't bring herself to chop off her own hair. She reasoned that she'd bought herself some time by selling the car and paying for the bus with cash. Besides, certainly she'd blend in better with a chic, stylish cut than with a butcher job. So she picked a busy, upscale salon and listened to the stylist prattle on about how his boyfriend was so far in the closet it would take an archeologist months to dig him out.

He looked at her in the mirror. "I bet you don't have boyfriend troubles, now do you?"

Sedona tuned back into the conversation and smiled mischievously. "Can't say that I do." She winked at his reflection and watched as comprehension dawned.

"Seriously, sweetheart? No way!" His scissors stopped mid-clip. "You don't even register on my lesbi-o-meter, and I always know!"

"Not always, apparently."

"Oh, honey, I want to live vicariously. Please tell me you have a gorgeous lover and the two of you jet off to some fantastically private getaway in the Caribbean every weekend."

"Sorry to disappoint."

"Well, as spectacular as you are, I can understand why you'd want to keep your options open."

Sedona watched her reflection in the mirror as her expression turned cool and guarded. *"Stay close to the truth,"* she heard Dom say in her head. *"Easier to keep your story straight."*

14

"I'm on the move a lot. No time for attachments, I guess."

"Well, when you're ready to settle down, somebody's going to get a helluva catch." He fluffed her hair, removed the cape protecting her outfit, and spun her in the chair, admiring his handiwork. "A shame to cut that beautiful mane, but Wigs for Cancer will love you forever, and you look fabulous, if I do say so myself. Short, sexy, and easy to care for, just like you asked."

"I'm glad it's for a good cause." Sedona meant it. She stood, reached in her pocket, and pulled out several bills, which she handed him.

"And you're a good tipper. Thanks, doll." He air-kissed her and busied himself sweeping up her hair.

Sedona looked away. It wouldn't do to dwell on it.

Outside on the street, she stepped into the middle of a large group of passersby, blending into the crowd, just another busy New Yorker on the way from one appointment to the next.

Back in the hotel room, Sedona pulled out her laptop and booted it up. She opened her Internet connection, grateful for the hotel's Wi-Fi access, and typed in www.whitehouse.gov. Two clicks later, she was staring at the president's public schedule for the week. "Thank God for openness and transparency," she mumbled.

Fortuitously, the president was on a barnstorming tour of the country. Tomorrow, he was scheduled to make stops at a series of colleges and universities across the Northeast and Midwest.

Sedona ran her finger down the screen, until it rested on a planned stop at the State University of New York at Albany. Then she opened a new browser window and pulled up Google Maps. "Handy. One hundred fifty miles and on a train route. Thanks, Mr. President," she said, around a yawn. She'd been on the move for almost twenty-four hours and worked a full day before that. By her calculation, she hadn't slept in a prone position for almost two days.

She could catch an Amtrak train out of Pennsylvania Station tonight, get a hotel room in Albany, and be in position in plenty of time for the president's arrival sometime early in the afternoon. Or she could try to get a good night's sleep here and get on a train first thing. At least that way she'd be alert and not out on her feet.

Would she be safer here or there? Could they already have tracked her to New York? And who the hell were "they"? Sedona set the laptop aside and walked to the windows to gaze out at the city lights twinkling against the evening sky. If only she knew who was after her, and what Tuwaitha had to do with it, maybe she could make some sense of all of this.

She rubbed her eyes, her decision made. She would order something from room service, draft a letter to the president and store it on the flash drive, sleep for a few hours, look at the satellite images with fresh eyes, and head to Albany to see the president.

CHAPTER TWO

Dawn broke, spilling shafts of weak sunshine across the bed. Sedona tilted the laptop screen away from the glare. She pounded the keys in frustration. Despite her best efforts, she could not enhance the satellite images without losing the already-shadowy figures altogether. The best she could do was to confirm that there were people and vehicles in once-restricted places in the Tuwaitha compound—a facility that she and her team secured and, supposedly, permanently sealed years ago.

If Tuwaitha was back in play, it could destabilize the entire region and dramatically shift the balance of power. Sedona could think of many different factions that might benefit from such an outcome—too many, in fact, to narrow down without a lot more information than she had in hand. Well, if all went according to plan, it would be the president's problem soon enough, and all that would be left for Sedona to worry about would be staying alive.

"Is that all?" She chuckled mirthlessly as she double-checked to make sure she had properly copied the contents of the flash drive onto her hard drive before ejecting it and hiding it in an unlabeled prescription pill bottle in her toilet kit. She powered down the laptop, set it on the bed, and headed into the bathroom for a quick shower. By the time rush hour hit its peak in Penn Station, she would be right in the middle of the bustle, just another commuter on her way upstate for a business meeting.

"What have you found out? Where is she?"

The man rubbed his temple and tightly gripped the phone. "We've got eyes out searching everywhere for her, sir."

"Which means you've got nothing."

"We found her car at a used-car lot in Baltimore an hour ago. It was clean. We immediately covered the airport, the train station, and the bus station. We wrapped the city in a blanket, but she had a head start."

"Because you failed to secure her at Fort Meade."

"I don't know how she could've known we were coming for her, sir."

"Obviously, she's smarter than you are."

The man ground his teeth but outwardly ignored the dig. "She hasn't used a credit card and her cell phone is turned off. We've investigated every place she was likely to go. But she has no living relatives and, as far as we can determine, no visible ties to anyone. No dependents, no husband or lover, no regular routine."

"Next time we talk, you'd better have her in hand."

"Yes, sir," the man said, though he knew the line already had gone dead.

⊰⊱

"I thought the audience was engaged and receptive, what did you think?" The president of the United States glanced over at his press secretary, a diminutive woman who was struggling to match his pace. He shortened his stride.

"I agree. The off-script comment about the successful leaders of tomorrow understanding the intersection of humanity and technology was a nice touch. Wish I'd written it."

"Sometimes, I just get carried away in the moment. Glad you approve. Let's add it at every collegiate stop."

"Yes, sir."

"Now, I'm going to make my Secret Service detail crazy." The president quickened his step and plunged into the crowd of surging bodies waiting behind wooden barriers just outside the auditorium.

The faces mostly blurred together as a sea of gloved hands reached out to touch him. He envied them their warm coats and gloves. It was freezing. But, like so many presidents before him, he chose to forgo an overcoat and gloves in an effort to appear more vigorous and youthful.

The president understood the risk inherent in diving into the rope line, but he prided himself on being an accessible leader, a man of the people. His wife hated that he took chances like this, and the head of his Secret Service team lectured him regularly about the potential for disaster and the fact that they simply couldn't adequately protect him in such situations.

As the president reached to his left, his right arm fully extended, he became unbalanced and stumbled forward. A woman appeared out of the throng directly in his path and steadied him, stopping his forward momentum with a hand on his left shoulder and the other hand on the right side of his chest.

"Thank you, ma'am," he said, smiling at her as he got his feet back under him. "That could've been embarrassing." She had arresting chocolate-brown eyes and a stylish haircut. He thought she was too old to be a student, but perhaps she was a member of the faculty.

"You're very welcome, Mr. President," she replied with a grin of her own, which revealed a deep dimple just to the left of her mouth. With the hand that still rested on his chest, she straightened the kerchief in his breast pocket.

Before the president could say another word, members of his Secret Service detail surrounded him on all sides, and the moment was over.

"Mr. President, we need to go now," the lead agent said in his ear.

Sedona turned up the collar on her overcoat and donned the pair of cheap sunglasses she had purchased that morning in Penn Station. Although she was on hyper-alert, she saw nothing and no one that raised alarm bells. More importantly, she didn't *feel* anything dangerous around her.

She allowed herself to be swept along with the crowd as it meandered toward a series of buses that would take them to outer parking areas or public transportation. It was cold out, and she contemplated the luxury of taking a cab over waiting for a public bus to take her back to the room she'd secured at the Marriott when she arrived in Albany.

"Cabbies remember faces. Stick to the bus. Overworked drivers, tired passengers caught up in their own stuff."

Sedona heard Dom's voice clear as a bell in her head, and she frowned. Damn him for being so practical, and so right. She sat down at the bus stop that would take her to Wolf Road.

She had no idea how long it would take the president to find the flash drive she'd dropped into the breast pocket of his suit jacket. "Hope you find it before you send the jacket to the cleaners," she mumbled.

It was the one thing she hadn't been able to plan with certainty. Positioning herself so that she could unbalance the president and then be in the right spot to catch him was as easy as bending over ostensibly to tie her shoe and then standing up again. Ensuring that he would be the one to take his kerchief out of the breast pocket, well, that was another matter. She briefly closed her eyes to ask for the only help she knew she could count on.

Archangels, angels, ascended masters, guides, please help me get this vital information to the president. Michael, since you're in charge of electronics, please ensure that the president is the one that finds the flash drive and that he reviews the contents. This I ask of you with your blessing, amen.

Sedona opened her eyes, satisfied, for the moment, that she'd done all she could. Now, all that was left was to wait. And shop. She'd noticed a large mall just down the street from the hotel. It would be wise to pick up a few more outfits and undergarments, since it didn't seem likely that she'd be going home anytime soon.

∽ॐ∾

"How was your day?"

The president pulled his wife into his arms. "Much better now." After all these years, he still thought she was the prettiest woman he'd ever seen. "Have I told you yet today how much I love you?"

"You have." She patted him on the chest. "But you can tell me again." She patted his chest again, a perplexed look on her face as her fingers closed over a slight bulge in his breast pocket. "What's this?"

"What's what?"

"This." Her brow furrowed as she reached into the pocket and pulled out a flash drive along with his kerchief. "Since when do you store data in here?"

"I don't." He took the drive from his wife's fingers and examined it. "I have no idea how that got in there." He walked over to a small, old-fashioned roll-top desk and opened it to reveal a state-of-the-art computer station.

"Oh, no you don't. You've been on the road all day. Now is our time."

"This'll just take a second, sweetheart." The president knew his wife wasn't buying it, but his curiosity was aroused.

"Of course it will. I'll just be over here—in the bed—when you're ready."

He hesitated for a second but couldn't resist the pull of the mystery. He sat down at the desk, powered on the computer, and plugged in the drive.

∾∾

Sedona snapped up the burn phone on the first ring. "Hello?"

"Sedona Ramos, I presume? This is the President of the United States. I'm sorry to be calling so late."

Sedona immediately recognized his voice and thought he sounded a bit bemused. She took that as a good sign. "Hello, Mr. President. It's not a problem, sir. Thank you for calling."

"Seems to me like you went to a heckuva lot of trouble to get this information to me. Want to tell me exactly how you managed that?"

"Do you really want to know, sir?"

"Actually, I am curious."

"We met in Albany, New York, this afternoon, sir. You were falling in my direction." Sedona waited for the president to sort through his recollections.

"Ah. The woman who stopped my fall. With your hand on my breast pocket."

"Yes, sir. That was me."

"Ingenious. I'm impressed." The president chuckled. "Although you're lucky the Secret Service didn't take you to the ground for touching me."

"It was a calculated and necessary risk, sir."

"You're very brave."

"Just doing my job, sir."

"I'd say this goes above and beyond." The president cleared his throat. "Tell me, Ms. Ramos, why bring this directly to me?"

"I have reason to believe security and the chain of command may be compromised in the agency."

"So you said in your letter. What makes you think so?"

"Sir, only analysts and operatives with the highest level clearance could access that system. To input that data and those images, someone would've had to have inside information. The fact that there were no names attached to the file tells me that it had to be someone who had the ability to override standard required protocols. The fact that my merely opening the file garnered the attention of a goon squad within minutes, armed to the teeth with the latest weaponry and technology, means that whoever is behind this is well organized, a seasoned professional with field experience and ample resources."

"Makes sense. So you know, I've had someone review all of the security footage from last night at Fort Meade. There's a curious blank spot between ten o'clock and ten thirty."

Sedona tried to keep the panic from welling up. The president had gone to the NSA after all. So concerned was she that she almost missed what he was saying.

"Before you worry too much, let me assure you that I used an outside expert I keep on my payroll for just such purposes. I have not contacted anyone from the NSA or any of my National Security advisors, and my man left no fingerprints in the system. No one but you and I know that he was in there."

"Thank you, sir."

"He also corroborates your account. He followed your keystrokes and verified everything you've said. For the record, like you, even he was unable to find a trace of the report in the system, although he was able to see that something had been erased."

"Yes, sir." Sedona chewed something over in her mind. "Sir, did your man also look up my personnel files?"

"Of course. I don't return just any phone call, you know."

Sedona could hear in the president's voice that he was smiling.

"I assume there was a picture of me in my files, which means you already knew where you'd seen me."

"Indeed, I did. But I wanted to hear you say it. Let's call it a little extra insurance. It's not every day that a beautiful woman saves my butt and manages to outwit my Secret Service agents at the same time."

Sedona knew she shouldn't be surprised that the president had investigated her, but she was a little taken aback by the lengths to which he had gone. "I'm glad I passed muster, sir."

"I'm glad you're on my side, Ms. Ramos."

"Always, Mr. President."

"I'd like you to come in, Ms. Ramos. I don't like that you're in danger."

"I'll be fine, sir. It's more important that you find out what's going on at Tuwaitha. If they think I've shared the information, they'll likely disappear underground, and we can't have that, sir. We need to catch them."

"I promise you, we will. Where are you now?"

Sedona hesitated. After all, this was the president. "Respectfully, it's better if you don't know, sir. I'm safe for the moment."

"I don't like it, Ms. Ramos."

"I'm sorry, sir."

"I won't issue you a direct order to come in, provided you make me a promise."

"What's that, sir?"

"Don't lose this phone. I'd like to know that I have a way to contact you."

"Yes, sir."

"Stay safe."

"That's my plan, sir. Goodbye."

⋘⋙

"Vaughn Elliott, is that you?"

Vaughn Elliott, former CIA agent and current recluse, closed her eyes, already regretting having answered the phone. "You were expecting someone else? To what do I owe the pleasure, Sabastien?"

"Don't I even rate a 'Hi, how are you?'"

"Is this a social call?" Vaughn pinched the bridge of her nose where a tension headache was starting to form.

"*Oui, et non.*"

"Which is it, genius? Yes or no? It's either a social call or I'm hanging up on you and going back to the beach. Three. Two. O—"

"Wait! *Merde.* Why do you have to make everything so hard?"

Vaughn smirked. "Because it's fun when it's you and because I told you when I set you up in D.C. as private cyber sleuth to the president that I wished you well, but that I was done with the game. Retired. What part of that didn't you hear? As I recall, I even said it in French so there'd be no misunderstanding." She held the phone against her ear with her shoulder while she went back to preparing herself a fruit salad.

"I got the message, but this is not about the Company."

"Then what?" Vaughn expertly skinned a kiwi, sliced it, and added it to the bowl.

"I want to, how do you say it…bounce something against you."

Vaughn laughed. "You mean 'bounce something off me' I presume."

"*Exactement. C'est ça.*"

"I'm listening."

It had been months since Vaughn last ventured to the mainland from her island paradise and almost that long since she had seen or spoken to anyone other than the locals. In spite of herself, she was almost glad to hear a familiar voice. She had recruited Sabastien Vaupaul to work for her when she caught him hacking into the CIA database and nearly derailing one of her operations. Most recently, he was instrumental in helping Vaughn recover Sage McNally and foil a plot to kill the US Senate majority leader.

"I received an unusual call from the president last night," Sabastien said. "First, he wanted me to verify the authenticity of some files he received outside of channels to make sure they hadn't been doctored."

"That doesn't sound particularly exciting."

"Maybe not. But then he asked me to hack into the NSA database to find the originals. I could tell that they had been there, but even I could not un-erase them."

"Maybe you're slipping."

"Not possible. And that is not all."

"Mmm?" Vaughn rinsed strawberries in the sink.

"He had me review the Fort Meade security footage from last night."

"What was he looking for?" Vaughn tried to keep her tone casual, though her curiosity was piqued.

"He would not tell me much, except that an NSA analyst was the one who discovered the files. Then, the analyst claims that the files disappeared from her system and she was paid a visit by some very unauthorized baddies. The president wanted to see if she was telling the truth."

Vaughn stopped slicing, the knife poised in mid-air. "Was she?"

"That I cannot tell you. What I can say is that there is a curious gap in the security tapes that takes place within minutes of the files disappearing from the system. I could see her at her desk working. I could follow every keystroke she made up until the point where she accessed that file. I watched her get up from her desk and go to a filing cabinet. She seemed agitated. She rushed back to the computer and was clicking keys, so that fits with her trying to recover the file. I could see her look up quickly, as if she heard or saw something. Her eyes widened. Then the tape goes all snowy. Nothing more until almost half an hour later and there is no sign of her again. I even went back into the system today. She did not report for work and never logged in."

"So how did the president end up with the file?" Vaughn stopped even pretending not to care.

"Again, I do not know. But he had me vet this analyst very thoroughly."

"Who is she?"

"I do not know if I should say."

"Why would you tell me all of this and then not reveal who she is?" Vaughn growled.

"*Mon Dieux*, Elliott, you are pretty surly for someone who does not have an interest in anything work-like."

"Shut up, Sabastien."

"Okay. But if I do, you will not get any more information from me."

"Just remember, I still maintain a healthy collection of weapons and I know where to find you."

"That is low, Elliott."

"But effective."

"Just so. But still, I really am not authorized to tell you that. It could mean my job."

Vaughn wanted to scream. "Then why are you telling me any of this?"

"Because I think this woman is one of what you would call 'the good guys' and I think she may be in a lot of danger."

"What makes you think so?"

"The president had me track this woman. There has been no activity on her credit cards, her cell phone is turned off, someone is monitoring her bank account, and her home and work phones are tapped."

"So what do you want from me?"

"I want to know how much danger she is in."

Vaughn rolled her eyes. "Without more information, I can't answer that. It sounds like she could be in deep, but then again, maybe not."

"Do you think she is dead?" Sabastien's voice was almost a whisper.

"I have no way of knowing." Vaughn knew it wasn't what he wanted to hear. His voice held genuine concern. Sabastien was someone who usually was so confident in his own abilities and immersed in his own geeky world that he was oblivious to the humanity around him. "What is it about this woman, Sabastien?"

"I do not know. She is very pretty. But it is more than that. There is an intangible quality about her. I cannot explain, Elliott. I can only say that I am troubled for her."

Vaughn considered. "Well, somehow the files ended up in the president's hands. That tells me that the woman managed to preserve the file or copy it before it disappeared. So we know she's resourceful and that she somehow got the file to the president. If she didn't do that from her work computer—"

"She did not."

"Then she obviously made it out of the building alive."

"True, but I have been monitoring all of her activity and she is simply gone. Not a trace of her anywhere and she has not been back to work."

"Does she have any field experience?"

"Oh, yes. She has been all over the world."

"Okay, then. I would say she's probably capable of taking care of herself and you shouldn't worry."

"Come on, Elliott. I am not a child. Do not dismiss me or my concerns."

Vaughn resumed rinsing the strawberries. "I'm not, Sabastien. I meant what I said. She sounds like she's got some training and a good head on her shoulders. Like I said, without knowing a whole lot more about what was in the files, I don't know what else I can tell you."

Sabastien heaved a deep sigh. "I do not know what I was looking at. And even if I did, it was top secret and you no longer have clearance. I could be arrested for treason if I shared the information."

"I don't want you to violate any rules or regs."

"But what can I do? How can I help her?"

Vaughn shook her head, although she knew Sabastien couldn't see it. "You can't right now. Sometimes there's nothing you can do."

"As you Americans would say, that sucks."

"I know. I know."

"I am sorry about Sage. She was a lovely girl."

Vaughn closed her eyes. "Too nice for me." She hoped her tone brooked no further discussion of her failed relationship with Sage McNally. Sage was better off on her own back in the states.

"It will likely piss you off when I say this, but I miss you, Elliott."

"You're right. See you around, Sabastien."

Vaughn disconnected the call but continued to hold the receiver, her thoughts and emotions jumbled at the mention of Sage's name. Better to think about Sabastien's mystery instead. Who was this woman and what the hell had she stepped into? "Not your problem, Elliott. Remember? You're done with all that."

Vaughn speared a piece of apple with a fork and bit into it. Not surprisingly, the sweetness of the apple could not replace the bitter taste in her mouth.

CHAPTER THREE

The helicopter hovered, its descent temporarily suspended, before touching down gently on the lush, green, rolling lawn at Camp David, the presidential retreat. When the rotors stopped spinning, two passengers emerged. One was a fit, sandy-haired man in his early sixties. The other was a tall, striking woman with glossy black hair and arresting blue eyes.

"Did the president say what this is all about?"

"No. Just that—"

"Katherine Kyle and Peter Enright, I presume. I'm Louis Dampier, the president's personal assistant. If you'll come with me, the president will meet you in his study."

Kate and Peter climbed into the back of the custom-built golf cart that would take them to the main house. Although it had been twenty-two years since either of them had been there, it was a ride they were both quite familiar with.

"Feel like déjà vu to you?" Kate asked, when they were settled on opposite ends of the well-worn leather sofa in the president's study. As press secretary to a previous democratic president, she'd been to Camp David many times. As a special assistant, Peter also had been to the retreat often.

"All over again," Peter answered.

"It's a little unsettling, don't you think? I mean, so much time has passed, and yet, in here, it's as if nothing's changed."

"Kate, Peter," the president said, striding into the room.

Both Kate and Peter quickly rose.

The president took Kate's hand. "You don't mind if I call you Kate, do you? President Hyland has spoken of you so often, I feel as if I know you personally."

"Not at all, Mr. President. It's an honor to meet you." Kate stood ramrod straight.

"No need to stand on ceremony with me." He turned his attention to Peter. "Your reputation precedes you, sir."

"As does yours, Mr. President."

"Touché." The president moved to a matching leather chair facing the sofa and motioned for them to sit. "I'm sure you're wondering why I summoned you."

"It has been rather a long time since I've been contacted on urgent business by a sitting president, sir." Kate took the lead. "I'm not sure how I can be helpful, but I'll do my best."

"Whatever you need, Mr. President," Peter added.

"That's exactly what Charlie said you would say."

"I'm not sure whether we should be flattered or concerned about our predictability."

The president laughed. "Let's get right to it, shall we?" He leaned forward. "You've seen the images on the news of the so-called 'Arab Spring' revolts from Tunisia and Egypt. Ben Ali is already out, and Mubarak is all but done, as well."

Kate and Peter nodded.

"Well, the unrest is spreading into Yemen, Iran, Bahrain, Libya and Algeria. Obviously, that's in addition to the wars in Iraq and Afghanistan, the situation between Israel and the Palestinians, the unreliability of Pakistan's allegiances... It seems all of the Middle East and North Africa is a tinderbox. At the moment, it's hard to tell how all this will shake out. The situation is too fluid, and there are too many players in the game."

"Sir, presumably the Arab Spring isn't a bad thing for the US."

"You're correct, Kate. Not in and of itself. But all that mayhem has spawned an unforeseen complication."

"Sir?"

"This is for your ears only." The president looked meaningfully at each of them in turn. "I trust that whatever we say in here, stays in here, except for persons I specifically authorize you to brief."

Again, both Kate and Peter nodded.

"A reliable source has discovered some unusual activity outside of Baghdad. It's a former Saddam nuclear site called Tuwaitha."

"I remember that name," Peter said. "Didn't our folks move something like five hundred fifty metric tons of yellowcake out of there a few years ago?"

"They did. The previous administration facilitated the transfer of all the material to Cameco, a uranium producer in Canada. Or so they thought."

"Sir, surely something as important as that would've been verified?" Kate asked.

"It was. According to testimony given at the time before the Congressional Intelligence Committee, every barrel was accounted for, and the place was shuttered. That's what makes this so troubling."

"What are you thinking, sir?"

The president rose and began pacing. "There are several possible scenarios, and none of them would be good news for us."

"Either someone was incompetent and some of the yellowcake got left behind," Peter ventured. "Or someone stole some of it and covered it up. Otherwise, the activity you've spotted involves something not tied to that event."

"Exactly."

"It's been three years, sir," Kate said. "If that yellowcake has been sitting there all along, why has someone waited until now to do something with it?"

"If it was incompetence, then it may be that the yellowcake is just now being discovered as our troops draw down."

"If it's either of the other two scenarios, it may be that someone is using the confusion in the region as a cover for whatever plan they have in mind," Peter said.

"And that's why you're both here." The president sat back down. "Normally, a report of unusual activity such as that which I've described would be included in my daily briefing either from the CIA, the Joint Chiefs, or potentially, Homeland Security. But that didn't happen here, and that's particularly troubling."

"So, exactly how did you come by the intelligence, sir?" Kate asked.

"Several days ago, I was surreptitiously slipped some information by a mid-level analyst from the NSA. This individual went to a lot of trouble and put herself at great risk to get the information directly into my hands."

The president swiveled his chair to gaze out the window, then turned back. "What she gave me, frankly, is chilling."

"What is it, sir?"

The president touched the buttons of a remote control and a portion of the wall slid open to reveal a large-screen display. "A series of current images of the Tuwaitha Yellowcake Factory." He pushed another button on the remote, and a large satellite image filled the screen.

Kate and Peter moved in to get a closer look.

"As you can see, the complex is abuzz with activity." The president pointed at a series of buildings. As he clicked through several long-range images, numerous vehicles and people appeared to come and go in a time-lapsed sequence.

"Sir, I'm sure you know that images can be manipulated," Peter said.

"Of course." The president dismissed the idea with a wave of his hand. "That's why I personally consulted with an independent expert. He assures me that the images have not been altered in any way."

"Why didn't your source just take her findings to her superior?" Kate asked.

"Apparently, she discovered the images quite by accident. When she tried to dig a little deeper, she immediately was locked out of the system."

"By accessing the file while logged in under her own username and password, she triggered some sort of alarm," Peter said.

"Exactly." The president nodded. "She's been on the run ever since."

"Any chance she's being paranoid, sir?" Kate asked. "And how do you know she's legitimate?"

"My technology expert was able to hack into the NSA database and retrieve her service record. Since I actually met her, although I didn't know it at the time, I was able to verify that she was the one who directly handed me the information.

"In addition, my expert has been able to determine that someone has been working very hard to find this woman. Her

32

phones are tapped, and her bank account activity is being monitored along with her credit cards. Someone is going to a lot of trouble to locate her." The president sighed. "So yes, she's legitimate, and no, I don't think she's imagining things."

"Where is she now?" Kate asked.

"Honestly, I'm not sure." The president held up his hand. "I know, that sounds crazy. But she was convinced that if whoever is looking for her determined that she'd shared the information with anyone, it would compromise our ability to identify and thwart whatever is going on at Tuwaitha."

"Sounds like she's putting herself in grave danger, sir," Peter said.

"Indeed, and I'm not happy about it," the president said. "She had me contact her via a burn phone. I'm hoping she hasn't dumped it. I plan to call her when we're done here and put her in contact with you."

"With us, sir?" Kate asked. "What is it you'd like Peter and me to do?"

"The whole thing stinks, and I'm particularly troubled that none of my direct reports has mentioned anything at all about Tuwaitha. Now, it might be that they don't know about it. But with something this sensitive, they certainly should be aware and, in turn, should have informed me right away.

"I have no way of knowing exactly what the activity at that facility is, although the location would logically indicate that it involves raw uranium. Given the extreme sensitivity of this matter, and the potential for catastrophic outcomes, we simply can't go charging in there."

"Of course not, sir," Kate agreed.

The president continued, "Are there dissident Iraqi elements creating dirty bombs? If so, why haven't my intelligence agencies heard any chatter or put a report on my desk about it? Did a quantity of yellowcake somehow get left behind in '08 and someone is trying to cover his ass by cleaning it up now? If so, again, why doesn't my intelligence team, with all its sophisticated equipment, know about it or think it's significant enough to bring to my attention? Is it conceivable that whatever is going on at Tuwaitha is unrelated to the yellowcake? Or is there another explanation?"

The president jumped up to pace again. "It seems inconceivable to me that one or more of my direct reports wouldn't know something about this. And since none of them has indicated an awareness of any activity at all in the area…"

"You're worried about an internal, covert operation being driven or sanctioned by some of your own people," Kate said.

The president's expression was grim. "I think we have to consider it as a possibility. That's why I need a team that's above reproach to investigate."

"You're looking for someone outside the normal chain of command."

"I'm looking for someone who's off the grid entirely," the president corrected. "Kate, I believe you're acquainted with former CIA agent Vaughn Elliott?"

Kate's eyebrows shot up. "How did you—"

"I'm the president."

"Of course, sir. Yes, sir. I know Vaughn, but she retired."

"I'm aware, Kate. And, officially, I'd like her to stay that way…"

"Yes, sir."

"She's proved herself many times over, and I know she's someone who gets results and who can be trusted implicitly. And, I imagine she still has other members of her band of merry men and women who would follow her into a burning building without asking a question."

"I wouldn't know about that, sir. Vaughn and I are social friends, not business colleagues."

"I know that too. That's why I'm banking on you being able to persuade her to take this assignment."

"Sir?"

"She knows you respect her privacy and her choices. If you ask her, she'll understand how imperative her participation is to the success of this mission."

"I don't know about that, sir, but I can try."

"I was hoping you'd say that." The president pulled a manila envelope from a drawer and handed it to Kate. "Give this to her. It contains a detailed mission briefing, along with other items she'll need."

"I'm assuming you've got something planned for me, sir?"

"Peter, over the years you've been an invaluable asset and a true patriot. Not just one, but many presidents have trusted you with their lives."

Peter shifted uncomfortably, and the president hurried on. "I know you've taken yourself out of the game."

"Not entirely, sir. I'm a consultant."

The president shook his head. "Not this time. I need you to get back on the field for this one. Elliott will require a lot of help. I want her to have the best. I'm sure I don't have to tell you what's at stake. We're talking about potential weapons of mass destruction here and I need the utmost discretion. I have no idea who are the good guys, and who are the bad guys, so I'm not taking any chances."

"Yes, sir," both Peter and Kate answered.

"There are instructions in the packet for communicating from the field. You're answerable only to me, and you'll have direct access to me, any time, night or day."

"Yes, sir."

"I understand Ms. Elliott has picked herself a nice, secluded retirement spot."

"That's a nice way to say she's in the middle of nowhere, sir." Kate laughed.

"I've arranged transportation for you. You'll find the rest of what you'll need on board the bird."

"Thank you, sir."

The president picked up his private phone. "Now let's see if I can convince the last member of your team to officially come on board." He dialed a number from a slip of paper he pulled from his pocket. "Ms. Ramos? This is the president. I'm glad you didn't throw away the phone. I know you think it best to stay away, but I've put together a very special, very unofficial team to look into Tuwaitha. I trust them with my life and I hope you'll trust them with yours."

Kate and Peter watched as the president listened and nodded.

"Yes, I understand. But we really need your expertise. You know Iraq and you know Tuwaitha. Ms. Ramos, your country needs you."

The president paused again to listen and waved dismissively. "The target on your back is all the more reason I want you involved in this on the inside. Believe me, we have the means to deflect any unwanted attention and to send these folks on a wild goose chase that will have them running in circles for a very long time...

"Where are you? Very well...I'm sending a small, private plane to pick you up. It will be completely off the radar. There won't be anyone official or anything at all to tie the plane to me or to any government agency. For all intents and purposes, it'll look like a private jet picking up a businesswoman on the way to a meeting. On board will be two people, Katherine Kyle and Peter Enright, both winners of the Presidential Medal of Freedom. They earned that by saving the life of former President Hyland. I've selected them and the other member of the team both because they're the best, and because they have no ties to any of the players who might have anything to do with the goings-on at Tuwaitha. They'll brief you on the rest of the details...

"The plane will pick you up in less than two hours. Thank you, Ms. Ramos. I'll look forward to meeting you on a more formal basis when this is all over. Goodbye."

The president hung up the phone and faced Kate and Peter. "Okay. She's on board, albeit reluctantly. Here's her contact information." He handed Kate the piece of paper from which he'd dialed her number, and then consulted his watch. "Better get going. The helicopter will take you back to Andrews, where a small plane will be waiting to take you to Albany, New York."

Kate and Peter raised eyebrows simultaneously. "Looks like we're making a stop in our old stomping grounds," Kate said.

"Looks like it."

"From there, you'll be taken to Elliott's compound. I'll leave it to you to figure out the best approach to use to convince her how important this matter is and how much we need her participation and expertise."

"Thank you, sir."

"Keep Ms. Ramos safe. I don't know who's behind this, but it's obvious they mean business."

"Yes, sir."

"Godspeed to both of you."

❦

The plane bounced twice, then taxied smoothly toward the private terminal at Albany International Airport.

"Are you sure it's okay for me to be here?" Jamison Parker, *New York Times* best-selling author and Kate's wife, shifted self-consciously in her seat.

Kate raised an eyebrow. "First, I cleared bringing you along with the president's people. Second, I paid for your flight to avoid any appearance of impropriety. Third, tomorrow is Valentine's Day. We've never spent it apart and we're jetting off to an island paradise. What part of that makes you uncomfortable?"

Jay patted Kate's cheek. "The part where you picked up a passenger at Andrews who hasn't been cleared to hear the details of this mission."

"We've got that covered, right Peter?"

"Yes, dear."

"I can't wait to hear this," Jay said.

"It's simple. Peter and I will brief our passenger on the plane, away from your sensitive ears. Once we arrive at our destination and get the social niceties out of the way with Vaughn, you'll politely excuse yourself. I'll come get you when we're done talking business and you and I will start our vacation. Alone. Together. On a semi-deserted island." Kate waggled her eyebrows. "Did I mention alone?"

Jay laughed. "You might have said it in passing."

"Okay, folks. We're clear to disembark," the pilot said.

"This'll only take a few minutes," Kate said to the pilot. She trotted down the stairs, across the tarmac, and into the terminal, leaving Peter and Jay behind.

Kate spotted Sedona right away. She was standing in one of the airport concessions pretending to read a magazine. She was well positioned with her back to the wall so that she could see the foot traffic in all directions. For someone who was being hunted, she looked remarkably composed.

Kate took stock of the people milling about and judged that likely none of them were paying undue attention to Sedona, so she approached casually, as if she were meeting a business colleague.

"Sorry it took me so long to get here," Kate said. She noted that although Sedona shifted so that her weight was on the balls of her feet, she made no move to run. "The boss wanted to make sure we had the most up-to-date information available."

Sedona made a non-committal sound.

Kate pointed to the briefcase she held in her hand, then to the magazine Sedona was holding with the president's picture on the cover. "I think he's much more handsome in person."

"I agree, although he's a little taller than I expected." Sedona put the magazine back on the rack, pushed off the wall, picked up her bag, and started to walk toward the door leading to the tarmac.

Kate, who expected Sedona to be more wary than she apparently was, took a second to catch up. When she did, she said, "I'm Katherine Kyle and this," Kate handed Sedona an envelope with the raised seal of the president's office on it, "is for you."

"Thanks."

Kate watched Sedona's profile as she tucked the envelope in her coat pocket and continued to walk. She furrowed her brow. "Don't you want to have a look at that?"

"Don't need to."

"Why is that?"

"I believe you are who you say you are, and that the president sent you."

Kate was positive the president hadn't provided Sedona with her picture. "And you know that because…?"

"Your energy," Sedona said, without breaking stride.

"My energy?"

"Yep." Sedona glanced at her quickly and continued to scan the terminal as they approached the exit. "Your energy is very clean and positive and there are many angels surrounding you. That wouldn't be true if you wanted to do me harm. Plus, Archangel Michael told me to trust you."

Kate nearly stumbled. Was this woman, a decorated NSA operative presently being hunted by people who clearly wanted to kill her, talking to her about metaphysical stuff? "Unbelievable," she muttered.

"Oh, and I googled you as soon as the president told me whom I'd be meeting." Sedona winked and pointed to the exit. "You coming?"

38

CHAPTER FOUR

Sedona bounded up the stairs and stepped inside the plane, pausing just long enough to let her eyes adjust to the change in lighting. She blinked as her gaze settled on a stunning blonde sitting in the front row. She was gesticulating with her hands and talking animatedly to a ruggedly distinguished man in the seat opposite her. The blonde looked up and smiled.

"Hi," she said as she jumped to her feet. "You must be Sedona. I'm Jamison Parker—Jay to my friends. Don't mind me, I'm not really here."

Sedona smiled in return—really, it was hard not to in the face of such vivaciousness. She noted that the numerous pictures she'd seen of Kate and Jay hardly did them justice. Sedona shook the outstretched hand. "Nice to meet you, or not, since you're not really here." She turned toward the gentleman. "Peter Enright, I presume?"

"Excellent powers of deductive reasoning."

Sedona noted his handshake was firm, but not overpowering. While she had no trouble finding plenty of information all over the Internet on Kate and Jay, she found precious little about Peter Enright. She found that intriguing, but not alarming. If he was CIA, as Sedona suspected he was, it would've been more surprising than not if her cursory search turned up much.

"We're good to go," Kate said to the pilot as she came up behind Sedona.

Sedona stowed her bag, took the seat next to Peter, and prepared for takeoff.

"I'm glad you're safe," he said. "Sounds like you've had a pretty harrowing time of it."

"Nothing I couldn't handle." Sedona shifted in her seat so she could see Peter's eyes. In them she saw intelligence and compassion. A quick peek at his aura revealed a man with a huge heart who likely trusted his gut hunches rather than any material information he received. There was a significant amount of purple in his field, so he clearly was allied closely with Archangel Michael as a fierce warrior. Yet, that compassion she saw indicated that he chose his battles carefully and only when provoked. And battle he must have done, judging from the cloudy area in his chest near his heart chakra. Sedona wondered what had happened to cause that.

"Sedona," Jay said as the plane taxied down the runway. "That's a pretty name. Any relation to the town?"

"Mmm. It's where I was conceived."

"Kate and I love that place. It's so beautiful. Magical, really."

"I think so too." The loving look that passed between Kate and Jay as their fingers interlaced wasn't lost on Sedona. She suffered a brief pang for something she once had, but knew she never would have again. Her back pressed into the seat as the plane left the runway and began its ascent. The increase in engine noise precluded any further conversation.

When the plane reached altitude and leveled off, Kate said, "Shall we get the briefing out of the way? It's a long flight. I'm sure Sedona would like to catch some shuteye."

"Sure," Peter said.

Jay held up a hand. "That's my cue to exit stage right." She unbuckled her seatbelt, kissed Kate on the forehead, and stepped over her and into the aisle. "It's really nice to meet you. I'm glad you're okay," she said to Sedona. To the group she said, "Let me know when it's all clear for me to come back." She walked to the back of the plane, lay down across two seats, and closed her eyes.

Sedona waited until Kate's eyes stopped tracking Jay. "First, it would help if I knew where, exactly, this long flight is taking us." Sedona looked at Kate, then at Peter.

"The team leader is a former CIA officer," Kate said. "Her name is Vaughn Elliott. She lives on a remote island in the Caribbean. We're going to see her now."

Sedona absorbed this information, pleased that the president chose a woman to spearhead the mission. She turned to Peter. "I like to know who I'm working with. Are you Company as well?"

Kate answered for him. "Peter worked for the New York State Department of Correctional Services for years and is an independent consultant with an expertise in weapons and technology."

"And?" Sedona allowed her skepticism to show. She looked pointedly at Peter. She watched as he made up his mind how much to share.

"And I was"—he emphasized the last word—"Company. Deep cover."

"I thought the credo was, once a Company man, always a Company man."

"I haven't been active or in the field for a long time."

Sedona wondered if that fact and the faraway look in his eyes had anything to do with the cloudy area in his aura, but his tone indicated he had shared as much as he intended.

"The president tells us you have some familiarity with Tuwaitha."

Sedona accepted the change in topic with equanimity. "I was there when we cleared the place out and shut it down. That's why I knew what I was looking at so quickly when the images came up on my monitor. It's also how I knew that something was very wrong."

"About that," Kate said. "If someone was trying to do something surreptitious, why put it in the NSA system where someone like you could find it?"

Sedona nodded, appreciating that Kate cut to the heart of the most vexing thing about the situation. She'd been wondering about that also. "I don't know, yet. On the face of it, it doesn't make any sense."

"How did you happen across the file?" Peter asked.

"I was working late at my desk in the NSOC." Noting their blank stares, Sedona clarified, "the National Security Operations Center. Nothing unusual there. My assignment was to review the latest batch of Arabic-language intercepts from Iraq. We were looking for evidence of an impending action the CIA got wind of a while back. So I was double-checking the translation of the chatter from our front-line analysts. As you can imagine, the stream of information is constant."

Kate and Peter nodded.

"I plowed through all of one set of files pretty quickly and I had nowhere to be, so I thought I'd help out and tackle the next set to give the late shift a head start. I got down to the last electronic file folder in the next batch. That's when it got hinky."

The co-pilot emerged from the cockpit with four bottles of water, and Sedona stopped talking.

"Anybody thirsty?"

Once he was gone, Sedona resumed her story. "Every file that comes through is identified both by the analyst that captured the information and by the person who requested it. There are no exceptions to this—it's standard protocol and required in order to upload the file and have it included in the folder."

"How are the contents of each folder determined?" Kate asked.

"Files are sorted first by conversation thread and secondarily by target, then by timeframe. Everything pertinent within a given period of time would be included in the folder." Sedona took a sip of water. "So if separate phone calls or meetings involve say, a total of eight people, all of those individual discussions would be their own file and would be included in one folder, prioritized by primary target of interest, then secondary target and on down the line."

"How many files were in the folder you were reviewing?" Peter asked.

"There were seven. But, as I started to say, the thing that made the last file in the folder unusual was that it identified neither the field agent nor the translator—where that information should have been, there was a series of numbers. In the middle of several pages of seemingly innocuous text were the images of Tuwaitha."

"Interesting," Peter said. "What were the other files in the folder?"

"Nothing special. Routine discussions about plans for minor incursions and actions. Some tough talk and bragging about stuff these guys were never going to do but that made them feel like big men."

"Was there anything at all that the first six files had in common with the Tuwaitha file?"

"Not that I can think of right now. Those files all were properly identified."

"Did you happen to copy those files?"

Sedona shook her head. "I had less than two minutes from the time I accessed the questionable document to the time those goons showed up on the floor—long enough to copy it to the flash drive, get to the filing cabinet to search for a physical copy of the file, get back to my desk to throw some things together, and get the heck out of there."

"You said the text surrounding the images was innocuous," Kate said.

"That's right."

"Does that mean it was like all the other documents in terms of content or are you saying it was gibberish?"

"I haven't had a lot of time to study it yet, but on the surface it looked like everyday conversation." Sedona yawned and rubbed her eyes.

As Peter started to ask another question, Kate interrupted him. "You must be exhausted. I know it's been a long few days and we've got a haul in front of us. Why don't you get some sleep. I'm sure we'll be going through all of this again with Vaughn."

Although she wanted to object, Sedona knew Kate was right. She was too tired to be of much use. "Probably a good idea." She retrieved a blanket and pillow from the overhead compartment and retired to an empty row to lie down. Nothing about anything that happened in the past few days made much sense. Perhaps some rest would bring clarity to her jumbled thoughts.

Can I get you something to drink?" Vaughn Elliott led the way into her living room. "Coffee? Iced tea? Something stronger?" She went to the wet bar in the corner and poured herself some iced tea. She knew she was stalling. It wasn't like her friend Kate and her wife Jay to drop in on such short notice and without an invitation.

The last time they'd seen each other was at Kate and Jay's wedding. Even Vaughn had to admit it was a beautiful affair, although not something she'd ever consider for herself. Sage was right—Vaughn had no time or space in her heart for a loving, committed relationship.

Vaughn shook her head to clear her thoughts and the small stab of pain at having failed, yet again, at sustaining a relationship. *Stay where your feet are.* She looked expectantly at Kate and Jay, who were settling themselves on the leather sofa.

"No thanks, we're fine." Jay answered for the couple.

"So, you were just in the neighborhood?" Vaughn arched an eyebrow to express her skepticism. She noted that Jay seemed suddenly to find something very interesting in the pattern of the Oriental rug.

"You know, I think I'm more tired than I thought." Jay yawned as if to punctuate the point. "If you don't mind, I'm going to turn in." She smiled that megawatt smile that Vaughn had seen on the back of book jackets in bookstores in many countries. It was dazzling, Vaughn had to admit.

"Of course. If there's anything you need that's not in the guest cottage, let me know."

"Thanks. I'll see you at breakfast." Jay leaned over and sweetly kissed Kate before disappearing through the open sliding glass doors and onto the path that led from the rear of Vaughn's home.

"That was subtle." Vaughn shook her head.

"That's why I never let her play poker," Kate said.

"Good idea." Vaughn turned her glass in the light, watching the liquid shift and swirl around the ice cubes. "So, want to tell me what this is really all about? Please tell me this isn't some sort of intervention meant to lure me back into proper society."

"Not exactly."

When Kate stood and faced her, they were eye to eye. There weren't all that many women about whom Vaughn could say that. Also unlike most women, Kate wasn't intimidated by what Vaughn thought of as her "penetrating stare." She sighed and ran her free hand through her hair. "What, then?"

"I was asked to come see you."

"By?"

"The president of the United States."

Vaughn groaned and swiveled her head to release the sudden tension in her neck. "Didn't he get the memo? I'm retired."

"He did. That's why he wants you."

"Is that so? Whatever it is, he can find some other out-to-pasture civil servant." Just to create some distance, Vaughn walked back to the bar and refreshed her nearly full glass.

"He specifically asked for you."

"Am I supposed to be flattered by that?" Vaughn's nostrils flared.

"I don't believe the president is in the business of flattery. He is, however, in the business of keeping the country safe, and he's asked for your help."

"That's low, Kyle. Appeal to my sense of duty, my patriotic nature? Beneath you, my friend." Vaughn wiped her hands on a towel and came out from behind the bar.

"Think what you want, but when you hear what's at stake, I'm confident you'll drop the surly attitude. Besides, it never works on me. You know that."

Vaughn offered a grudging smirk. What her friend said was true—Vaughn had tried many times over the years to get the psychological upper hand with Kate when they competed at tennis or racquetball at the court club in D.C. where they'd met. In Kate, Vaughn found her competitive match. It irked her no end, but earned Kate her respect.

Vaughn sat on the edge of a chair arm. "Better spit it out."

When Kate finished, Vaughn blew out an explosive breath. She debated whether or not to tell Kate about her conversation with Sabastien. After all, it was clear they were talking about the same woman. She decided against it, since technically Sabastien had no business telling her anything. Instead, she said, "This is no small thing."

"Exactly. As I told you up front, that's why the president asked me to approach you."

"I'm not sure I'm what he needs," Vaughn said, almost to herself.

"He's obviously sure," Kate countered.

"What you need is an expert in raw uranium and nuclear production."

Kate moved back to the sofa and sat down. "You can add one of those to the team you put together."

"I've never been in Iraq."

"Not a problem."

Vaughn narrowed her eyes. "Why did the president send you? You and I have never mixed business with pleasure. It's one of the reasons I've kept you in my life." Vaughn saw Kate's minute flinch and realized she'd wounded her. She wished she could take the words back. Kate was someone whose company she genuinely enjoyed and whose friendship she treasured.

Kate schooled her expression. "No doubt that's why I'm here. The president anticipated that you'd be less than enthusiastic. He calculated that, based on our friendship, you'd hear me out. I knew it was a risk, but I felt that the situation warranted my taking that chance." She jutted out her chin.

"I'm sorry, Kate. I don't mean to take this out on you. It's just... It's been a couple of years, and I've gotten comfortable in my own little world, you know?"

Kate nodded, but Vaughn noted that she didn't make eye contact. It occurred to her that Kate probably didn't want to be here asking this of her any more than Vaughn wanted to be asked. She traced the condensation on the outside of her glass as she decided how much she wanted to share with her friend.

"My last assignment didn't exactly go smoothly." Vaughn and Kate never had discussed business, despite the fact that Vaughn knew quite a bit about Kate's career. Most of it was a matter of public record and readily available via a web search—the rest Vaughn had read in the case file about the simulated death and kidnapping of President Charles Hyland in 1989.

On the other hand, Kate could've searched everywhere and not found a reference to Vaughn. Even the record of the Edgar Fairhaven and Brian Pordras trial for the attempted assassination of the Senate majority leader and Sage's abduction had been redacted to protect her involvement and identity. Vaughn looked over at Kate to gauge her reaction. What she saw was polite attention.

"I lost a good friend. That seems to happen a lot around me." Vaughn thought of Sara and closed her eyes to prevent a tear from leaking out. After all this time, she still mourned the loss of her first love.

"It's a rough business, Vaughn, although I'm sure that's little consolation to you." Kate's voice was gentle. "The president is fully aware of your record of service. He has enormous respect for

46

you. He never even considered anyone else for this assignment."
Kate got up, went to where Vaughn sat, and put a hand on her arm.
"I know what it's like to have those you care about ripped away
from you."

Vaughn could see in her eyes that Kate understood something
about loss. Then she remembered the story of the attempted
murder of Jay and the two months it took her to recover her
memory and return home to Kate.

Kate squeezed Vaughn's arm once, then broke contact.
"Sometimes, you have to soldier on just because it's the right thing
to do, even when all you want to do is hide away from the world
forever."

Vaughn cleared her throat. "I assume you have briefing papers
for me to look at?"

For the first time since Jay left the room, Kate smiled. "I
thought you'd never ask. Oh, and I also brought along a couple of
friends I'd like you to meet…"

❦

"The way I see it," Vaughn was saying, "we've got multiple
issues to sort through."

Sedona took the measure of the woman sitting across the table
from her. She was handsome with strong features. She also was
haunted. Not in the physical sense, of course. But Sedona could
see the damage around her heart chakra. Vaughn had suffered
great loss in this lifetime and she carried the burden in her aura.
While she wondered what had caused that kind of pain, Sedona
didn't get the sense that Vaughn was the type of woman to
encourage exploration of personal issues and Sedona never would
violate anyone's privacy by "looking" to determine what had
happened.

Sedona mentally shook herself to refocus on the conversation.

"…What exactly is the activity at Tuwaitha?" Kate asked.

"Who's behind it?" Peter chimed in.

"What threat does it pose?" Vaughn threw in, as she wrote the
issues on a large pad of paper.

"Why don't the president's top advisors know about it? Or, if
they do, why aren't they reporting about it?" Peter asked.

"What's the connection to the NSA? How did they have access to the computers and the ability to override standard protocols?" Vaughn scribbled.

"And who wants me dead?" All heads turned in her direction and Sedona held each of their gazes in turn. "Although, presumably those would be the same individuals who are behind all of this."

"Right," Vaughn said, the marker she was using stuttering over the page. Sedona thought she noted a fleeting look of compassion.

"I think those are the major questions," Kate said, breaking the awkward silence.

"Mmm." Vaughn capped the marker. "We're going to need some help." She looked at the faces in the room. "Are we all agreed that, given Sedona's status, this is the safest place for our initial command central?"

When everyone nodded, Vaughn took out her cell phone and dialed a number. "Sabastien? How quickly can you get here?" Apparently pleased with the answer, Vaughn hung up and dialed again. "Justine?"

Sedona watched as a series of emotions crossed Vaughn's face. Clearly, this was someone with whom she shared more than a passing work acquaintanceship. The more she saw of Vaughn, the more intrigued Sedona became.

CHAPTER FIVE

Y ou aren't any closer to finding her than you were the night she slipped through your grasp. This is completely unacceptable." The man's voice was eerily calm. This stood in stark contrast to the bulging vein in the middle of his forehead. He dusted some imaginary lint off the cuff of his impeccable steel-gray suit.

"Sir, we're doing everything we can. I've got a dozen men combing through her life and another dozen retracing every step she's taken for the past year. We're looking for any patterns, any clues, anything at all. If it's there, we'll find it—and her. It's just a matter of time."

"Time," the lone woman at the table chimed in, "is a luxury we cannot afford. She's eluded us for almost a week. We have no idea what she saw, what she knows, and whom she might have told. I say we pull the plug."

"Are you nuts? We can't fold now. This has been in the works for years. We go forward as planned." The little man with the odd accent practically foamed at the mouth.

"Enough!" The conference room's final occupant rose from his chair at the end of the rectangular table, his voice rich and deep. "Use whatever resources you need to hunt down this woman. Find out where she's been, what she knows, whom she's been in contact with, and kill her. No loose ends. The objective and the plan remain the same. Have I made myself clear?"

Vaughn surveyed the faces around the table on the sun-lit patio as the conversation flowed around her. Kate was talking with the latest arrival, Lorraine King, a former deep-cover CIA agent Peter asked to bring in. Although Vaughn had never met her before, some of her exploits were legendary, including her late 1980s infiltration of a shadowy multinational organization called the Commission. It was only after Peter made the introductions that Vaughn made the connection between Peter, Kate and Jay, Lorraine and the Hyland case file. When Vaughn read the file during her training with the Company, all non-civilian names were redacted. That explained why she was unaware of Peter or Lorraine's involvement.

Vaughn scanned the rest of the table. Jay and Peter were trading good-natured jabs. Sabastien had managed to procure a seat next to Sedona, who appeared to be listening politely as he prattled on about some sub-routine he wrote. Vaughn still was trying to get the measure of this woman. Sedona was beautiful in an unselfconscious way. It wasn't just her looks. There was something almost ethereal about her. Vaughn caught herself staring and looked away.

"Right, Vaughn Elliott?"

Vaughn shifted her gaze to Sabastien, who obviously thought she was listening to his story. "Whatever you say, genius." She resisted the urge to laugh as he puffed out his chest. Vaughn couldn't be sure, but she suspected that his efforts to impress Sedona would be wasted.

"As much fun as it's been to break bread with all of you, my wife and I have plans." Kate stood and took Jay's hand.

"I've been promised an afternoon on a private beach and some scuba diving. How can I resist?" Jay asked.

After everyone said their goodbyes to the couple, Vaughn escorted Kate and Jay into the house and to the front door. Jay hugged Vaughn and stepped outside. "Are you sure you don't want to stay here?" Vaughn asked Kate as she lingered behind.

"Thanks, but you're going to have a full house now. The hotel will be fine for us. Besides, I promised Jay a romantic getaway."

"I still say we could use your perspective."

"It seems to me you've got plenty of folks more suited to this assignment than I am. Still, if there's anything I can do to lend a hand, I'm only a phone call away."

"Okay. Have fun."

"Always," Kate said. "Be careful out there."

"Always." Vaughn closed the door behind Kate and was surprised to find Sabastien waiting in the foyer. "Yeah?"

"Why did you not tell me on the phone that Sedona was here?" he said in a harsh whisper. "You knew I was worried sick about her safety and yet you played stupid."

"That's dumb, not stupid," Vaughn said. She started to push past Sabastien, but he stood in her path. "If you're going to become Americanized, though I don't know why you'd want to, then at least learn the proper idioms." She shoved him aside. "And for the record," she tossed over her shoulder, "she wasn't here when you called me."

He caught up to her and put a hand on her arm. "But she was here when you called me back and asked me to come."

"Yes."

"What does she know of me?"

Vaughn rolled her eyes. "Is that what this is about? Your ego? You can share all the tales of your glorious triumphs. I haven't told her anything about you."

"That is not what I meant, Elliott." Sabastien glanced in the direction of the sliding glass doors that led to the patio and lowered his voice even further. "Does she know I am the one who researched her for the president? Is she aware I know all about her and that night?"

Vaughn softened her stance and patted Sabastien on the shoulder. She should have given him more credit. "No. I haven't told anyone about that."

"Do you think we should? Tell, I mean."

"Good question." Vaughn considered their options. If she and Sabastien said nothing, surely the information eventually would come out. When it did, there might be a lot of hard feelings. As much as she didn't want any part of all this, she had agreed to take on the assignment and be team leader. That meant instilling trust among the troops. "We have to tell her."

"How?"

Vaughn pursed her lips in thought. "I don't know yet, but it needs to be soon." She noted the trepidation in Sabastien's eyes. "Leave it to me."

"Thank you, Elliott." Sabastien kissed her on both cheeks and moved away before Vaughn could smack him. "You are the best."

"If you do that again, you're a dead man. Where's your gear? Why don't you do something useful and get yourself set up in my office."

"Right." Sabastien ran off toward the living room.

While he more often than not grated on her last nerve, Sabastien simply was the best at what he did and Vaughn knew she was lucky to have him on her team. As she anticipated, he showed up at her door with massive amounts of technology in tow. There were eight hard-sided cases of stuff in all and one tiny suitcase for his clothes—quintessentially Sabastien.

"It's 1300 hours now," Vaughn said, when she returned to the patio. "Why don't I show you all to your rooms so you can get settled in? Let's meet in my office in half an hour. Sabastien is getting his equipment set up. Once he's ready to go, we'll plan a course of action and see what he can tell us."

Peter, Lorraine, Sedona, and Justine rose from the table and followed Vaughn into the house. "Lorraine and Justine, if you don't mind, I thought I'd put you in the cottage. There are two bedrooms out there, but you'll have to share a bathroom." Vaughn gestured to her left, toward the back of the house.

"Works for me," Lorraine said.

"I'm easy," Justine added.

"I heard that about you." Vaughn winked.

"Be careful or I'll start telling stories and you know I have plenty of those."

Vaughn feigned fear. "Peter, you and Sabastien can take the two rooms down that hallway." She pointed to a corridor that split off from the living room to the right. "Take whichever room suits you best, Peter. Sabastien isn't picky."

Finally, Vaughn turned to Sedona, who was watching her with that same unnerving intensity Vaughn noticed earlier. "I thought I'd put you in the room next to mine, since you're the only one on the radar so far." She was interested to note that Sedona didn't show any outward reaction. "I'm sure you're completely safe here, but I don't like to leave things to chance, if that's all right with you."

"It's your house," Sedona said. "You make the call."

Vaughn still didn't know what to make of her. Sedona was either the coolest customer on the planet, or else she hid fear really, really well. Vaughn searched for a word to describe the way Sedona made her feel—*discomfited* came to mind. "Okay then," she said. "This way."

There were three laptops, four twenty-three inch monitors, a mobile printer, a large-format color printer, and various and sundry other electronic devices spread over the large teak desk in Vaughn's office.

"I'm impressed," Sedona said, as she surveyed the array of equipment.

"What? *Merde.*" Sabastien rubbed the spot on the top of his head where he'd just slammed it into unforgiving wood. He extricated himself from underneath the desk. "Ouch."

"I'm sorry," Sedona said. "I didn't mean to startle you."

"You did not. I mean, you did but..."

Sedona thought Sabastien's blush was endearing. "If you want me to wait outside until everyone else comes—"

"No." Sabastien smiled sheepishly. "That is, it is not necessary. I am almost finished here."

"Anything I can do?"

"No. I have got it within control."

Sedona chuckled in spite of her best effort not to.

"I said something sideways again, did I not? Elliott is always correcting me." Sabastien fiddled with one of the Ethernet cables. "What was it this time?"

"The expression is 'under' control, not 'within' control."

"Oh."

Sedona perched on the side of the desk. "Where are you from?"

"Originally?"

Sedona noted that Sabastien continued to worry the cable. Sedona didn't need to be psychic to know that he was more comfortable with equipment than with people. "Yes."

"Paris, France. But my father also had a place in Switzerland. Really, we travelled all over the world."

"Sounds exciting."

"More like exhausting." Sabastien's shoulders visibly relaxed.

"How do you know Vaughn?"

"That is a long story."

"I've got time."

Before Sabastien could answer, Vaughn appeared in the doorway. "You all settled in?"

"Wasn't much to settle," Sedona answered.

Vaughn had changed into a pair of worn jeans and a t-shirt. While the jeans fit her well, Sedona mused that she preferred the shorts Vaughn wore earlier—they showed off her well-developed quad muscles to perfection.

"What have you done to my nice, neat office, genius?"

"You told me to set up."

Sedona watched the dynamics between Vaughn and Sabastien. It reminded her of what she imagined it would be like to have a sibling. Vaughn treated Sabastien like a younger brother.

"Listen, before everyone else gets here, there's something you should know." Vaughn stepped fully into the room and held Sedona's gaze.

"Okay."

"The president told you—"

"Wait! Elliott, perhaps I should leave the room?"

"No, Sabastien. Stay where you are."

Sedona wondered at the look of misery that crossed his face.

"As I started to say, the president told you that he'd vetted you and reviewed your account of what happened the night of the incident at the NSA."

"Yes." Out of the corner of her eye, Sedona watched as Sabastien literally crawled back under the desk.

"Well, the computer expert the president referenced is that geek hiding like a coward under my desk." Vaughn gave Sabastien's backside a nudge with her foot. "You can come out now, coward."

Sedona turned this information over in her mind. That meant Sabastien knew a great deal about her, including details about her personal life, all of which would've been included in her personnel files. The NSA was notorious for its thorough scrutiny of employees. Every hire was required to undergo a rigorous background check, psychological screening, and interviews with multiple managers. He saw all of that.

"I am sorry," Sabastien said, wringing his hands. "I was not trying to pry. It was my job."

Sedona realized discomfort must be showing on her face. She smiled wanly. "It's okay. I guess if someone had to rifle through my life, I'd rather it was someone I knew than some complete stranger."

"It feels a little weird, though. No?"

"A little."

"If it is any consolation, your credit record is excellent."

Sedona laughed. "Gee, thanks. Good to know."

Vaughn cleared her throat. "In the interest of full disclosure, Sabastien called to talk to me about your case before the president asked me to help."

"I never revealed your name." Sabastien's face was bright red. "Honest."

"I believe you," Sedona said.

"He was upset because it seemed like you were in a lot of danger. He wanted my opinion as to whether or not you were okay."

"And?" Sedona tried and failed to read what was in Vaughn's eyes.

"I told him the truth. I didn't know. But it seemed to me that you were resourceful enough to make it out of the building and get the information directly into the hands of the president. That's no mean feat. So I suspected you knew how to handle yourself."

"I see."

"So you are not mad?" Sabastien asked.

"You were looking out for me, right?"

"Yes. Exactly."

"Then how can I be mad?" Sedona looked from Vaughn to Sabastien and back again. "Will you excuse me a moment?"

Sedona walked quickly down the hall and out onto the deck that overlooked the ocean. She grabbed the wooden railing and took several deep breaths, trying to calm herself. As an employee of the NSA, she wasn't privy to her own personnel file, so she had no idea how thorough the information was. Did Sabastien read her psych evaluation? Did he know about Rachel? Could he see her pain on the page? And if so, had he shared any or all of that with Vaughn?

She wasn't sure which was more disconcerting, knowing that Sabastien might have seen her life laid bare, or the possibility that he shared those private details with Vaughn.

"You know—" The voice behind her startled Sedona. "Sabastien really was worried for your safety and well being."

"I'm sure he was." Sedona continued to look out at the ocean. She wasn't ready to face Vaughn just yet.

Vaughn came along side her. "Whatever you're thinking, you can stop now." Vaughn placed her hand on the railing adjacent to Sedona's, but refrained from touching her. "Sabastien didn't tell me anything other than the circumstances of that night and the fact that you'd been in the field many times. That's all. I swear."

Sedona finally turned enough so that she could see into Vaughn's eyes. She was telling the truth. "Did you get the sense that Sabastien knew a lot more?"

Vaughn appeared to weigh the possibility. "I've known Sabastien a long time. He's not a curious kind of guy. He does what he's tasked to do. Nothing more. He's no voyeur. People usually don't interest him. It's all about the data—the machines."

Sedona nodded. That jibed with what she had observed of him.

"But I have to say, it's the most worried about another human being I've ever seen Sabastien. When it comes to women, he's a little like a child. I suspect he's not your type, so if you're not interested, please be kind and don't break his heart."

Sedona stood there with her mouth open as Vaughn walked away.

✥

"Since we can't be sure when the images Sedona saw were taken, I've asked Sabastien to get us some fresh images of Tuwaitha. Also, some additional footage from the area at the NSA where Sedona worked," Vaughn explained as the team gathered around behind the computer screens.

"You got into the NSA's security system without setting off any alarms?" Sedona asked. She stood just to Sabastien's right with her hand on the back of his chair.

"I did." Sabastien sat up a little straighter. "When I was in there for the President, I left myself a back hallway."

"Back door," Vaughn said.

"*Quoi?*"

"Back door, Mr. America. It's a 'back door,' not a 'back hallway.'"

"As you say." Sabastien waved Vaughn away and returned to the task at hand, his fingers flying across two keyboards.

"Okay. What are we looking at?" Peter asked.

"As soon as I am done borrowing this Russian satellite, coming up on the far left, you will see an aerial view of Tuwaitha. The two right screens will be inside the NSA."

"You're hijacking a Russian satellite?" Lorraine asked.

"I prefer to think I am leasing it."

"How long before they notice?" Justine asked.

"A minute or two at most."

"What do we need to key in on?" Vaughn turned to Sedona, who was paying avid attention to what Sabastien was doing. Her brow was furrowed in concentration.

"I'll know it when I see it, but I would focus on the two large buildings toward the back of the complex. The rest of the structures are for storage and administration."

"Okay, Genius. You heard the woman." Vaughn positioned herself behind Sabastien's left shoulder. She caught a hint of Sedona's perfume. It was clean, fresh, and enticing. Vaughn moved farther away from her.

Several images filled the two left screens. Sedona moved in for a closer look. "There," she pointed to a spot on the second screen. "Can you get us a different view of that?"

"I will try."

"If you can somehow get a ground view, or at least zoom in so we can distinguish what those trucks are and what's on that rooftop…"

Sabastien manipulated the mouse with one hand while clicking several keys on one of the keyboards. The view on the left monitor changed. As it did, a series of loud beeps erupted.

"*Merde*."

"What is it?" Lorraine asked.

"We tripped a sensor," Peter explained.

"On the satellite system?"

"No. It is not coming from there." Sabastien's voice was tight as his fingers worked furiously at the keys. Within seconds, the screens went black. He sat back, sweat beading his forehead.

"What just happened there?" Justine asked.

"Somebody did not appreciate us poking around." Sabastien said.

"Why did the screens go black? Did we lose the satellite link?" Sabastien shook his head.

"Someone on the ground blocked us," Peter offered.

"Yes." Sabastien agreed. "But that should not have been possible."

"What are you saying?" Vaughn asked.

"Whoever this is, they have very sophisticated equipment. Big bucks," Peter said. "The ability on site to detect and scramble a satellite taking pictures from space."

"But I have never heard such a thing is possible," Sabastien said.

Vaughn had never seen Sabastien baffled by technology before, and his expression worried her. Peter, too, looked grim.

"The technology's been around," Peter said, "but very few people know about it."

"Any idea who might be on the short list?" Lorraine asked.

"Nope. All I know is that the price tag is exorbitant."

"How expensive?" Sedona asked.

"More than the economies of many countries I could name."

"That eliminates some dissident Iraqi group as the source of the activity," Justine said.

"Unless they're being backed by some other deep-pocketed source."

"Let's worry about that after we deal with the more immediate problem," Vaughn said.

"What's that?" Sedona asked.

"We're flying blind with no visual intel on Tuwaitha."

"I did not say that, Elliott." Sabastien smiled a boyish grin. "I was able to capture some still images." He turned as one of the printers spit out several sheets of paper.

CHAPTER SIX

The man sprinted out of the elevator and down the hallway, barely pausing at the receptionist's desk to be acknowledged. When the receptionist nodded at him to go in, he burst through the heavy oak door. "We have something."

Disconcerting pale blue eyes glowered over the top of a pair of reading glasses. "After so much time, it better be good."

"I think you'll be well pleased."

The expression in the man's eyes hardened even more. "I'll be the judge of that."

"The new equipment you had installed worked. At 1345 yesterday the system detected an intrusion."

The man behind the desk showed no reaction except to put both hands on the desk, palms down, his fingers slightly curled. "And?"

"It blocked access to the satellite."

"And?" The man leaned forward.

"It registered the satellite and tracked the signal back to an address."

"Where?" Now the man was practically vibrating out of his seat.

"A house on a remote island in the Caribbean."

"Who owns it?"

"We don't know."

"What does that mean?"

"We're still tracking it down. We think it belongs to someone who doesn't exist."

"But you have the address."

"Yes, sir."

"Give it to me." The piece of paper in his hand, the man rocked back in his chair. "And it took you twenty-four hours to tell me about this because…"

"Sir, we wanted to be sure what we had." Sweat started to stain his underarms. "We didn't want to bother you with a potential false reading. Also, we thought you'd prefer to know once we had more information about the owner of the house."

"You know what your first mistake was?" The man asked, his voice perfectly pleasant.

"Sir?" The sweat trickled down his sides.

"Thinking." The man pulled out a World War II vintage .45 caliber Ruger with a short-nosed silencer.

"Sir?" The pain lasted only a second.

❧

"Miss Vaughn?"

"What is it, Michel?" Michel and his father did maintenance work and odd jobs for Vaughn. Michel often came over to talk to her. Vaughn liked him—a lot. He had a curiosity about the world and an innocent point of view she envied.

The slight boy's deep chocolate skin was slick with sweat and he bent over to catch his breath.

"Remember," he began, pausing to gulp in air. "Remember you told me and Papa always to keep our eyes open and to tell you if ever we saw or noticed anything out of the ordinary?"

"Yes." Vaughn looked at Michel more closely. He was disheveled. Vaughn instantly surveyed the area around the front of her home and touched the gun tucked into the back of her shorts. "Where are you coming from?"

"The airport. I ran all the way, as fast as I could."

Vaughn raised her eyebrows. The airport was three miles away.

"I was bringing Papa something to eat," he continued. "He was working his shift at the airport rental counter." Michel sucked in another breath. "Six men. All white, all with mean faces. One with a scar. They rented two SUVs and asked about the road leading here. Three big bags. They wouldn't let Papa touch them, but they seemed heavy."

Michel blinked his big, brown eyes at Vaughn. "Papa thought you would want to know, so he helped me slip out the back when the men turned away. He said to tell you he's delaying them as long as he can and he disabled the GPS units in the cars and gave them bad directions."

"How long ago did all this happen?"

"I came straight away."

Vaughn calculated that the group would be about fifteen minutes away, assuming they had GPS capability on their phones. *Shit.*

"Did I do good, Miss Vaughn?" Michel's chest finally had stopped heaving.

She patted him on the head. "You did great, Michel. Your Papa too. Tell him not to take any more chances, okay? I want the two of you to stay inside until tomorrow. No exceptions."

"But Papa's shift will not be over for another five hours."

"I know. Please, Michel. This is very important. Go right home, close the blinds, and don't answer the door for anyone." Vaughn could see the confusion in his eyes. She put her hand on his arm. "Do you understand?"

He nodded.

"Your Papa will be home soon. Go right now. Stay off the road and out of sight. Run up the beach, instead."

Vaughn turned to go back into the house.

"Miss Vaughn?"

"Yes?"

"Are you going to be okay?"

Vaughn winked. "You bet. But I may not see you guys for a while. I want you to stay away from my house until I tell you it's okay." She reached down and gave Michel a quick hug. She really did like this kid. "Now get going."

She waited until he'd run around the back of the house toward the beach. Then she took out her cell phone and dialed a number. "Alain? It's Vaughn. I need you to do something for me, and then I need you to go home right away and stay out of sight until those men leave the island. Please don't ask me questions, we don't have time."

❖❖

"Are you sure about this?" Sedona asked. "This isn't really necessary. When they realize no one is here, they'll search the place, gather whatever intel they can, and take off."

"Maybe that's the way you work in the NSA, but where I come from, we don't take any chances." Vaughn's fingers worked swiftly and surely as she packed the explosives and carefully molded them to the inside of her desk drawer.

Sedona *was* sure, but she had no intention of explaining to Vaughn her connection to Archangel Michael and the fact that she'd already asked for, and received, guidance about the impending attack.

"This is your home. Why would you be willing to destroy that?"

"Because she feels violated. This was a haven and once those men cross the threshold, her heretofore separate worlds will collide."

Sedona acknowledged Archangel Michael's answer in her head, but she wanted to know if Vaughn would tell her.

"Okay. Time to go." Vaughn affixed the blasting cap into the C-4 and pocketed the key-fob-sized remote control.

"Guess not," Sedona mumbled.

"What?"

"Nothing."

Vaughn took her by the arm and hustled her out the door and around to the side of the house. They found the others waiting by the separate three-car garage. Everyone was there except for Sabastien.

"He's not done yet?" Vaughn asked.

"I am here!" Sabastien hurried up, out of breath. "I am here." He dragged three large bags behind him.

"Is it done?" Vaughn asked.

"Oui. Everything is in place. I just need to get the rest of the equipment."

"I'll help you." Sedona started to head back into the house.

"No. I'll do it," Peter offered. He and Sabastien took off.

"Make it quick," Vaughn called after them. "T minus four minutes. We need to get out of here." Vaughn faced the rest of the group. "Can you three get all this stuff into the garage and load the 4x4? Here are the keys." Vaughn tossed the keys to Justine.

"Where are we going?" Justine asked.

"You, Lorraine, Peter, and Sedona are going to the airport. Head due east on the beach for about six miles, then turn south. That will take you to a back access road. It's the long way around, but it's less conspicuous. Someone will be there to open the gate for you. His name is Jacques. He's a pilot. The plane is being prepped right now. Go with him."

"What about you and Sabastien?" Lorraine asked.

"We've got something we need to do. We'll catch up to you later."

"Nothing doing," Sedona said.

"I don't have time to argue with you." Vaughn's eyes flashed. "We all stay together."

"The Jeep can't hold all of us, and, in case you've forgotten, I'm calling the shots here."

"We stand a better chance…" Sedona stopped talking when Justine touched her lightly on the arm and subtly shook her head. "Right." Sedona slung two bags over her shoulder and used enough force to open the side door to the garage that it slammed against the building, echoing loudly behind her. At the moment, she was too angry to care.

"You two go around back. Keep the coms open, but maintain silence unless absolutely necessary."

"You want anyone alive?"

"Only long enough to find out what they know. Then we waste them."

Vaughn's left eye twitched and she tightened her grip on the handle of her Glock. The gesture was empty, since she and Sabastien were situated several hundred yards away and down a slight incline behind a craggy rock formation, but it made her feel better. "How many rooms can we see at once with this thing?" She jabbed the laptop monitor with a finger.

"I did not have a lot of time to set up, so only six." Sabastien manipulated a joystick with his right hand and the view changed.

With a few clicks of the mouse with his left hand, the screen split to show views of Vaughn's office, the living room, the library, the kitchen, her bedroom, and outside her front door.

"Do we have sound in every location?"

"*Oui.*"

"Good job."

"Did you just compliment me?" Sabastien spared Vaughn a sideways glance. His face lit up with almost childlike wonder.

"Don't push your luck." Vaughn frowned. She really did appreciate Sabastien's many skills, despite her gruff manner with him. She supposed she ought to tell him more often. Wasn't that part of what drove Sage away? Vaughn's inability to connect on a deep level with anyone? Her 'emotional inaccessibility?' She shook her head to clear it. It wouldn't do to dwell on something she felt powerless to change. She tuned back in to what Sabastien was saying.

"But you can only hear sound from a single location at a time."

"Okay." Vaughn pointed to the man who appeared to be in charge. "Stay on this guy in terms of sound."

"Walt, Scott. You two go left. Frank and I will go right." The man giving instructions pointed his gun at the door lock. "Everybody ready?" When he saw assenting nods, he fired, splintering the lock.

Vaughn growled.

"I am sorry about the intrusion into your house, Elliott." Sabastien's tone was sympathetic.

Vaughn did not want to think about it now. So instead, she did what she did best—she focused on the job at hand.

The two teams in the main house methodically swept through the rooms. "All clear here."

"Here too." The lead man tapped his earpiece. "Nick? Anything in the outbuildings?"

"Negative."

"Okay, get in here and we'll turn this place upside down."

The heat rose in Vaughn's chest and radiated outward as she watched these strangers paw through her things, turn over drawers and use switchblades to slice open upholstery. She struggled to keep her breaths even and her temper under control. This was her sanctuary—the place where she'd come to escape the very world these thugs represented.

"I do not know how you are watching this. It is breaking my heart and it is not even my home." Sabastien averted his eyes from the screen.

"I need to ascertain their proficiency and exactly what it is they're after." Vaughn's finger twitched on the remote. "Can you zoom in on that?" She pointed to the section of the screen that showed her office. "I want to see the kind of files they're looking for and the level of their computer skills." She already had determined that their weapons and communications equipment were state-of-the-art. That was consistent with the technological ability to track Sabastien's satellite reconnaissance at Tuwaitha and confirmed what she already knew—these guys were part of the same outfit.

Sabastien manipulated the joystick and the image zoomed in on Vaughn's computer monitor. The two of them watched in silence as one of the underlings sat down and started clicking keys. In less than a minute, he had broken Vaughn's password.

"*Merde.*"

"I thought you said this system was hacker proof." She looked accusingly at Sabastien.

"No system is completely foolproof, although in this case, this man is no fool."

"What is he doing now?"

"Looking for hidden files and keystrokes," Sabastien said.

Vaughn waited only a moment longer, until all six men were huddled together in the office. "Get down," she said to Sabastien, her voice husky with emotion. When the team leader pulled out his cell phone, she ducked and depressed the red key on the remote.

The explosion lit up the sky, showering the debris of Vaughn's life in a wide swath extending outward. When the dust settled she asked, "You okay?"

"*Mon Dieu*, Elliott." He was shaking.

"Are you hurt?" She looked him over.

"No."

"Okay, then. Let's get out of here." She jumped up and pulled him with her. Without a backward glance, she set off at a jog down the path and toward the four-wheeler she had hidden in the underbrush. There would be time later to mourn the loss of her personal paradise. Right now, they needed to regroup and figure out the next steps. One thing was clear—whatever Sedona had stumbled into, she had made some powerful enemies.

✎∽∾

"When was the last time you heard from them?" The woman pinched the bridge of her nose as she sifted through the documents on her lap. The limousine hit a pothole, forcing her to lunge forward to stop the cascade of paper onto the floor. She glared at the driver in the rearview mirror.

"Three hours?" she screamed into her Bluetooth. She listened for a moment. "Absolutely not! If we send another team in there, we risk compounding this disaster. How many extraction points and times have they missed?" She closed her eyes at the answer. "Do we have any eyes on the ground? Any way to get a visual without using traceable technology or sticking out like a sore thumb?" She frowned. "Don't start flashing a lot of money around, but find some local whose wife needs an expensive surgery or something. Let me know what you find out."

She clicked off the Bluetooth and laid her head back against the seat. This was not good. Not good at all. Out of the corner of her eye, she saw the Capitol come into view and gathered up her papers. She would have to deal with it later.

✎∽∾

"Alain, Michel," Vaughn called as she knocked on the door of the modest bungalow.

Michel peeked through the wooden blinds, his big eyes blinking at her.

"It's okay. Let me in." Vaughn had instructed Sabastien to stay out of sight. There was no point making this any more complicated than it already was.

The door cracked open and Vaughn stepped inside. "Where's your father?"

"I am here, Miss Vaughn." Alain came into the room, wiping his hands on a rag. "I came home straight away, as you suggested once I secured the chartered plane for you."

"Were you able to keep it off the books?"

"Yes, Miss Vaughn. There will be no record of the flight or the passengers."

"Thanks, Alain. You did good." She could see the questions in his eyes but knew that Alain would not press her for information that she was not willing to give. Still, she would have to tell him something. Even if six nefarious men hadn't shown up at the airport looking for directions to her place, and even if the fireball from the explosion hadn't been visible in the sky for miles around, the hole in the ground where her house had stood was undeniable proof that something was amiss.

"Miss Vaughn?" It was Michel who broke the awkward silence.

"Yes?"

"Are you a good guy or a bad guy?"

Vaughn rocked back on her heels as though she'd been slapped.

"Michel," Alain warned.

Vaughn held up a hand. "It's okay." She crouched in front of the boy. "Why do you ask?"

"On TV, I saw this movie with Jason Bourne. I think he was a good guy, but everybody thought he was a bad guy and they were all trying to kill him."

"I see." Vaughn pretended to consider the matter. "In that case, I guess I've got a lot in common with your friend Jason."

"So… You're a good guy then but people don't know it?"

Vaughn cupped Michel's chin in her hand and stood up. "Something like that. But this isn't a movie, young man, and I need you to do something for me."

His eyes got wide. "Anything."

"I need you to keep this our secret. No one can know anything about this, okay?"

He straightened up as tall as he could. "You can count on me, Miss Vaughn." He made a motion as if to zip his lips as she released his chin.

"Go on now, Michel. You've bothered Miss Vaughn enough."

The boy reluctantly headed down the hall toward his room, but stopped halfway there. "Miss Vaughn?"

"Yes?"

"Will I ever see you again?"

Tears sprang unexpectedly to Vaughn's eyes and she hurriedly blinked them away. "I don't know, Michel. I hope so."

He ran back to her and threw his skinny little arms around her waist. Without thought, she returned the gesture. It was Alain who pried Michel's arms loose and shooed him away.

"I'm sorry about that."

"He's just a boy," Vaughn said. "And his question was fair." She looked Alain in the eye. "Those men will never threaten or bother anyone on the island again. If anybody asks, there was a gas leak in the stove, but it would be best if the constable didn't open a full investigation." She waited for this to sink in. "Do you understand me?"

"I do." His eyes were solemn and sad. "Where will you go now?"

"I don't know. I have some things I have to do." She reached into her pocket and pulled out a slip of paper with a phone number on it. "This is for you. If you ever need me, call this number."

"Okay."

"If anyone comes around asking questions about who lived in my house—"

"I will tell them I don't have any idea, as will everyone else on the island."

"You're a good man, Alain. And you're raising a fine boy. Keep him out of trouble."

"I will certainly try."

Vaughn clapped him on the arm, letting her fingers linger for a fraction of a second. He and Michel were the closest thing she'd ever had to a family. As with the house, she would process all of these losses later. In the middle of battle, there is no time to grieve.

CHAPTER SEVEN

S edona sat in the last seat in the back of the plane, apart from the rest of the group, her arms folded tightly across her chest. She couldn't remember the last time she'd been this angry. The problem was, she wasn't sure why she was so steamed or what to do about it. She leaned her head back against the headrest and closed her eyes.

"You're pissed because you're worried about the dame."

"Dame? Really, Dom?" she asked the question in her head. *"What are you, some 1950s gumshoe? What 'dame'?"*

"The Elliott dame."

"That's ridiculous. Vaughn is a big girl. She can take care of herself."

"You got that right. But I think you're a little sweet on her and so you're worried. It's kinda cute."

"You don't know what you're talking about."

"So you say. I guess we'll see. Lemme know when you figure it out."

Sedona opened her eyes and watched out the window as a puffy, white cloud drifted by. As she usually did after a chat with one of her guides, she weighed and measured the truth of the information. Could Dom really be right? Was she attracted to Vaughn?

Certainly Vaughn was an attractive woman, but Sedona met many good-looking women. None of them were Rachel and none of them ever would be. That, alone, was enough to negate any romantic consideration. The familiar wave of pain clutched at Sedona's heart. It hit her with such force that it nearly knocked the wind out of her. She sucked in a deep breath through her nose and slowly let it out through her mouth.

Archangel Azrael, please, heal my heart. Please, bring me comfort and relief from this grief. I have a job to do right now. I need to be able to focus completely on that. Please take the pain away so I can concentrate on the tasks at hand.

"Are you okay?"

Sedona started. Justine was standing over her. "I'm fine." She said it perfunctorily and more sharply than she intended.

"Mind if I sit down?" Justine gestured to the empty aisle seat.

"Not at all."

The silence lasted less than a minute. "I know you weren't happy with the way things went back at the house."

Sedona shrugged. "It's Vaughn's op. She can run it any way she wants."

Justine nodded slowly. "I've known Vaughn a long time. She's been through a lot. Heck, we've been through a lot together."

Sedona turned to directly face Justine. Had she and Vaughn been an item? Were they still? How could she have missed that?

"It's not like that," Justine said, as if she could see the questions in Sedona's mind. "Vaughn and I were professional colleagues. We were also personal friends."

"Were?"

"Are, I guess. But I haven't seen Vaughn in a while. No one has. After the last op, she pretty much disappeared. She didn't want to be found."

Sedona considered how much she should ask. She wanted to know everything, but she wasn't sure that would be Vaughn's desire. "Did the op go badly?"

Justine chewed her lower lip. "Yes and no. It's complicated."

"You don't have to tell me."

"The main objectives were achieved. A major international plot was foiled, a kidnap victim was rescued, and some very bad operators got put away for a long time."

"But?" Sedona asked quietly.

"But the price was high. Vaughn lost a good friend in the process, and she very nearly lost her own life."

"I'm sorry."

"Me too."

It felt to Sedona as if Justine wanted to say more, but was unsure whether it was appropriate.

"Anyway, this is just by way of explaining to you that Vaughn has mixed feelings about accepting this assignment. I don't think she ever intended to get back in the game. If the president himself hadn't asked, I don't think she would have."

"I see. So, in some measure, it's my fault she's not enjoying a Mai Tai on her back deck overlooking the ocean right now."

"I didn't mean it that way," Justine said.

"I know. But it's the truth."

"I'm sure Vaughn doesn't see it that way."

Sedona wasn't so certain.

"Okay, folks. We're starting our descent. Better get those belts fastened," the pilot announced.

Sedona looked out the window at the crystal clear ocean below. She wasn't even positive where they were or where they were going. Somehow, that seemed fitting.

"Kate. It's Vaughn." Vaughn switched the cell phone from her left hand to her right as she maneuvered through the gate to the marina and down the steps to the dock, where a powerboat was idling in a slip. Sabastien trailed behind her.

"Hey. Miss us already?"

"You wish."

"I can hardly hear you. What's all that noise?"

"It's a boat engine. Listen, something's come up. I'm sorry, but I think it'd be best if you cut your vacation short."

"What's going on?"

Vaughn briefed Kate on the events of the day. When she was done, there was silence on the other end of the line.

"Kate? Are you still there?"

"I'm here. I feel like this is my fault for getting you into this," Kate said. "You blew up your own house? Oh, Vaughn."

Vaughn closed her eyes. She didn't want to hear the sorrow or sympathy in Kate's tone. She didn't want to think about what she'd done at all.

"Yeah, well. I signed up for this gig." She cleared her suddenly dry throat. "As far as I could tell, they never made contact with anyone after they arrived at the house, but I can't be positive about that, and I don't want to take a chance with anyone making a connection between your presence on the island and me. I know it sucks," Vaughn rushed on, "but I can't be sure they won't send another team. Also, we're going to be on the move, and I'm going to need someone to brief the president for me. Will you do that?"

"Sure. I'll just let Jay know that we need to pack up. She's going to be really disappointed. We spent the day diving on the other side of the island near the coral reef. It was magical."

"Yeah," Vaughn said quietly, "that was one of my favorite places to dive."

"Damn, Vaughn. I know you wouldn't have destroyed the house if you didn't think it was absolutely necessary—"

"It was." Vaughn didn't mean to snap, but Kate was beginning to sound like Sedona. Vaughn frowned. She wondered if Sedona still was as angry as she appeared to be when the 4x4 pulled out of the drive. *Why do you care?* Vaughn tried to shrug it off. The problem was she did care. In fact, she cared quite a bit about Sedona, what she thought, how she felt... Vaughn stowed a duffle bag under one of the bench seats, kicking it into place with more force than was necessary. "Listen, I've got to get going."

"No problem." Kate's tone was clipped.

Shit. "Like I said, Kate, I'm really sorry. These guys are pros, and whoever they're working for doesn't seem to be on a budget. I just think it's best not to tempt fate, you know?"

"Gotcha. We'll get on a flight for the States tonight. I'll fill the president in as soon as I can get an appointment." Kate was all business now.

"Right." Vaughn wondered how many more allies she was going to piss off before the day was over. "I think it's best if I reach out to you, rather than vice versa. That way we can keep the communications more secure."

"Of course."

"Kate—"

"Stay safe, Vaughn."

Vaughn held the dead line away from her ear. "What a crappy day."

"What is that, Elliott?" Sabastien was squinting in the bright sunshine.

"Nothing. We need to cast off. Are you ready?"

"Ay, ay, Captain." Sabastien gave a mock salute. "You own this boat?" He looked around and whistled appreciatively. "It is beautiful."

"Yeah. Now sit your ass down. This is going to be a bumpy ride." By her calculation, they could reach the mainland just before nightfall and meet up with the rest of the group for dinner. By then, Vaughn mused, she might have figured out a plan.

"Apparently it's nothing but a hole in the ground with teeny tiny bits of furniture strewn here and there." The woman's hair blew wildly in the sharp breeze off the Potomac. She pulled up the collar of her Burberry coat.

"That's most unfortunate. Any sign of our team?" The man with the pale blue eyes stared off into the distance.

"Nothing. I think we have to assume they're lost."

"You think?" The man emphasized the *k*. As he turned to face her, she could see the flint in his gaze.

"Astin. Those men were all battle-tested war heroes. They were hand picked for the assignment. Whatever was going on at that place and whoever owned it, it's obvious the Ramos woman—and I emphasize that we're assuming the satellite intrusion has to do with the Ramos woman—has some powerful allies of her own."

"Again," Astin said, "most unfortunate. Did we at least get a report from the field prior to losing contact?"

"The last check-in occurred shortly before they arrived onsite. Nothing after that. No data was uploaded, no cell phone transmissions were received."

"So you're telling me we have absolutely nothing."

"I didn't say that." The woman risked reaching out and touching him on the sleeve. At one time, they had been more than colleagues—they were young, passionate lovers, both on the path to greatness. But that was a long time ago.

Astin recoiled. "Out with it then."

The woman swallowed her regrets. "All right. Our source was able to relay that at least seven people had arrived within several days of the satellite incident."

"Interesting. Do we have pictures?"

The woman shook her head. "No, but we believe the group included two men and five women."

"And this source has not seen them since?"

"No. It's as if they disappeared. Perhaps our men took them out?"

"If they had, they'd still be alive, now wouldn't they?" Astin pushed off the railing and started to walk away.

"Wait!"

He turned to face her.

"What's next?"

"You'll know when you need to know. In the meantime, do be a dear and get that oil pipeline through your damn committee, will you?"

The woman stared after him, wondering what had happened to all their young, idealistic dreams and when it had come to this.

❧❧

Sedona picked at her salad as the conversation washed over her.

"Are you okay?"

Justine nudged her arm and Sedona mustered a smile.

"Fine."

"Well, that poor piece of lettuce certainly isn't. I think you've stabbed it to death by now."

That surprised a laugh out of her. "Yeah, well, I always say, 'The only good lettuce is a dead lettuce.'"

"Catchy."

"I'm thinking of copyrighting it so no one else takes it."

"Better hurry. That'll be a hot one." Justine reached over and speared a cherry tomato off of Sedona's plate.

"Hey!"

"What? You weren't eating it." Justine made a face as if to emphasize just how good the tomato was. "Want to talk about it?"

"About what?"

Justine rolled her eyes. "Okay. Let's try something else. Can I ask you a few questions?"

"That depends."

"On?"

"What's the topic?"

"Background."

Sedona stopped even pretending to eat.

"I'll go first," Justine offered. "I'm an East coast girl. I live in Maryland when I'm home, which isn't nearly often enough. I had no aspirations to be a CIA officer. They found me. I was a trauma nurse working out of an insanely busy emergency room. Lots of gunshot wounds and stabbings. Blood and guts everywhere. I guess they thought that would be good preparation for war zones and ops gone bad."

"So they just approached you out of the blue?" Sedona asked.

"Pretty much. I was doing triage on the late shift on a particularly busy night. I'd just finished sewing up some gangbanger on his third visit in a week. I walked out of his bay and over to the sterile sink to wash myself up. This man came up alongside me and took me by the elbow. He asked if he could buy me a cup of coffee, even as he was already leading me toward the cafeteria."

"That was pretty presumptuous."

"No kidding. I was about to tell him to go pound salt when he pulled out this very official-looking ID. He said something very trite about making me an offer I wouldn't want to refuse. He promised to get me away from that depressing hospital. Told me I could do something good and important for my country. The rest, as they say, is history."

"Just like that?"

Justine shrugged. "Pretty much. I quit the next day. Two days after that, I was in training. Six months after that, I was on my first assignment—an op in Cairo. That's where I met Sara and Vaughn."

Sedona's head snapped up. "Who's Sara?" She could feel the shift in Justine's energy before she saw Justine squirm in her seat.

"I probably shouldn't—"

"That's okay. It's none of my business." Sedona could feel the war raging within Justine. "Really. It's all right."

"Your life may depend on Vaughn. I guess that entitles you to know something about what makes her tick."

Justine squirmed some more, and Sedona resisted the urge to let her off the hook. She very much wanted to know more about Vaughn—a lot more. She doubted that Vaughn would talk freely about herself. That just didn't fit with the stoic, self-contained person Sedona had seen thus far.

"Sara was Vaughn's best friend, her college sweetheart, the one constant in Vaughn's life." Justine stared down at the table. "She was killed a couple of years ago, right in front of Vaughn's eyes, and Vaughn couldn't stop it."

Sedona gasped and put her hand to her heart. "Oh, my God. That's horrible."

"Vaughn's never forgiven herself. That event changed her in profound ways. I don't know that she'll ever be the same again."

Sedona quickly processed this information. It explained a lot. The holes in Vaughn's aura, the leakage from her heart chakra, the emotional wounds that Sedona saw when they first met, her gruff nature. So much pain. Sedona closed her eyes against it. When she opened them again, Justine glanced at her with a knowing look.

"That's such a sad story," Sedona said quietly. "I hope you're wrong about the last part."

"I hope so too," Justine said. "But I haven't seen any signs of it." She put her napkin on the table. "Your turn."

Sedona took a deep breath, buying herself time as she decided how much she should say. Fortunately, she was saved from having to say anything at all.

"Okay, folks. We've got a lot to figure out, so we might as well get started." Vaughn leaned her elbows on the table. "Here's what we know. There's clearly something going on at a closed nuclear facility in a war zone. Someone, or more likely, a group of people really doesn't want anyone poking around. Somehow, this is connected, at least peripherally, to the NSA or someone at the NSA. Whoever has a stake in this has got large amounts of money and access to seriously advanced technology. They've also got real pros, probably with military experience, on their payroll." She looked around the table. "Am I missing anything?"

"That about sums it up," Lorraine said.

"So where do we go from here?" Justine asked.

"Seems to me the one solid lead we have is the facility itself," Peter said. "It's the one place we know for sure we'll find more clues."

"True," Vaughn agreed. "But it's a big risk. We already know they've got the technology to detect a satellite focusing in on the place from space. I think it's a safe bet they could track humans on the ground with no trouble at all."

"I'm not sure we have an alternative. If we can't use advanced technology ourselves to get a look, we're going to have to do it the old-fashioned way." Sedona gestured to Sabastien. "I assume without actual human intervention, there is no more effective means to get a look at Tuwaitha, right?"

"Just so."

"Anyone else?" Vaughn asked. "All right. I guess that's settled then. I'll contact the powers that be and get us the gear once you all come up with a list of what we'll need." She made eye contact with each member of the team. "Next stop, Iraq."

CHAPTER EIGHT

We can't go in there without an expert in uranium enrichment," Peter said. He and Vaughn stood outside on the veranda of the condominium that had once functioned as one of Vaughn's safe houses. "We won't have the first clue what we're looking at. It's not enough to know who's running the show over there, or even who's behind this. We have to know what it is they're doing and how serious a threat it poses."

"I agree, but you understand my reluctance."

"I do. It means bringing in someone none of us knows. We'd be taking a chance on making ourselves vulnerable."

"I think it's fair to assume that if these people have the kind of resources we believe, and if what's going on at Tuwaitha involves the facility's original purpose, which is uranium refinement and production, they must also have scientists onboard who are running the operation over there."

"True," Peter said, "but they can't have every uranium enrichment specialist on their payroll. Maybe we should wait until we get over there and then reach out to someone in the Middle East."

"As opposed to an American, you mean?"

"Well, we already know that whoever is running the show has a connection to the NSA. The team that trashed your house was speaking English with an American accent…"

Vaughn nodded, her respect for Peter growing. "You're right. There'd be much less of a risk by going foreign." She let the idea sit for a minute, considering all the angles. "Not only that, but it would mean we wouldn't have to carry the person with us. We'd pick him up over there, which would also limit our exposure."

"That was my thinking."

The more time she spent with him, the more Vaughn realized what an asset it was to have a seasoned veteran like Peter to strategize with. He was good. Very good. A critical thinker who paid attention to the big picture and always seemed to be looking several steps ahead. It was a luxury she hadn't often had in the field and one that most definitely would come in handy now.

"Okay. I'll shake the trees and see if I can come up with a list of potential names," Vaughn said.

"I'll call Kate with an update if you want. She's going to talk to the president tomorrow. It looks like we're going to need some supplies, the sanction to slip unofficially into and out of Iraq, and some resources."

Vaughn pondered that for a moment. "Do you think the president wants to know that level of detail? I suspect he might prefer to have plausible deniability."

"Yeah. Now that I think about it, you're right. If he doesn't have actual knowledge of our plans or our whereabouts, he can honestly disavow any connection to us if things go sour."

They were both quiet then, as the very real possibility of getting caught or killed hung in the air between them.

"Hey. Why does it feel like a funeral out here? I mean, it's not like we're heading off to the most volatile region in the world to stop some evil plan to blow up humanity or anything," Lorraine joked, as she stepped out onto the veranda to join them.

"Nope. After all, that would be crazy, right?" Peter said.

Lorraine elbowed Peter in the ribs. "You're not going to make me save your life again, are you?"

"Heaven forbid. That pause for thought was just me trying to decide if I brought enough clean underwear," Peter said.

"Oh, no wonder you're so serious. That's a critical question, for sure."

Vaughn could see that Peter and Lorraine had real chemistry. She wondered if that was only professional. While she knew the broad outlines of the Hyland case, she suspected there were a lot of things that weren't in the file. In addition, Lorraine's reference to saving Peter's life intrigued her, as did the fact that he didn't seem to have any problem having been saved by a woman. Was that about the Hyland case too? Her curiosity drove her forward.

"I always like to know who I'm going into battle with," she ventured. "It's obvious you two know each other pretty well. If you don't mind my asking, how did that come to be?"

Peter and Lorraine looked at each other. It was Lorraine who answered. "I'm assuming you read the Hyland file as part of your training with the agency?"

Vaughn didn't see any sense denying it. "Yes."

"I figured. Every agent under the age of fifty I've ever met must have been forced to read that bleeping file."

"Well, it was legendary." It wasn't often that Vaughn felt like a fan girl, but if she were honest, Lorraine was the closest thing to a role model she had ever followed. Not that she would admit that out loud.

"Face it, King, you're a rock star." Peter poked Lorraine good-naturedly in the ribs.

"Somebody had to save you from yourself." She turned to Vaughn. "Mr. Macho over here was the oft-redacted person who orchestrated the hostage swap at the Lincoln Memorial. He nearly got himself killed in the process. Going in there without a vest. What were you thinking?"

A light went on for Vaughn as she remembered a detail from the Hyland case. "You were the agent that found and turned the doctor in charge of the president's supposed 'death'," she said.

"Correct." Peter wagged a finger at Lorraine. "As I recall, I was also the one who took out the unexpected guest—the last sniper. At the time I believe he might have been aiming at you."

"I don't know about that," Lorraine replied.

Yes, Vaughn thought, *these two definitely have chemistry.*

"Can I ask a question, if you don't mind?" All heads turned to see Sedona standing silently in the doorway.

Vaughn wondered how long she'd been standing there and how much she'd heard. Sedona had the unnerving habit of appearing like a ghost out of nowhere, completely undetected. Perhaps that would come in handy where they were going, but at the moment, Vaughn found it just plain disconcerting.

"Sure," Lorraine said.

"Are you two, by chance, married?"

That startled a chuckle out of Peter and Lorraine. Vaughn raised an eyebrow, marveling at the directness of the question she only dared ponder in her head. She watched with interest as unspoken communication passed between Peter and Lorraine.

In the end, it was Peter who answered. He reached out and took Lorraine's hand, squeezing it tenderly. "Yes. We've been married for close to twenty years."

Now, when Vaughn looked at them side-by-side, all pretext swept away, she plainly could see the adoration for each other in their eyes.

Sedona smiled at them. "I thought as much."

"What made you think so?" Lorraine asked. "We've kept it a closely guarded secret all this time so that no enemy combatant could use it as a weapon against us or perceive it as a weakness to be exploited. Even the president isn't aware of our marital status."

"I used my superpowers," Sedona breezily said as she walked back inside.

Vaughn and the couple stared after her. "What the heck was that all about?"

"I have no idea, but by God, I like that girl," Lorraine said.

"I like her too," Peter agreed.

Vaughn squirmed uncomfortably as the couple turned to her, waiting for her opinion. *I like her too. A lot more than I want to.* Vaughn's heart kicked hard and she felt alarm bells go off in her head. "She's certainly...different." Vaughn didn't like the knowing way Lorraine looked at her. "If you'll excuse me, I've got a lot to do to get us ready for our trip." She turned on her heel and retreated to her room.

Behind her, she heard Peter say, "What do you think is going on there?"

Vaughn was wondering the same thing.

The sand between her toes still carried the warmth of the day, even at sunset. Sedona stuffed her hands in her shorts pockets as she walked along. The sounds of the ocean lapping against the shore and the gulls calling soothed her jangled nerves as the wind pushed against her body. The breeze felt good on the exposed skin between the waistband of her shorts and the cropped top she wore.

What was it about Vaughn Elliott that so unsettled her? She wasn't the first strong, attractive woman Sedona had met since Rachel. She wasn't even the first female deep-cover agent Sedona had encountered. But there was something different about her, something Sedona couldn't easily define or dismiss. Something that got under her skin.

Archangels, angels, ascended masters, guides. Please help me to understand why Vaughn affects me so and please help me to know what it is, if anything, I'm meant to do about it. This I ask of you with your blessing, Amen.

"Hey!"

Sedona bent over and picked up a shell from the sand. She turned it over and placed it in the palm of her hand, marveling at its perfection.

"Hey!"

A hand grabbed Sedona by the arm from behind, startling her. She hadn't heard anyone approach. Reflexively, she stepped back hard onto the place where she estimated the person's instep to be.

"Damn it!" The hand tightened on the inside of her elbow, pressing against the ulnar nerve.

Sedona whirled to face her attacker, her other hand forming a fist. Before she had a chance to strike, she was wrapped tightly against the other person's body, her arms effectively pinned, unable to fight.

"Let go of m…" Her voice trailed off when her mind registered that it was Vaughn. Vaughn, whose eyes flashed fire and whose nostrils flared in anger.

"What the hell do you think you're doing?" Vaughn's voice was a barely restrained growl in her ear. She made no move to let go of Sedona.

"I could ask you the same thing." Although she refrained from smashing her heel down again on Vaughn's instep, she, too, did not back down.

"You're being hunted all over the globe and you just go trotting off down a wide-open, isolated beach by yourself?"

"I'm not in any danger here. Hell, no one knows where we are," Sedona shot back. "Even I barely know where we are."

"Very funny. It's my job to keep you safe, damn it."

"The hell it is."

"Don't you get it? There are real people out there who want you dead."

"Of course I get it. I can fully well take care of myself."

They were nose to nose, their bodies pressed hard together. Sedona could feel the heat of Vaughn's stomach against her bare midriff. Before she could register anything else, Vaughn's lips crushed against hers.

Sedona stiffened then yielded, the pulse pounding in her neck, her heart beating harder than she could ever remember. Her mouth opened under Vaughn's insistent assault. Her body melted into Vaughn's heat.

Sedona wanted to touch skin, but her arms remained pinned. She groaned as Vaughn's tongue teased her, challenging her. When Vaughn shifted to run her hand down Sedona's bare belly, Sedona's legs faltered.

It wasn't until she felt the button on her shorts release that Sedona fully understood where this was going. She clamped down on Vaughn's hand and broke off the kiss.

"No," she croaked against Vaughn's lips. Vaughn's hand went completely still. She pulled back and Sedona could see the haze of unbridled desire in her eyes. "No. I-I can't…"

"I'm sorry." Vaughn shoved off and backed several steps away. "I had no right… I didn't mean… You're not safe out here. You need to come back to the condo. I'll meet you there." Vaughn spun around and ran back toward the condo.

Sedona stood rooted to the sand, her lips tingling, her legs swaying unsteadily, her chest heaving, her body rebelling against the chill left behind by Vaughn's absence. She tried in her mind to process what just transpired, but she couldn't form a coherent thought. Whatever it was, if it happened again, Sedona wasn't sure she had the willpower to stop it.

"They've gone completely off the grid."

"That's not what I want to hear."

"I know, sir, but it's the truth." The young man with acne and big owl eyes pushed back from an array of computer equipment to face his visitor. He rarely got visitors down here, in the place he called "the bat cave." That would have been unsettling enough, but this particular visitor made his palms sweat. He'd heard the stories. This was not someone to whom you gave bad news.

"Explain."

"Well, sir. You said there were at least seven people we were tracking—two men and five women. We have definitive ID on one of them, Sedona Ramos. I reviewed satellite images of a ten-mile-square radius around the explosion site. Nothing. I looked at every surveillance camera on the island, including ones in the airport terminal. No such group appeared anywhere in a 24-hour period following the explosion.

"So I considered the possibility that they might have split up. I looked for smaller groups. Still, I found nothing out of the ordinary—some tourists, some islanders—no one that looked remotely like our group. Then I hacked in and examined boat charters, airline tickets issued, private planes chartered. Still, nothing. Because we had a single name, I went through Ramos's bank records, credit card history, phone records, et cetera. I tried to use the GPS on her cell to track her. Zilch." The young man looked up and blinked. "I'm sorry, sir. I know it's not what you want to hear, but there's simply nothing to go on."

"Yet."

"Sir?"

"There's nothing to go on, yet. I expect you to keep on this until you have better news for me. Do I make myself clear?"

"Yes, sir. But what about the tap on the Senate committee chairman's lines? Don't you still want to know if I hear anything about the oil pipeline?"

The man frowned and narrowed his eyes. "You have only one priority right now, do you hear me? I'll assign the other matter to one of your colleagues. Now, I strongly suggest you get back to work. The next time we have a chat, I expect you'll have better news for me."

The young man swallowed hard. "Yes, sir." He really, really hoped one of the "magnificent seven," as he'd taken to calling them, slipped up soon and left a technological trace. But just in case, he had a bag packed and ready to go in his trunk. His mother would take care of the cat.

❖❖

"Okay. Here's where we are right now," Vaughn began. She looked around the room at everyone…except Sedona. She simply couldn't make eye contact. She wasn't sure what she'd find there, and she was equally unsure whether or not she wanted to know. "I've asked Sabastien to lay out a few possible routes for us to take to get in-country without detection."

She cued him, and he began manipulating the mouse. A series of maps appeared on the wall, each with a red trail. There was a map leading from Turkey, one from Iran, one from Syria, one from Kuwait, and one from Saudi Arabia.

"As you can see, coming in from Iran presents the shortest route. That means the least exposure."

"It also means insertion in a very hostile country," Sedona said.

Vaughn made a point of intently studying the map. "True. But I believe the risk is worth limiting the amount of time it takes us to get to the target."

"Maybe," Lorraine spoke up, "but Sedona has a valid point. Even though it would take us longer to get to our destination through either Turkey or Kuwait, we'd be traveling through friendly territory at the outset. Between us, we might even have enough contacts to ensure safe passage and some additional support in terms of protection and resources."

Vaughn nodded in acknowledgment of the logic of Lorraine's argument.

"If we go in through Iran and we get caught, the likelihood of our getting out alive or without becoming an international political football are slim and none," Justine said. "That's a helluva risk."

"Peter? Wanna weigh in?" Vaughn asked.

He studied each of the maps in turn. "You're right, Vaughn, that the Iranian option has the advantage of keeping our time on the ground to a minimum. But I agree with the others—the stakes are too high and so are the risks." He leaned back in his chair. "I say we figure out between us how many contacts we have in Kuwait and Turkey. Syria is too hot at the moment in terms of political temperature, and Saudi Arabia gives me a hive."

Clearly outnumbered, Vaughn capitulated. "Okay. We're going to need good, solid, reliable contacts wherever we drop in. These have to be sources with some serious juice—access to high grade weapons and ammo, transportation, food supplies and some technology." She grabbed a legal pad and a pen. "Let's go around the table and see what we've got. That should help us figure out whether we're taking the high road through Turkey or the low road through Kuwait."

Fifteen minutes later, it was clear that the extent of the group's collective experience made either option viable.

"Listen," Lorraine said, "if we decide to come down from the north, we're going to have to contend with the mountains in Turkey and unpredictable winter weather. If we take the southern route and slip in through Kuwait, we can get all the way to the border on the waters of the Persian Gulf. There are plenty of merchant ships that would grant us passage for the right coin, and the weather would be less of a factor. In fact, if we could find the right vessel, it might even take us up the Tigris all the way to Baghdad."

"I've got some long-time buddies who stayed in Kuwait to pick up private business contracts after they retired. I could call in some favors," Peter offered. "These folks cross the border regularly both by land and on the water." He looked at Lorraine. "If you can get us through the Persian Gulf to say, Umm Qasr, I think I can take it from there, assuming we don't luck into a ship that'll take us the rest of the way. It wouldn't be anything for my contacts to let us hitch a ride into Baghdad. After that, we'd have to figure out a way to go the last twelve or so miles on our own."

"Sedona, didn't you say that you were at Tuwaitha when they shut the place down?" Justine asked.

"Yes."

Vaughn thought Sedona sounded subdued. She knew it was her fault but had no idea what to do about it. She fiddled with her pen and stared at the table in front of her.

"How did your group travel in and out?"

"Mostly Hummers. There were still active IEDs everywhere, so we had native guides and armored vehicles."

When silence followed, Vaughn was forced to look up. Sedona was looking right through her. She swallowed hard. "Okay. Well, the chances of us having an armored Hummer at our disposal are pretty slim. What are our other options?"

"I wish you wouldn't dismiss my input so readily, Vaughn." Sedona said. "In fact, I may be able to get us a lift in one of those Hummers."

Sedona's posture was rigid, unyielding. Vaughn flashed back to her pliant flesh, the heat of her mouth, just an hour earlier in their encounter on the beach and her face flushed.

"Okay. If you think you can get it done, that would be great. Sabastien has procured us some untraceable burn phones. I suggest we all get to work on putting together a network of sources and resources. Sedona and Peter, you take care of our ground transportation. Lorraine and Justine, you two concentrate on getting us a ride through the Persian Gulf. Sabastien, you're in charge of figuring out what kind of technology we're going to need and making sure we have it. I'll take care of getting us as far as the Persian Gulf and our weapons. Let's target being on the road two days from now. Everyone okay with that?"

When she heard no objections, Vaughn stood, signaling that the meeting was over. She made sure to linger behind long after Sedona left the room. When she finally emerged, Justine was waiting for her.

"Wanna talk about it?"

"About what?"

Justine sighed. "I've known you a long time, my friend. Something's eating you and I'd wager a month's salary it has something to do with our Sedona Ramos, who, by the way, is also curiously brooding."

Vaughn continued to walk. "You don't know what you're talking about."

"Don't I?"

"I'm not brooding."

"Okay. If you say so."

"I say so, now drop it. Don't you have something important you need to be doing?"

Justine stepped forward and stood in Vaughn's path, forcing her to stop. "I thought I was doing it."

"What? Being a pain in the ass?" Vaughn knew her tone was caustic. She didn't care.

Justine recoiled as if she'd been slapped. "No," she said, quietly. "Being your friend."

"I don't need a friend right now. I need someone to get us through the Persian Gulf." Vaughn looked at a point on the wall past Justine's head. She didn't want to see the hurt on Justine's face. She knew it was there. But hadn't prior conversations with Justine just like this on the last mission led to Vaughn's breaking Sage's heart? If Vaughn gave in and admitted that she had feelings for Sedona, Justine likely would encourage her to explore them, with potentially the same consequences as the last time. No. She refused to travel the same path with Sedona. There was nothing for it but to ignore what happened on the beach and move forward with the mission.

If only Vaughn could get her rebellious body and mind to comply.

CHAPTER NINE

Ahmed? It's Sedona," she said, in perfect Arabic. "How are you? How is your wife doing? Did everything go okay with the baby's birth?"

"Insha'Allah. Sedona Ramos, the baby is two and a half and walking already. You would fall in love with her."

"I'm sure I would. Listen, I'm in a bit of a bind and I need a little help if you can swing it. I'm going to be back in your neighborhood in a few days and I sure could use a lift." Unspoken between them was that Sedona would compensate him well for his assistance.

"You are coming here? The Americans are coming back? I thought you were all leaving the country."

"Yeah. This is more of an unofficial visit."

"Surely you are not sight-seeing?"

"In a manner of speaking. I'm showing some friends around. I want to be sure I keep them safe and make a good impression."

"I see. Exactly when would this be? I'm certain I can work something out for my old friend."

"That would be great. I'm thinking it would be this coming Thursday, if that's possible."

There was a pause on the other end of the line, and Sedona could hear muffled voices. She imagined Ahmed talking it over with his cousin Umar. The two men—barely more than boys—had been assigned to help the Americans interface with the local tribesmen and Iraqi forces tasked to guard Tuwaitha during the dismantling process. It was Ahmed and Umar's job to ferry the Americans anywhere they needed to go. The pair had taken a special liking to Sedona. Occasionally, they even brought her to their homes to enjoy a meal with their families. She adored Ahmed's wife and three kids and the feeling was quite mutual.

"Okay, Sedona. For you, we will make it happen. Where would we be meeting you and how many people?"

"You're the best, my friend. There will be six of us and some gear. Meet you at the usual spot in Baghdad? I'll let you know more specifics as soon as I know them."

"It will be good to see you. My wife and children will be so pleased. Will you have time to come to the house?"

"I don't know, Ahmed. That will depend on our schedule. I think this will be a quick trip and I don't want you to go to any trouble." In truth, she did not want to put him or his family in any jeopardy. She wondered if he had any knowledge of the current goings-on at Tuwaitha, but now was not the time to ask. She would wait and see what kind of reception she and the team got in person.

"Insha'Allah, I will see you soon."

"Yes, you will."

When Sedona disconnected the call, Peter was watching her, an enigmatic smile on his face.

"What?"

"You continue to surprise me," Peter said.

"Oh?"

"There's a lot more to you than meets the eye."

Sedona shrugged to hide her discomfort. "What you see is what you get."

"I don't think so. For instance, your Arabic is better than most people who've lived in-country for years."

"I'm a quick study. And you didn't tell me you knew Arabic."

"I have many skills. Don't deflect." He winked. "Then there's the matter of the way you seem to read people—even near strangers—with such ease."

"I told you—superpowers."

"Right. How could I forget?" Peter tapped his finger against his forehead and pretended to concentrate. "I'm trying to divine what else those superpowers entail, but I'm stumped. Want to help a guy out here?"

"A girl likes to leave some mystery." Sedona stood and stretched. "I took care of our ride. What have you been up to?"

"Watching you work."

"Wonderful. Are you planning to contribute anything useful?" Sedona teased. She really liked Peter. He was so easygoing. His aura was so strong with Archangel Michael, it was clear he was a warrior and fiercely protective, but this tender, lighthearted side intrigued her.

"Girls rule," Peter countered. "My wife tells me that every day. It's just my job to support you."

Sedona perched on the edge of the table. "Can I ask you a personal question?"

"Do I have a choice?" Peter sat on a chair facing her.

"Of course."

"I have a feeling I'm in good hands." Peter winked at her. "Ask away."

Sedona thought about how she wanted to phrase the question she'd been pondering since the first time she met him. It seemed she would have to give something if she wanted to get something in return. She took a deep breath. How much did she want to reveal of herself? She felt as though she could trust Peter implicitly. But, just in case, she decided to do what she always did in such situations—consult the angels.

"Archangel Michael, this is a question of discernment. Can I trust this man with all of who and what I am?"

She waited for the reply. As often was the case with Michael, the answer was quick and brief.

"Yes."

"You asked about my superpowers." Sedona licked her lips. "Would it freak you out to know that I can 'see' you?"

Peter's eyes narrowed. "In what sense?"

"In every sense, really. I have…abilities…a lot of other people do not."

"You're psychic," Peter said.

Sedona winced at the bluntness of the assessment. "Yes, that's true. I am. I am clairvoyant, clairaudient, clairsentient, claircognizant, and I spend quite a bit of time talking to angels and spirit guides."

"As in, you see dead people."

Sedona laughed. "Yes. But mostly I deal with the angels. Angels are not departed spirits. Angels did not evolve from human form."

"I see." Peter seemed to absorb this. "Why are you telling me this?"

Sedona blushed. Had she made a mistake in revealing so much?

"Listen, I didn't mean that I have a problem with it. Quite to the contrary. I'm just curious why you are entrusting me with this. You don't strike me as the kind of person who shares readily of herself."

"You're right about that. For one thing, Archangel Michael says I can trust you."

Now it was Peter's turn to laugh. "Good to know I'm trustworthy."

"For another, I saw something in your aura the first time I met you." Sedona watched the look of wariness cross Peter's face, and she hurried on, "I wasn't specifically looking. But it's very prominent." She got up and walked over to him. "That's what I wanted to ask you about." She ran her fingers over his chest. "It's an area of disturbance right here." She touched the spot where the hole in his aura disturbed his field.

Peter flinched.

"I'm sorry." Sedona dropped her hand. "You don't have to tell me if you don't want to."

"No. It's okay." Peter sighed. "It was 1989 and my friend Kate"—he looked up at her—"you met her."

"You mean Katherine Kyle."

"Yes."

"She was in a lot of trouble. Kind of like you are now." His eyes came to rest on her. "Anyway, it all got very ugly and it involved a shootout."

Sedona flashed on a glimpse of the *Time* magazine story from that period written by Kate's wife, Jay. "I read about that."

"Probably. Anyway, I got caught in the crossfire. If it hadn't been for Lorraine..." His voice trailed off and he cleared his throat. "If it hadn't been for her, I would have died in the rotunda of the Lincoln Memorial. I nearly did anyway."

Sedona touched the injured area again and met his eyes. This time he didn't flinch. "I'm so sorry."

"It was a long time ago."

"It still hurts you, not just physically, but emotionally and spiritually." She paused. "Would you let me help you?"

"How so?"

"I can ask Archangel Raphael, who is in charge of healing, to repair some of the damage to your aura, and maybe even to some of the physically damaged tissue, if you're willing. If not, that's okay. I understand not everyone believes in this."

"Sedona," he said gently, "I've lived a long time and through some truly harrowing situations. Too many, in fact, not to believe that there's something much bigger than me out there watching out for me. I'm game if you are." He smiled. "What do you need from me?"

"Nothing, really, although it would be helpful if you took a few deep, cleansing breaths and cleared your mind."

Peter did as requested and Sedona closed her eyes with her hand hovering several inches from Peter's shirt.

Archangel Raphael, this warrior is in need of some healing. Please bring your beautiful, emerald green healing light into his chest. Please send your healing energy through my hand and guide me so that we might bring him some relief. Sedona felt the power surge through her right hand and let go of control, allowing Raphael to guide her. She continued in this manner until she felt the power leave her.

When she removed her hand and opened her eyes, Peter was looking at her with awe.

"Are you okay?" she asked him.

"That was fabulous. I have no idea how you did that, but I feel...lighter."

"Good." Sedona patted him on the shoulder and moved away. "Make sure you drink plenty of water for the rest of the day. It'll help with the healing process." Then she turned and left the room.

"Yes. Six total. Right." Vaughn stared out the window, the burn phone in one hand, while the fingers of her other hand massaged her temple, where a pounding headache made it nearly impossible to think.

She tried to focus on the conversation. "No. Nothing commercial. I either need a private, off-the-books charter or some kind of cargo transport." She listened for another second. "Yeah, DHL will do. How much?" Her eyes widened. "I could buy your whole damned company for less than that... Yeah, yeah. All right. It better be comfortable—I'm not as young as I used to be. I get stiff easily. And Sparky? From there I'm going to need a helicopter and a pilot with experience in Navy Seal-like moving drops. You got someone that fits the description? It needs to be someone you'd trust with your own life... Don't mess with me... Remember, you owe me, Sparky... The Persian Gulf. I'll tell him where when the time comes... Yeah, I miss you too. Kinda like a toothache. See ya."

Vaughn hung up the phone. That's when she noticed Sedona. She was sitting outside on the ground, her legs crossed in a lotus position, her face turned up toward the sun. Vaughn's stomach flipped.

"She's something else, isn't she?"

Vaughn whirled around at the sound of Peter's voice. He came up alongside her and pointed at Sedona.

"I just booked us a flight plan."

Peter didn't acknowledge the shift in conversation. Instead, he stood looking out the window as Vaughn had been before she was interrupted.

"Did you hear me?"

"Yep. I did," Peter said. "Do you have a problem with Sedona?"

"What?" Vaughn blustered. "I don't know her well enough to have a problem with her."

"Then why do you seem so ill-at-ease around her? You're awfully tough on her."

"I don't. I'm not." *I don't know what to do about her.* Vaughn walked to the other side of the room, away from the windows. "Do you have any aspirin? I've got a killer headache."

"No." Peter continued to watch Sedona. "She's a special woman, Vaughn. If you haven't figured that out yet, you should try spending a little time with her."

98

Vaughn nearly choked. The last thing she needed right now was to spend more time with Sedona. The woman confounded and bewitched her and she couldn't afford to lose focus. This mission was critical. Lives were at stake—including Sedona's.

"Did you hear me say I booked us a flight plan?"

"I did." Peter finally seemed to concede and turned his attention to Vaughn.

"Sabastien is taking care of getting us new identities. We'll fly first to London commercially, but on two different flights. You and Lorraine will be leaving from Miami and traveling as husband and wife."

"That's original." Peter smiled.

"I like to stick as close to the truth as possible. It leaves less room for error."

"Agreed."

"Sabastien and Justine will also be on your flight. They'll be posing as boyfriend and girlfriend."

"Hmm. A bit of a stretch."

"We could make them business colleagues, but I'm throwing Sabastien a bone here."

"Okay. What about you and Sedona?"

"I'm taking responsibility for her. After all, as far as we know, she's the only one of us they've been able to identify. She's still the primary target. As team leader, it's my job to keep her safe." She said it as dispassionately as she was able and schooled her face into a neutral expression. She lost Sara on an op and she nearly lost Sage—she'd failed every important woman in her life for whom she'd been responsible on a mission. That wouldn't happen this time. She'd see to it personally.

"Uh-huh."

Peter's tone indicted that he wasn't buying the explanation, so Vaughn plowed ahead. "The two of us will take another commercial flight. We'll fly from Atlanta, but it will arrive at Heathrow at roughly the same time as your flight."

"You really think that's a good idea?" Peter asked. "That cuts you off without any backup. At least take a different flight from Miami. That way we're close by if anything happens."

"It's too obvious if we all show up at the same airport. I'm sure they're going to have people monitoring air travel."

99

"You said it yourself," Peter pointed out. "Apart from Sedona, they don't know who they're looking for, and possibly not even how many of us there are."

"I say it's too risky. I can take care of her." *I need to take care of her. I have to prove I can do this, otherwise, I shouldn't be here.*

Peter held her gaze. Vaughn refused to flinch. "Are you sure that's what's driving your decision?"

"What else would it be?" Vaughn's face reddened. "If you don't trust me to run the show, take it up with the president."

Peter held up his hands in surrender. "Take it easy. I'm not questioning your abilities or your credentials here." He softened his tone. "I just want to make sure we think everything through. After all, as you said, there's a lot at stake. I've always been a big believer that it's helpful to talk things over before finalizing a plan. That's just the way I work. If that's a problem for you, tell me now."

Vaughn ran her fingers through her hair and closed her eyes. She'd always been a team player, but this was different. How could she explain it to Peter? It would sound ridiculous and selfish. "No. No, you're fine. I'm just tired and I've got a headache that would fell an elephant at two hundred yards."

"Lorraine usually has some ibuprofen with her. You might ask her when we're done."

"Thanks."

"Where are we going from London?"

"I've got an old friend who deals with a lot of cargo—some of it unofficial. He's got us six seats on a DHL cargo plane to Kuwait International Airport."

"That ought to be comfortable," Peter said sarcastically.

"I warned him that I'm not as young as I used to be. He assured me the plane is modified to accommodate situations like ours."

"He does this kind of thing often?"

"I didn't ask. He didn't tell," Vaughn said. "From the airport in Kuwait we'll take a chopper to the ship in the Persian Gulf."

"What kind of ship?"

"Justine still has contacts in the medical field. One of her buddies is in charge of humanitarian aid to war-torn countries. In a stroke of pure genius and incredibly fortuitous timing, she was able to find a Red Cross supply vessel that's heading to Baghdad in our timeframe."

Peter whistled. "Sometimes, it's better to be lucky than to be good."

"Tell me about it. Still, we're not officially welcome, so we'll have to drop in under cover of darkness and stay out of sight."

"Nobody's going to hear a helicopter buzzing overhead and wonder what's going on?"

"They would…if the chopper was going to buzz overhead. We'll lose our air transport several miles before we reach our destination. We're going to drop a small pontoon boat and take that to get to the ship. The security chief is the only one who knows we're coming. He'll facilitate our getting on board safely."

"Sounds like a solid plan, and it also means you don't need my help getting from Umm Qasr to Baghdad."

"Nope. We'll go right up the Tigris courtesy of the Red Cross. How did you and Sedona make out with the ground transport from Baghdad to Tuwaitha?" Vaughn asked.

"Sedona took care of it. By the time she was done, there was nothing for me to do but sit there and watch her work."

Vaughn arched an eyebrow in question.

"Her Arabic is better than most native-speakers. It seems she made some friends when she was in country decommissioning Tuwaitha. We've got a ride from the same guys who used to ferry her and her team around in 2008."

"She trusts them?"

"From her end of the conversation, it sounded to me like they considered her family. She seems to have the ability to worm her way into people's hearts." Peter looked toward Sedona, then back at Vaughn. A smile played on his lips. "You really should see if Lorraine has something for your headache. I can ask her for you, if you want." He inclined his head toward the window. "In case you're too busy."

Vaughn followed his line of sight. Sedona still sat as she had been. Vaughn wondered exactly what it was she was thinking that resulted in such a look of serenity. She wished she could feel that too.

❦

"It's time to make some decisions," Astin Trulander, president of Calico Petroleum said. He hadn't wanted to convene another meeting so soon of "The Four," as they called themselves, but he had been ordered to do so, and he saw little choice in the matter.

"What's our status with the Ramos woman?" Randolph Quinn asked.

"*Our* status," Astin sneered at the little man. Since Astin had a dislike of all things Irish, he'd always resented the little prick's presumptuous nature and distrusted him on principle. The fact that his ex-wife also was from Ireland might have had something to do with that. It might also have had something to do with the fact that Quinn was essentially an uneducated street urchin who had spent his whole life making and setting off bombs in the mean streets of Dublin. Until the most recent peace agreement, he had been the Irish Republican Army's top bomb maker—a terrorist on Interpol's ten most wanted list. "The only reason you're here is because Grayson wants you here. If it was up to me—"

"Enough." Homeland Security Secretary Daniel Hart's baritone reverberated off the walls. "Astin is correct. As in all wars, a good general needs to reassess the battle plan."

Astin ground his teeth. Hart never passed up an opportunity to work in subtle reminders that he was a military man—a veteran, tested on the field of battle during the first Gulf War. He was the only holdover Cabinet appointee from the previous administration. The president cited his valor in that conflict and his reputation as a skilled tactician as reasons for retaining him to oversee the US security apparatus. In so doing, the president unwittingly gave them the perfect insider.

"The work onsite is progressing on schedule, I can tell you that," Randolph said, his brogue making the 'can' sound more like 'kin.' "I'm told we'll be ready within the month."

US Senator from Texas Emily Kincaid, Chairperson of the Senate Energy Committee, shook her head. "It's no good. By then, the whole thing could blow up in our faces."

Astin stared hard at the woman he once planned to marry. He wondered what he had seen in her. *Probably just a young stud's hormones. She was a looker and you were looking.* "We can't stop now," he said out loud. "There's too much at stake. We've been ordered to proceed."

"Then why are we here?" Hart asked.

"We're not getting anywhere with our search for Ramos, or the mysterious bunch that arrived on that island shortly before the satellite incident."

"They couldn't have just disappeared into thin air," Emily said.

"Actually, you're wrong about that, lass. I've been doing it for years." Randolph smiled and Astin wanted to wipe the cocky grin off his face with his fist.

"The point is," Astin said, "since we don't know where they are, we need to anticipate where they're going."

Hart nodded in agreement. "I see where you're heading with this. The Ramos woman must have gotten a better look than we thought at those images. That's why she was trying to get another peek at Tuwaitha." Hart drummed his fingers on the table. "You think she'd head to Iraq?" He directed the question to Astin.

"She tried to get more images of the place and failed. Going there in person is the next logical step."

"I think it's more of a leap than a step, Astin," Emily said. "Even if she were behind the satellite episode, what makes you think she's capable of taking it any further? She knows she's being watched. It's why she's being so careful. If I was her, I'd lie low. She's got to be scared out of her mind."

"She's not you, Emily," Astin snapped. And there it was—the reason he'd been turned off by her in the end. She lacked a spine.

"We have to assume she had something to do with the satellite deal," Hart said. "That means either she's remarkably resourceful, or she's recruited some friends. If that's the case and they have the wherewithal to take out six of our best soldiers in an explosion of that magnitude, it's a safe bet that she's not done causing trouble."

"I say, let 'em come to Tuwaitha. We'll take 'em out before they ever get close. My boys will handle it," Randolph said.

Astin bristled. "We've already had to send seven of 'your boys' back to the Irish ghetto they came from for calling attention to themselves. Pissing on the wall of the mosque? What part of 'be inconspicuous' didn't your men understand?"

"You and your uptight southern ass. The boys was just having a bit of fun, that's all."

Astin stood and shoved his chair back. He towered over Quinn. His fist quivered at his side.

"Sit down, Astin," Hart said. "Both of you, simmer down. This isn't getting us anywhere."

Astin itched to knock Quinn into next week, but he recognized that Hart was right—this wasn't getting them anywhere. He sat back down. "Daniel, what kind of resources can you put in the field to take care of Ramos and anyone she might bring with her?"

"I can have a team standing by within forty-eight hours. I'll also alert forces at every border into Iraq. That's easy—I'll just label her a jihadist. It'll save us using other resources."

"Do it," Astin said. "The order stands as before for Ramos, and anyone else with her. Initiate a permanent solution. I'll inform Mr. Grayson tomorrow." He gathered his papers and rose. "If you'll excuse me, I've got another meeting to get to." He stuffed the papers in a leather briefcase. "The next time we see each other, it should be to celebrate the successful annihilation of our pest problem."

CHAPTER TEN

T he president sat across from Kate, his expression grim. Vaughn's report forced him to face the very real probability that Americans were at least partially responsible for whatever was going on at Tuwaitha.

"I have to say, this was not the news I was hoping for."

"I know, Mr. President."

"She blew up her own house?" He shook his head in wonder. "I don't think I could've done it."

"I imagine that was one of the reasons you selected Vaughn to lead the team, sir. She's as strong as they come."

"Mmm. Still, I feel horrible about that."

"I know Vaughn, sir. I suspect it was more important to her that she prevented the intruders from completing their mission, while suffering no casualties to her team. The house was secondary."

"Yes, I believe you're right about that. You said that when you spoke with her, she mentioned a boat."

"Yes, sir."

"Any idea where they were headed?"

"No, sir."

The president swiveled in his chair so that he could retrieve his iPad from the desk behind him and see the map that was open on the screen. He swiveled back and put the iPad on his lap, running his finger from the green pin that represented Vaughn's house, to the nearest landmasses accessible by boat. There were several possibilities. "Depending on what kind of boat she was using, assuming it was a personal boat and not a larger vessel, she could've gone any one of several places. None of those include the United States mainland."

"I don't think she wanted to operate domestically if she could avoid it, sir."

"I understand that and I respect her judgment. In her part of the world, it's much easier to take care of incidents like the one with those intruders without a lot of unwanted scrutiny. Speaking of which, was there any backlash? Any legal ramifications?"

"Not that I'm aware of, sir." Kate smiled. "Vaughn was much beloved on that island. I think many people would've stepped up to protect her privacy and her reputation. I wouldn't be the least bit surprised to find out that the explosion had been classified an unfortunate accident, and that there was no mention of any casualties in the blast."

"Good." The president nodded to himself. "Good." He refreshed the iPad screen. "I don't suppose she outlined their next steps for you?"

"No, sir. I'm not sure Vaughn had gotten that far."

"Hmm. Even if she had," the president ventured, "I doubt she would've shared that information." He recognized Kate's quizzical expression and continued. "Plausible deniability. If anything goes wrong that calls attention to the mission and I don't know what they're up to, I can honestly say I had no knowledge."

"That makes sense."

"Unfortunately, it also means I'm in the dark about what may well be the most important operation of my presidency to-date."

Kate started to say something then clearly reconsidered.

"What is it, Kate? You know you're welcome to speak freely here."

Kate frowned. "Then let me ask you a hypothetical question."

"Okay." The president leaned forward.

"If I were, say, to give you my best guess as to what was happening now, based on my close relationship with Peter and my knowledge of how he thinks and works and the similarities I see between him and Vaughn, would that affect your plausible deniability?"

The president laughed. "Hypothetically speaking, since any information from you would involve only pure conjecture and supposition, I'd say there would be no harm in entertaining hypothetical scenarios."

"In that case, sir. I'd look...here." Kate reached over and adjusted the map's coordinates so that it showed a view of the Middle East. She pointed to Iraq."

The president's mouth made an *O*, though he said nothing for several seconds. "Huh. In such a case, I'd be worried that they might not have everything they needed." He tapped his chin thoughtfully with his finger.

"Sir, I can imagine what you're thinking, but I wouldn't recommend it. This team is very resourceful. Anything you might do or supply, no matter how indirect, would leave a trail. I'm sure that's exactly what they are trying to avoid for your own good."

The president bit his lip. He knew Kate was right, but he still didn't like the idea of leaving people in the field without any visible support or backup.

"If it makes you feel any better, sir, I'm sure if it became absolutely necessary to the security of this country, they would ask for assistance."

"That's small consolation, Kate." The president closed the cover to the iPad. "In my time in office, I've come to discover that sitting on my hands and doing nothing is often harder than taking action."

"Understood, sir."

The president stood and walked Kate to the door. "Do you think you'll be hearing from our friend again anytime soon?"

"We left it that she would contact me when necessary, sir. So it's anybody's guess."

"If you do talk to her, please tell her 'Godspeed' from me. My thoughts and hopes rest with her and her team."

"Yes, sir, I'll be sure to pass the message along. I'm sure they'll be happy to hear that."

"I'll look forward to your next update."

"Yes, sir."

After the president bid Kate goodbye, he leaned against the door. The situation at Tuwaitha could be the defining moment of his presidency, not to mention a catalyst for a nuclear attack and, potentially, the largest war since World War II. How Vaughn and her team handled the mission could mean the difference between war and peace, heroism or ignominy. However the events of this action turned out, the president understood that the fate of his career and his legacy rested on the shoulders of six civilians acting without portfolio. He only hoped he had chosen well.

୶ଊ

Sedona let the rising sun warm her face. She listened to the rhythm of the waves and imagined the crystal clear blue waters cleansing her of any lower energies, any remnants of shadows.

She pictured the sun as God's golden light filling her from within. As she did every morning and night, she cleared, grounded, and protected herself, calling on the archangels and ascended masters to help her along the way. Her mother taught her long ago that shielding herself psychically and spiritually was every bit as important as protecting herself physically.

She took in a deep, cleansing breath, then another, and another. On each inhale, she imagined herself breathing in the essence of the Universe—Divine white light and perfect love. With each exhale, she imagined herself eliminating a gray mist that represented any negativity or fear.

She invoked Archangel Michael to cut any cords of fear. She asked Archangel Michael, Archangel Raguel, Archangel Jophiel, Archangel Haniel, and the Ascended Masters El Morya and Lady Nada to turn on the spiritual vacuum cleaner and vacuum away any lower energies or remnants of shadows that might be in her field. She imagined the pure waters of a beautiful waterfall washing away any lingering energies. Then she called upon Archangel Metatron to use his geometric shapes to clear and open all of her chakras.

She sensed a now-familiar energy behind her, but chose to ignore that for the time being, especially since the part of the routine that remained—protecting herself—was quick and essential to her well-being.

When she finished a few minutes later, she acknowledged Vaughn's presence. "If you've come to yell at me for venturing out on my own—"

"I didn't," Vaughn said. She came up alongside Sedona. "May I sit down?"

"Sure." Sedona noted that Vaughn left a healthy barrier of space between them.

"I came to tell you we'll be shipping out shortly."

"Okay." Sedona continued to watch the waves roll in and out.

After a lengthy silence, Vaughn asked, "What were you just doing?"

"Meditating. I do this every morning and night. Why?"

"You...you looked so peaceful. I wondered what you could be thinking that put that expression on your face."

"Now you know." Sedona imagined that someone like Vaughn—a woman of action, not words, would reject the idea of taking the time to go deep within.

"Please don't get defensive about it. I-I was thinking I wish I had something in my life that made me feel as serene as you looked."

"Oh." Sedona finally shifted her gaze to Vaughn's profile. The sun gilded her tanned skin. The sight nearly took Sedona's breath away. She swallowed hard. "Y-you could do that, you know."

"Meditate?"

"Yes."

"I doubt it. Sitting still like that isn't in my DNA."

"No?" Sedona turned fully toward Vaughn. "What do you do when you're on a sniper assignment and you're waiting to pull the trigger? You wait for just the right conditions. The correct wind speed, the proper trajectory, the perfect angle. No doubt you regulate your breathing before you pull the trigger. Am I right?"

"Yes on all counts, but..."

Sedona was amused that Vaughn seemed surprised by her intimate knowledge of the craft. Dom taught her well. "But, what? What you go through in those moments leading up to the kill is a form of meditation."

Vaughn shook her head. "Somehow I don't equate preparing to take a life with the peace I saw on your face just now, or yesterday afternoon, either."

Sedona smiled. "So, you've been spying on me?" She watched as an appealing blush crept up Vaughn's neck to her cheeks.

"No. I happened to glance out the window yesterday afternoon."

"Sure."

"Anyway, we'd better get back and gear up." Vaughn stood abruptly. She put her hand out to help Sedona up.

Sedona took the outstretched hand. It was strong and supple and the contact sent a frisson of unexpected warmth to Sedona's belly. They were nose to nose, their hands still connected, palm to palm. Sedona could feel Vaughn's breath on her lips, see Vaughn's chest rising and falling in a quicker than normal rhythm. She knew her own heart was matching that beat.

This time Sedona was the one who pulled Vaughn close. She hesitated only for a fraction of a second before tightening her grip on Vaughn's hand and pulling her against her body. This kiss was every bit as electric as the first, and maybe more so. This time, it was Sedona who set the pace. Her free hand found Vaughn's ass and squeezed. Vaughn's moan only served to increase the heat between them.

She felt Vaughn moving the hands that still were joined between them until they were pressing against both of their centers. Sedona gasped at the exquisite pressure and freed her hand. She wasn't sure whether she undid Vaughn's zipper or whether Vaughn did it herself, but it didn't matter. Her fingers slid into Vaughn's warm wetness, and she was lost. She was vaguely aware of Vaughn breaching the barrier of her shorts and panties, the simultaneous strength and gentleness of her fingers inside her. She devoured Vaughn's mouth with her teeth and tongue and stroked her until they both exploded.

Neither of them withdrew. They leaned against each other, forehead to forehead, breasts heaving, bodies still quivering. The shock of what they'd just done left Sedona speechless. Never in her life had she wanted and taken with such animal intensity and without conscious thought. She couldn't even imagine what had propelled her down this path. All she knew was that this connection—whatever it was—between her and Vaughn, was too powerful to be ignored or willed away. The thought frightened her more than the dangerousness of the mission they were about to embark upon.

❧❧

Astin detested this place—the gray walls, the rancid smells, the desperate people. But to refuse a command to "visit" with his maternal uncle, the infamous former business magnate and power broker Wayne Grayson, was akin to cutting off his own balls with a butter knife.

He fussed with the buckle on his bolo tie while he waited for prisoner number 77722 to be led into the visitor center at the maximum-security federal prison.

Finally, after what seemed like an eternity, the frail-looking man in the orange jumpsuit, his hands and feet shackled together, shuffled over to the opposite side of the booth and picked up the phone. Even through the scratched Plexiglas, Astin could see the menace in Grayson's expression. It sent a shiver through him.

"I don't like what I've been hearing lately, boy." Grayson leaned forward, close to the glass, his head tilted to the side to hold the phone because the length of chain on the shackles wouldn't allow him to easily raise his hand to his ear.

Not knowing what to say, Astin said nothing.

"Our people are dying with alarming regularity, mostly at your hands, the way I hear it." Grayson emphasized the *your* by jabbing a bony finger at the partition. "What the fuck is wrong with you?"

Astin squirmed. It shouldn't have surprised him that his uncle had other sources on the outside, but he thought he'd been discreet. "They were underperforming."

"Sit up straight, punk."

Astin pushed his ass back in the seat and threw his shoulders back.

"You listen to me." Spittle formed at the corners of Grayson's mouth. "Only a complete idiot would think that killing the messenger helps motivation. All that does is keep people from wanting to work for you."

"You used intimidation all the time."

"I used finesse. I used leverage. I didn't run around like a goddamned cowboy firing off my six-shooter to prove the size of my penis. Have I taught you nothing?" He was so close to the Plexiglas that the last word left a fog on the surface.

Astin flinched. "They didn't get the job done. We needed results."

"There's a little word called subtlety. Perhaps you've heard of it? Instead of offing these people, you find their weaknesses and exploit them."

Astin willed himself to sit still. He knew the telltale signs—a lecture was about to begin.

"The poor slob you shot in cold blood in your office last week, for instance. You know, the one who gave you the information about the origin of the satellite intrusion?"

The light dawned for Astin and he remembered the man standing across the desk from him. "It took him twenty-four hours to report the breach and when he did, he didn't have the name of the owner for the place where the intrusion originated."

"You sniveling idiot! He brought you the best lead you have to date. Do you really think anyone else is going to want to bring you an important piece of information that may not be everything you want it to be? No! They're going to avoid you like the plague. In the end, you'll have nothing and no one left to blame but yourself."

"What would you have me do? I had to make an example of him."

"Bullshit!" Grayson shouted.

"Is there a problem here?" the burly guard asked, coming to stand next to the prisoner.

"No, sir. Just excited about some family news."

"Well, keep it down over here."

"Yes, sir."

When the guard moved away, Grayson lowered his voice. "If you want to own these people, find their weaknesses. That man owed seventy-five thousand dollars in gambling debts. He'd been evading his bookie for months. If you had taken the time to know that, all you would've had to do was threaten to tell his bookie where to find him if he didn't come up with a name attached to that house."

Astin stared slack-jawed at his uncle, wondering how in the world he could've known all that. First, who the man was and what information he had come up with, second, that Astin had shot him to death for failing to identify the owner of the house, and third, that the man owed money to a bookie. It was one thing to know in the abstract that Grayson talked to other people on the outside. This…this was something else. Clearly, Astin had underestimated his uncle's reach.

Grayson continued, "When my sister asked me to take you under my wing—to be a father figure to you—I agreed. I thought you could be the son I never had. Now I wonder if all those lessons were wasted on you."

Astin's left eye twitched. It always had, ever since he was a young boy and discovered that disappointing Uncle Wayne usually had dire consequences. He knew he never quite measured up to his uncle's standards. Yet he was beholden to his uncle for everything he had—his company, his house, his lifestyle, his present position in the most powerful organization in the world. No matter that he was a grown man, a distinguished businessman in his own right— he forever would be in the shadow of this ghost sitting across from him. It was time to say what he'd come to say so he could get out of this godforsaken place and back into the real world, where he was the boss.

"We're putting a team in place to intercept and eliminate Ramos and whoever is helping her. Daniel says we'll be operational within twenty-four hours. He's also designating her as a terrorist. Troops will be looking for her at every border leading into the active zone."

"And if she gets past you again?"

"She won't. We'll have that place sewn up tight as a drum."

"You'd better be right about that, Astin. We've worked too hard and there's too much at stake for you to screw up again. If there's the slightest glitch, I'm holding you personally responsible."

"There won't be."

"I hope you're right. Because if it turns out otherwise, you'll be shredding paper as an errand boy for one of my companies in some third-world country for the rest of your days. Do you understand me?"

"Yes, sir."

"It's a good thing I loved my sister."

"Yes, sir."

"I know what you're thinking, Astin. 'The old man has been locked up for twenty-two years and he'll be stuck behind bars for the rest of his life, he can't touch me.' Don't underestimate me, boy. That would be a very foolish mistake." Grayson pointed the bony finger again. "Those who have aren't around to tell the tale."

"Yes, sir. I won't let you down."

"See to it." Grayson stood, signaling that the meeting was over.

Astin couldn't get out of there soon enough. Someday, the old man would get what was coming to him and Astin would finally, finally be free.

CHAPTER ELEVEN

Sedona kept her hands busy by cleaning her Glock-40. Her fully packed duffle bag and briefcase sat on the floor next to the bed.

She and Vaughn had walked back to the safe house from the beach in complete silence, their arms close but not touching.

It should have felt awkward, but Sedona was too shell-shocked to notice. What happened in those few wild moments was so out of character, so unexpected, she had no idea what to do with it.

"Hey," Peter said, as he knocked on the doorframe. "Mind if I come in for a second?"

Sedona put down the cloth with the silencer in it. "Not at all." She motioned for Peter to sit. "What can I do for you?" She prayed that he wasn't here to talk about her and Vaughn. It occurred to her that she hadn't paid any attention to their surroundings. She had no idea if the two of them had had complete privacy or not. That's how out of her mind she had been. She frowned. The whole episode was surreal.

"You okay?"

"Huh?" Sedona looked up sharply. "I'm fine. Why?"

"You just seem a little distracted."

"Well, let's see." She started counting off items with her fingers. "Some unnamed party is doing a bang-up job of trying to kill me. Because of me, five other people's lives are in danger. Vaughn had to blow up her own house. And we're about to fly into a war zone." She smiled kindly at Peter and let her hand drop. "Personally, I can't imagine why I might seem off balance."

Peter laughed. "That's fair, except I take issue with some of your points. First, our lives aren't in jeopardy because of you—

115

they're in jeopardy because of whoever is behind whatever is happening at Tuwaitha."

Sedona started to interrupt, but Peter held up a hand to forestall her. "Please, I'm on a roll here. Second, Vaughn chose to blow up her house. We don't know that she didn't have other options available to her. Third... Well, I don't have a third, but if you give me a few minutes I'm sure I can come up with something."

Sedona affectionately bumped Peter's shoulder. "I'm sure you could." She went back to cleaning the barrel of the silencer. "Is that why you're here? To lift my spirits?"

"No." Peter bumped her shoulder back. "But is it working?"

Sedona thought for a second. "Yeah, you know? Actually, it is." And that was the truth. "So, if that wasn't your primary objective in coming to see me, what was?"

"I have a question for you."

"Shoot." Sedona picked up the disassembled gun and pretended to hand it to him.

"Oh, very punny."

"It wasn't my best, but it'll have to do."

"What I wanted to ask you is, is it really necessary for you and Vaughn to fly from Atlanta instead of Miami like the rest of us?"

Sedona knew her face registered the surprise she felt at being asked the question. "Peter, this is Vaughn's op. I wouldn't presume to second guess her decisions—"

"No. No. That's not what I mean," Peter said. He searched for the words. "What I'm asking you is, in your...other capacity...can you see if splitting up is really necessary in order for you to go undetected?"

"Ah." Sedona nodded. "Wow. That's different." She scooted back against the wall. "I've never been around anybody on an op who sought that kind of advice." In truth, she'd never told any of her colleagues about her abilities. For once, it felt good to be considered for all of who she was.

"Is that something you can do?"

"Yes. Give me a second." Sedona closed her eyes and took several deep, cleansing breaths. *Archangel Michael, I need crystal clear advice. Would it be safe for all six of us to travel on the same aircraft out of Miami?*

"Yes."

"We'd be fine if we all took the same flight."

"You're sure?"

Sedona shrugged. "It's not me. It's Archangel Michael. I got a clear yes."

"Okay."

"Why are you asking me this?"

"I know Vaughn believes it's her job to keep you safe, but I feel pretty strongly that the best way to do that is to stick together. If you two go off by yourselves and fly via Atlanta, there's nothing any of the rest of us can do if something goes wrong. Not only that, but we'd have no way of knowing." Peter shook his head. "I can't explain it. I just don't feel comfortable splitting up like that."

"You're someone who relies on your gut."

"In my experience, sometimes that's all you've got," Peter conceded.

"You do realize you're intuitive, right?"

"As in gifted like you are? Not a chance."

"Maybe not as intuitive as I am, no. But you have abilities. You probably never recognized them as such, but I'd wager you've been using them all along."

Peter seemed to think about that. "I don't know. I suppose if you consider trusting hunches while under fire, I guess I have a little of that."

"Yes, you do." In the lull in the conversation, the full implications of what Peter asked sank in. "You want me to challenge Vaughn's decision on the travel arrangements based on abilities she doesn't even know I possess?"

"God, no. I would never leave you exposed that way." Peter put a comforting hand on Sedona's arm. "No. I'll take care of it. I just wanted to be sure I was right in my assessment."

"You were looking for a little insurance."

"Something like that. I already had the conversation with Vaughn once."

"How did that go?" Sedona could just imagine how Vaughn would feel about being second-guessed.

"About the way you'd expect. She blew me off."

"So what makes you think you'll get a different reaction this time?"

"I don't know that I will, but it just feels to me like I ought to try again."

Sedona slid off the bed and stood up. As much as she didn't want to see Vaughn right now, she knew she couldn't leave Peter to deal with the situation alone. He was right. They were better off traveling together. She just had no idea how to convince Vaughn of that without explaining more than she was ready to reveal.

"What are you doing?"

"I'm coming with you of course."

❦

"Absolutely not." Vaughn stood with her arms folded across her chest.

"I understand how you feel—"

"Don't give me that. You have no idea how I feel." Vaughn watched as Sedona's jaw clicked shut. She realized that Sedona might have misinterpreted her meaning. She wanted to add that this wasn't personal—she was speaking only about the travel arrangements—but now was not the time.

"Vaughn," Peter said. "Nobody is questioning your authority or your right to make decisions."

"The hell you aren't." Vaughn pointed her finger at him. "We had this discussion once, as I recall. I told you then and I'll tell you again—if you don't like the way I run things, take it up with the president."

"What the hell is going on in here?" Justine strode into the room and stood in the middle of the group with her hands on her hips. Lorraine and Sabastien were close on her heels. "I can hear you all the way on the other side of the condo." She looked first at Peter, then at Sedona, and finally at Vaughn.

"We were just discussing the travel arrangements," Sedona said. "Peter and I believe we should all leave out of Miami."

"Vaughn insists that she and Sedona should go out from Atlanta, instead," Peter said.

"It's my responsibility to keep Sedona safe." In her mind's eye, Vaughn saw a glimpse of Sara opening the explosives-laden casket and then Sage, her body battered, her eyes filled with fear.

Never again would she rely on anyone else to protect someone so important to her. "This is how I choose to do it."

"In other words," Sedona finished, "Vaughn seems to think it should be her way or the highway."

Vaughn recoiled at Sedona's unflattering summation. Didn't she see the danger? At this critical juncture, Vaughn didn't want any distractions, that included by other members of the team. If it was just the two of them, her focus would be razor-sharp. "There can only be one person in charge of an op. Period. I'm that person. Sedona is the only known factor. The two of us traveling together presents a lower profile than six of us. That's how I see it, and that's how this is going to go down. Case closed."

"I understand your logic, Vaughn," Lorraine jumped in, "but I think Sedona and Peter are right on this—it makes more sense to stay in proximity to each other so that we all have backup—you included. If you isolate yourself by going out of Atlanta and something goes wrong, we have no Plan B."

"Sedona is the only one with experience at Tuwaitha. She's our most valuable asset on this mission," Justine added. "Without her, we have little chance of succeeding, not to mention that we lose our ground transportation from Baghdad. These guys are right, Vaughn. It's all of our jobs to protect Sedona."

Vaughn wanted to scream. She'd been in the field as long as any of them, with just as many successful ops under her belt. Why couldn't they accept that this was the way she wanted to handle the trip? However, the fact that Lorraine thought she was off base gave her pause. After all, Lorraine was the agent Vaughn wanted to be all those years ago. She was the gold standard for CIA agents. But she also was married to Peter. Would she side with him for that reason? Vaughn didn't want to think so.

She looked around the room at each of them. She clearly was outnumbered. "So, which one of you wants to be in charge? You figure it out and let me know." She stalked out of the room.

"What did I miss there?" Lorraine asked. "What was that really about?"

Sedona blew out an explosive breath. Although she hadn't "looked," she could guess at part of Vaughn's disquietude, since she was feeling it too. She was off balance. The episode on the beach was a mistake. It changed the dynamics between them, and therefore the dynamics of the group. That led to clouded judgment. Did Vaughn want them to travel separately purely because of the mission? Or was it more personal than that? Either way, Sedona couldn't allow one or two moments of passion to jeopardize the operation. Should she tell the group? Did they have a right to know what was eating Vaughn?

"The woman just blew up her own house. I think we ought to cut her some slack," Peter said. "I'd be out of sorts too."

"I've worked with Vaughn on several ops. I can tell you I've never seen her lose her cool before." Justine looked directly at Sedona as she said it, and Sedona blinked.

She wondered if Vaughn had said something to Justine about their tryst and then discounted it. That didn't fit Vaughn's profile. It wasn't the first time, though, that Justine made a comment that led Sedona to think she might know more than she should. She flashed back to her discussion with Justine on the plane. What had made her think Sedona wanted to know so much more about Vaughn? It occurred to Sedona that perhaps Justine had some intuitive abilities of her own.

Sedona wanted to volunteer to go talk to Vaughn, but she wasn't sure that would help the situation.

"Ah, if I may," Sabastien shyly interrupted, "I think I might have a solution that would work."

"I'm all ears," Peter said.

"Well, since we know that someone is looking for Sedona, we could give them what they want."

"And that helps, how?" Lorraine asked.

"I am not saying this well," Sabastien said, shifting nervously from foot to foot. "What I mean is, I could fix it so that whoever is chasing Sedona thinks they know where she is. I could create a misperception."

"You mean a misdirection." Sedona laughed and went over and kissed Sabastien on the cheek. "That's brilliant."

Sabastien blushed. *"C'est ça.* I could create a false paper trail of credit card activity that would have them think she is someplace far, far away from her actual location."

Peter nodded. "I've used tactics like that before. It might work, and it would make the travel arrangements less of an issue."

"It would certainly take a lot of the pressure off, at least temporarily," Lorraine agreed. She looked fondly at Peter. "It worked for a while when you did that with Kate. Where was it you had us thinking she'd gone?"

"Ironically, it was Sedona and then Flagstaff."

"Well, it seems that would be fitting," Sedona said. "Do you really think they'd buy it? I mean, me using my debit card after all this time? They probably know I've intentionally gone dark. Wouldn't that be too obvious?"

"Whatever they think about it, they'd at least have to investigate," Justine said. "Any distraction is better than no distraction."

"What if you had run out of cash and you were desperate? You would have to do something for money," Sabastien said.

"Where would I use the card?" Sedona asked.

"Since they showed up at my house," Vaughn said quietly from her position in the doorway, "we should assume they've made the connection between you and the satellite pictures we tried to get."

Sedona's breath caught at the sight of her. She looked almost haunted. "Vaughn, I'm—"

Vaughn waved Sedona away before she could finish the sentence. She walked into the room and sat down on the edge of a table. "If they have a brain between them, whoever they are, they'll figure out that you're going to try to get more intel on Tuwaitha. So it doesn't make any sense to try to have them chase their tails in the US. It stands to reason that you'd head to the site."

"But that is where we're going," Sabastien said. "Why would we want to give them a real destination?"

"Who said anything about that?" Vaughn countered. "We know there are at least five countries through which Sedona might enter Iraq. We considered them ourselves."

"All we have to do," Peter picked up the thread, "is help them to pick the wrong entry point."

"Precisely. Sabastien, let's have Sedona travel to Istanbul, Turkey via New York and Frankfurt," Vaughn said. "What day would you all think we should have her fly?"

⊷⊱

"Can I talk to you?" Justine asked.

Vaughn looked over her shoulder at her friend. "You're really predictable, you know that?"

"I've been called worse." Justine joined Vaughn on the balcony. "And you haven't answered my question."

"Would it make a difference if I did? You've obviously got something to say, which I knew you would, so let's hear it."

Out of the corner of her eye, Vaughn could see Justine's furrowed brow. She recognized that she had been hard on her friend since the moment Justine arrived on the island. She wasn't sure she could explain the reason herself. Maybe it was that having Justine around reminded her of her failed relationship with Sage, a relationship that Justine had encouraged. Or maybe it was that being around Justine conjured memories of Sara. Whatever the reason, Vaughn found herself angry all the time whenever Justine was around.

"First, let me say that whatever bug you've got up your ass about me, you'd better get over it." Justine poked her finger in Vaughn's chest. She vibrated with anger. "You're the one who called me for this op, not the other way around. If you don't want me here, just say so. I'm happy to go back to my nice, quiet life."

Vaughn closed her eyes. It seemed that everything these days was a confrontation and she was tired of fighting friends. No doubt she would be better served if she saved that for their common enemies. "I want you here," she conceded.

"Okay." Justine removed her finger from Vaughn's chest and gripped the railing, instead. "So what the hell is your problem?"

"Which one?" Vaughn barked a laugh.

"Nice deflection. That self-defeated, martyr tone doesn't suit you, Vaughn. And it sure as hell is a far cry from the Vaughn I know."

"Maybe I'm not that girl anymore. Has that occurred to you?"

"Bullshit." Justine pivoted to face her. "I let it go when you moved to the middle of nowhere. I cut you slack when you never answered my phone calls or e-mails after Sage left. I even made excuses for you with mutual friends."

"I never asked you to reach out to me and I certainly never asked you to make excuses for me," Vaughn said, still looking straight ahead.

"You didn't have to. You're my friend. Helping each other out is what friend's do. But maybe you've forgotten that."

Vaughn winced. "Maybe I never knew it to begin with. I told you a long time ago that I was a lousy friend. You chose to stay anyway. Don't blame me because I came as advertised."

Justine grabbed Vaughn by the arm and swung her until they faced each other. It was then that Vaughn could see just how deeply she'd hurt her friend.

"I'm done making excuses for you, Vaughn. I'm done cleaning up your messes because you checked out of life when Sara died."

Vaughn flinched as if she'd been slapped.

"I lost my best friend too. But you were too busy feeling sorry for yourself to notice. You were too busy wallowing in your misery to realize that the world went on without you and yes, without Sara."

Tears formed in Vaughn's eyes and she blinked. She acknowledged the corresponding tears in Justine's eyes.

"I'm sorry if that hurt. I'm sorry you couldn't save Sara. I'm sorry she's not here right now. If she were, she'd kick your ass from here all the way to Iraq without the benefit of a plane. She'd kick your ass for treating Sage so badly."

Vaughn dropped her chin to her chest. Justine was right about all of that.

"And she'd surely kick your ass for the way you're behaving toward Sedona."

Vaughn's head snapped back up. "What does Sedona have to do with anything?"

"Ah. That got a reaction out of you, didn't it? Now we're getting somewhere."

"I don't know what you're talking about."

"I'm talking about the fact that the sparks between you two are hot enough to start a forest fire and yet, I know you. She'll just be more collateral damage when you're done because you refuse to rejoin the human race. You refuse to come back to the land of the living."

"You're way off base." Vaughn's voice shook with emotion.

"Am I? I don't think so. I saw you follow her down to the beach two days ago. I saw the look on your face when you came back alone. Then I watched you follow her again this morning and I watched your expression when you returned together."

Vaughn's eyes closed involuntarily. She had hoped they'd slipped back unnoticed. She should have known better.

"You're torn up. I could see it in your face. Sedona doesn't know you yet, so she doesn't know what that look means. I've seen it before. You're attracted to her. Your heart draws you toward her. But you're so closed off, you've already determined that any relationship between you can't happen."

"Are you done psychoanalyzing me yet? In case you haven't noticed, we're in the middle of an op. There's no time for the personal." Vaughn's face was inches away from Justine's now.

"Really?" Justine leaned back. "That's rich coming from you."

"What do you mean by that?"

"Explain to me exactly what strategic advantage there is to having Sedona defended by one person when she could be defended by five."

"It's my jo—"

"Oh, my God. Please don't give me that tired bullshit about Sedona being your responsibility. Admit it, you're afraid she'll end up like Sara and it'll be all your fault. Wake up, Vaughn. We're all in this together. We're a team, and you're not utilizing the incredible resources you've got around you. I've never seen you make such wrongheaded decisions in the field."

Justine clenched and unclenched her jaw. "I strongly suggest you take a minute to sit with yourself and figure out what this is really about. And then get your head back in the game. We can't afford to get on that plane this afternoon without the Vaughn I know to lead us."

Vaughn could only watch after her as Justine retreated into the condo.

"And by the way?" Justine called over her shoulder, "I'm pretty sure Sedona can take care of herself."

CHAPTER TWELVE

Sir, I have something for you. I think you'll be pleased."
Steven Ochs, the acne-faced, owl-eyed computer geek,
folded, then unfolded his hands. He took in the trappings
of the office from his seat across from the infamous Astin
Trulander. The place was impressive. Still, he'd heard stories of
people who came in here to give this man news and never came
out. He wasn't one to put stock in gossip or rumors, but somehow,
he believed this one. He'd felt that kind of vibe when Trulander
came to visit him in the bat cave.

"I'll be the judge of that," Trulander said.

"Yes, sir." Steven picked up the manila file folder he held on
his lap. Unfortunately, his hands were shaking so badly that the
papers slid out before he could transfer the folder to the desk.

"You idiot," Trulander thundered.

Steven's hands shook harder. "I-I'm sorry, sir." He got down
on his hands and knees and collected the papers and stuffed them
back in the folder. With both hands on the folder this time, he
placed it on the desk.

Trulander snapped it up impatiently and whipped it open. He
perused the top document, then the next and the next. His eyes
were gleaming. "How sure are you that this information is
accurate?"

Steven, who still was getting up off the floor, swallowed hard.
He believed with all his heart that his next answer could make the
difference between going home to his cat tonight or exiting the
office in a body bag. "Accurate in what sense, sir?" He slid back
into the chair.

"How many senses of accurate are there?" Trulander boomed. "Either the information is good or it isn't. Which is it?" His face was turning purple.

Steven sat on his hands to keep them from shaking worse than they already were. "I..." It came out as a squeak, and Steven cleared his throat to try again. "I'm absolutely certain that the debit card used belongs to Sedona Ramos, sir. I can also verify that the card was used to purchase airfare from New York to Istanbul, with a stop in Frankfurt, Germany. The purchased ticket lists John F. Kennedy International Airport as the originating airport and the flight is a British Airways flight scheduled for a 7:15 a.m. departure the day after tomorrow."

Trulander stroked his chin. "And if I asked you again whether you truly believe Ramos will be on that flight, would you stake your cat's life on it?"

Steven was glad he was sitting, because his knees went weak. Trulander knew about Spock? "Um, statistical probability indicates—"

"I don't give a rat's ass about statistical probabilities." Trulander slammed his palm on the desk for emphasis. "I asked you a simple question and I expect a direct answer. Would you swear on your kitty-cat's life that Ramos will be on that plane?"

Steven thought his head would explode. He had a fifty-fifty chance of being right. What if he picked the wrong fifty? "Well, sir, if it was me and I'd paid that much for a flight, I'd certainly get on it."

Trulander continued to stare at him, his fingers drumming on the desk. "I sincerely hope you're right. If you're not..." He let the implication hang in the air.

"I hope so too, sir," Steven mumbled. "God, I hope so too."

"Get out."

Steven rose shakily to his feet and stumbled out of the office.

"I'm not buying it. It's too easy," Daniel Hart said. His voice vibrated in direct correlation to his footfalls on the treadmill at the exclusive gym.

"I agree with you. She's too savvy, with too much field experience, to make a careless mistake like using a traceable debit card." Orlando Niger, deputy director of the NSA and fellow Gulf War veteran, ran effortlessly on the adjacent treadmill in the otherwise empty facility.

"I'm curious," Hart said. "Did you ever meet this woman?"

"I did. It was at a dinner in the director's honor a few months ago."

"What was your assessment?"

"Apart from the fact that she's one sweet-looking piece of ass that I wouldn't have minded tapping?"

Hart chuckled. "Yeah, apart from that."

"Smart. Resourceful. Driven. Not easily intimidated or rattled."

"Too bad she's on the wrong side of this."

"Yeah. It's a damn shame." Niger powered down the treadmill and toweled off. "What's your plan?"

"That ass, Trulander, actually believes Ramos will be on the plane from JFK. He wants me to put resources there."

"Are you going to do it?"

"For the moment, I don't have much choice. Grayson insists that we give this asshole enough rope to hang himself—let him continue to think he's the big man." Hart decelerated to a walk. "So I'm tasking a minor team with airport and flight duty."

"And the rest? What do you suppose Ramos is really up to?"

Hart shook his head. "I wish I knew. I do think Trulander is right about one thing—she's probably headed to Tuwaitha."

"Since she gave you a Turkish route, it seems doubtful that she's heading into Iraq from the north."

"Exactly. We'll cover it, but I'm focusing more resources on the other possibilities. My guess is she'll try to sneak in either through Iran, which would be damn ballsy, or Kuwait, which would be less convenient, but also less risky."

"That's a lot of area to deal with. You've got enough resources to cover it?"

"That's where you come in, my friend. I need you to get a little creative for me."

"How so?"

"Ramos has been absent without leave for at least a week now. I need you to 'find' some documents on her hard drive that indicate she was in communication with some of the targets of the voice intercepts. That would explain her being on the run."

Niger's mouth dropped open. "You want me to elevate her to the terrorist watch list."

"More than that." Hart smiled wickedly. "I want you to make her an imminent threat to national security. By tomorrow morning, I want every TSA agent, every police officer in every jurisdiction, every border agent, every soldier at every military checkpoint from here to Iraq actively looking for her. I want our military bases in Iraq on high alert and her picture disseminated to every embassy so that if she tries to seek asylum in any country in which we have a diplomatic presence, she'll be arrested on the spot."

"You're going to use the resources of the government so we don't have to be everywhere."

"I knew there was a reason I made you my second-in-command in C Company twenty years ago. You're a sharp guy, O."

"I can do this, but I'm going to have to be careful about it. The debacle with the Tuwaitha file required some really fancy footwork. I can't take a chance on another snafu."

"That was most unfortunate."

"Especially for the jerk who accidentally sent the file instead of leaving it in the usual drop location—the spam folder."

"He certainly won't be making that mistake again."

"Too bad for his wife, who was nine months pregnant at the time of his 'accident'."

"She'll get survivor benefits. That's more than he got." Hart slapped Niger on the back. "I have confidence you'll get this taken care of discreetly."

"I'll see to it personally. I always did enjoy creative writing."

The drone of the engine and the propellers lulled Sedona to sleep. Her legs were stretched out in the aisle of the small plane for the short flight to Miami. She had the row to herself, which was more than fine with her. She'd been sure to get on first and find a seat. Her emotions were too raw; she needed the space to try to untangle the jumble of feelings swirling in her heart.

Every time she nodded off, she saw Vaughn's face enraptured and felt Vaughn's muscles contract around her fingers. Sedona jerked awake and crossed her legs. That line of thinking and the visceral memory would not do either of them any good where they were headed.

Besides, she had absolutely no indication that Vaughn wanted anything more to do with her. They had not spent a single moment alone together since that morning on the beach. And the dust-up over the travel arrangements had done nothing to improve either of their moods.

What was it Vaughn had said? "You have no idea what I'm feeling..." or something like that. Sedona recognized the truth of that statement. Vaughn's expressions and her demeanor gave away nothing, and Sedona refused to use her other senses to ferret out the truth. If Vaughn wanted her to know what she was thinking and feeling, then she would share it on her own. If not, so be it.

The problem was, Sedona didn't know how *she* was feeling about what had transpired. Obviously, she was attracted to Vaughn in a way she hadn't been attracted to anyone other than Rachel.

Rachel. What would she have thought of this situation? Tendrils of guilt swept through Sedona. Until Vaughn, there hadn't been anyone who touched Sedona's heart and few who touched her body. On those rare occasions when Sedona craved female company, she paid for it. That way, there were no emotional entanglements, no misunderstandings, and no danger of anyone stealing Sedona's heart and then dying on her.

Sedona swallowed a cry and turned toward the window. How was it possible, after three years, that Rachel's loss still hurt so much? And how could Sedona even think about any kind of relationship with Vaughn when her heart would always belong to Rachel—her lover, her life-long best friend, her soul mate?

Her eyelids grew heavy again, and this time, Sedona allowed herself to succumb to sleep. She would need the rest, because once they got where they were going, it was anybody's guess when the next downtime would come.

Vaughn scanned the crowd in the Miami airport. There was the usual complement of TSA agents and cops. No one seemed to be paying them particular attention.

She insisted that Justine and Sabastien go through security first, a full two-and-a-half hours ahead of the scheduled flight. Vaughn and Sedona would go next, an hour and forty-five minutes before the plane took off, and Peter and Lorraine would go last, half an hour after that, in case anything went awry. In that case, Peter and Lorraine would have an opportunity to break off the plan and find an alternate route to Kuwait. Under that scenario, the rest of the mission would fall to them.

Sedona walked beside Vaughn, and Vaughn noted that she seemed perfectly at ease. Vaughn knew she couldn't be, but she admired the acting job just the same. Neither one of them had said a single personal thing to the other in the two hours they'd been alone together since arriving at Miami International.

"All clear so far," Vaughn whispered into the coms. The tiny piece of plastic in her ear was almost too small to see. The transmitter on her hip appeared from the outside to be an iPod. Next to her, Sedona bopped to imaginary tunes on an identical iPod, her headphones tuned, instead, to the com frequency Sabastien had set for all of them. They made the decision not to give Sedona a microphone, since that would be difficult to explain if they got stopped.

To facilitate her ability to defend Sedona, Vaughn had Sabastien spoof the identity of a Deputy US Marshal transporting a high-value protectee to witness protection. This enabled her to carry her Glock-40 on her hip and her Walther .380 in an ankle holster. It also made it legal for her to check the rest of the group's weapons, and resulted in a decreased level of scrutiny for her. In addition, it forced the TSA agents to give her and Sedona a wide berth.

"Ten-four," Peter answered. "Everything still looks quiet outside security."

"All is well in the gate area," Justine reported.

"See you all on board," Vaughn said, signing off. She lightly grasped Sedona by the elbow and steered them toward a Starbucks. It was a red-eye flight, and she was going to need some help to stay vigilant.

୶ଡ଼

Orlando Niger chewed his fingernail to the nub as he waited for the changes to the file to upload. He considered himself risk-aversive these days, so this bit of late-night creative writing and file replacement gave him hives. Still, he owed his life to Daniel Hart for saving him from a sniper's bullet, and it was time to repay the debt.

When Daniel approached him and recruited him several years ago, Orlando hadn't fully understood the extent of the commitment, nor the reach of the organization to which he was pledging his allegiance. Now, it was too late to back out. He was in too deep, and he knew too much. The best he could hope for was to make himself indispensible. Turning Sedona Ramos into a reviled terrorist would go a long way toward accomplishing that goal.

He heard the quiet ding signifying that the file upload was done. Now all that remained was for Orlando to "discover" it. He would bring it to his boss's attention, a man for whom neither he nor Daniel had much use. He was a pompous, self-important stump of a man who cared little for the nitty-gritty details of his agency's work. That was the type of thing for which he had a deputy director, as he often reminded Orlando. His boss would then elevate the information to the appropriate authority's attention. That authority, of course, would be Daniel Hart. And it would be done.

By late tomorrow morning, there wouldn't be any place that Sedona Ramos could hide.

୶ଡ଼

Wayne Grayson finished his evening exercises in the yard at the federal penitentiary and headed back inside.

"Your lawyer wants to see you," the stocky guard on the door reported. "Don't bother going back to your cell. We're taking you to the meeting room."

Grayson showed no emotion, he simply shuffled along with the gait of a man who spent too long behind bars and aged before his time. Those who had watched him for a long time knew not to be deceived by this. His eyes and his mind were razor sharp. Behind bars or free at large, this was a man to be feared.

When he entered the private meeting room where lawyers met with their clients, his lawyer already was seated at the table.

"Stanley, you're looking well-fed."

The lawyer looked up at him and blinked. "I have some documents for you to review." He slid a folder across the table.

Grayson cracked his knuckles and caressed the folder like a lover. He opened to the first document, which was a request to have his sentence commuted by the president. He smiled. "That's rich," he mumbled.

He impatiently thumbed through until he got to the middle of the pile. Then his eyes lit up. There was the transcript of that nebbish nephew threatening the computer geek's cat. Grayson cackled. "What an ass." Still, at least this time the idiot didn't kill anyone. Yet.

"Do you want me to do anything about him?"

"Hmm?" Grayson was engrossed in the rest of the word-for-word transcription of every conversation, live or on the phone, Astin had conducted in the last week.

There were the usual blustering threats and the bone-headed business decisions. Those didn't bother Grayson. He expected as much from his younger sister's only boy. She had him as an out-of-wedlock teenager when she could barely take care of herself. She came weeping to her big brother, begging him to take the boy in and make something of him.

Grayson loved his sister, so he tried to teach her son the ways of the elite business world. But the boy had about as much aptitude for business and social interactions as a baboon, and it quickly became clear to Grayson that he would have to find some place to stash Astin where he would do no harm. The little oil company Grayson Enterprises picked up in a hostile takeover seemed the perfect place.

Grayson's unfortunate arrest and conviction for treason for the kidnapping and attempted murder of President Hyland created a new set of challenges. It was nothing insurmountable—Grayson certainly could continue to lead the organization from his jail cell—but he would need a figurehead. A stooge. Astin was the perfect candidate.

No doubt Astin thought he actually was in charge. For years this worked to Grayson's advantage. But not anymore. He broke the cardinal rule, which was to leave no trace. He was getting sloppy and it had to stop.

It was a shame, really, but Grayson had carried him along as long as he could. He was sure his sister would understand from her perch in Heaven.

"I asked, do you want me to do anything about him?"

Grayson focused on the lawyer. "Not yet." He read further. "Hart is handling the actual search?"

"Yes, sir. He tells me the lady suddenly has become of great interest to Homeland Security. Seems she's a terrorist."

"How interesting," Grayson smirked.

"She's moved to the top of the 'imminent threats list' and is presently being hunted by every law enforcement officer from here to Baghdad."

"She must be very dangerous." Grayson's smile widened. "What is the current status?"

"Beginning tomorrow morning, there won't be anyplace that woman can go that she won't be recognized and apprehended."

"Excellent, Stanley. I do love when you bring me good news."

"Yes, sir."

"Is there a separate team in place at the facility, just in case she gets that far?"

"Yes, sir. There's an elite eight-member squad strategically stationed around the perimeter. I'm assured she won't be able to get in."

"I want to know the second she's finished. And Stanley, I do mean finished. No messy loose ends, like a trial."

"Understood, sir."

"What about the group we think she's traveling with?"

"Anyone she's allied with will be considered aiding and abetting a terrorist, of course, and will be dealt with accordingly."

Grayson nodded his approval. "Make sure the same instructions apply to them, as well."

"Of course, sir. Anything else?"

"How's that oil pipeline coming? Has Kincaid gotten it through her committee yet?"

"She's mustering the votes as we speak, sir."

"Tell her to hurry it up. All of these things must be perfectly timed, otherwise this will have been a wasted exercise. I do so hate to cause thousands of potential deaths and a possible war for no reason."

"Yes, sir. Is that all?"

"For now, Stanley. For now."

CHAPTER THIRTEEN

Vaughn watched Sedona sleep. She was curled up facing the window, but her profile was fully visible. Her face was relaxed, her mouth turned up in a half-smile. Vaughn couldn't remember ever seeing such beauty. She deliberately turned the other way.

The problem with long flights was having too much downtime. Up until now, it had been easy to avoid thinking about the events of the past few days. But here, flying over the ocean at 37,000 feet, there was nothing but time to think.

"What the hell is it about me and damsels in distress?" she muttered. First, it was Sage and the race across the desert sands of Mali to find and save her. Now, it was Sedona. Was she simply attracted to women who needed her? Could it be that these two situations were her way of recreating the scene with Sara and coming up with a different ending?

"Good Lord." Vaughn ran her fingers through her hair. Was that it?

Sedona groaned in her sleep and Vaughn automatically put a hand out to soothe her. Immediately, she settled back down and Vaughn removed her hand.

Sedona was not Sage—that much was certain. It wasn't just that one was dark where the other was light. Sedona was battle tough. Sage was softer and gentler. Sedona was edgy. Sage was bookish.

But they shared some qualities too. Both were intelligent, resourceful, observant, and analytical. Both were attractive, although in very different ways. Vaughn glanced at Sedona once again. Oh, yes. She was definitely exquisite. Vaughn wondered what she would look like without her clothes on. A lightning bolt of desire flowed through her and she stifled a moan. She reminded herself that they were on assignment and that, when this was over, they would go their separate ways.

Vaughn replayed the conversation with Justine. Was she right? Was Sedona destined to be collateral damage? Was Vaughn incapable of real love anymore?

Certainly it was true that a part of her died with Sara. How could it not? Sara was the yin to her yang. She was the balance. She understood Vaughn in ways no one else could. Vaughn was lost without her and suspected she always would be. So yes, Sara's death irrevocably changed Vaughn. For that, she offered no apologies.

What, then, was this thing with Sedona? Was it anything at all? A few moments of passion on the beach hardly counted for a relationship. Vaughn glanced at Sedona again. She wondered what Sedona thought was between them. Sedona hadn't seemed to be in any rush to discuss what happened either. Was she even looking for a relationship?

That was pretty presumptuous. Vaughn laughed at herself. Maybe she was getting ahead of herself. Perhaps sometimes a tryst really was just a tryst.

⤚⤙

The director of the NSA chewed on an unlit cigar. "You're sure about this?"

Orlando Niger tried not to roll his eyes. "Yes, sir. Our internal affairs team discovered the incriminating documents on her hard drive this morning. They had the translation independently verified. There is no question of the communication's authenticity or that it came from Ramos's computer."

"I see. Well... Damn. Well... It's a shame. Her record up until now was exemplary."

"Sir, with all due respect, we need to move on this now. We have no idea where this woman has gone. The documents seem to indicate she may be heading to the Middle East with vital, top-secret details about our information-gathering processes and technology. If she reaches her destination, this could be catastrophic. Not only that, but it would be a huge stain on the agency's reputation. This could be a major blot on your record." Niger knew an appeal to the director's vanity and ego would likely push him to action. "I'm just trying to protect your legacy here."

The director put down the cigar and scanned the report once again. "Okay then. If you're sure, I'll give a call over to Homeland Security and send this up the flagpole."

Niger breathed a sigh of relief. "Thank you, sir. I know you're doing the right thing."

On the way out of the office, he glanced at his watch—it was 9:27 a.m. Once Hart had the official report, it would be only a matter of minutes until the order would be given and alerts would go out. Within the hour, there wouldn't be any place in the world Sedona Ramos could hide.

Heathrow Airport was a mass of people scurrying to and fro. The first thing Sedona noticed was the unusual number of cops swarming around. The hair on the back of her neck stood up and a chill ran through her. She glanced to the side. If Vaughn was alarmed, she didn't show it.

Archangel Michael, is this trouble for me? Immediately, her body was suffused with heat. This was another way that Archangel Michael communicated with her. Her gut tightened and she nodded imperceptibly. *Okay. Thank you, Michael, for being with me. Please protect me and give me crystal clear guidance as to how to proceed.*

"Vaughn," she said quietly, her lips barely moving.

"Yeah."

"We have a problem."

"What do you mean?"

Sedona debated what to say. If Peter were walking with her, she would've been straightforward. Somehow, she didn't think that this was the proper time to tell Vaughn about her abilities. Still, she wanted to be as honest as she could be.

"Do you see the increased police presence?"

"Probably standard protocol these days."

"I don't think so." Sedona wrapped her arm inside Vaughn's elbow and tugged.

"What are you doing?"

"Do you trust me?" Sedona's eyes pleaded with Vaughn.

"Y-yes."

"Okay." Sedona pulled them up short and kissed Vaughn passionately on the mouth. She turned them so that Vaughn completely blocked her from the view of passersby.

At first, Vaughn resisted and Sedona could feel the shock running through her. Then she yielded. Sedona struggled not to get lost in the kiss. When the cop who had been looking in their direction passed, she released Vaughn.

Vaughn stumbled back a step. "What the hell—"

"Get Peter and Lorraine on the coms. Tell them to do a little poking around. Those cops are looking for someone specific." She inclined her head to indicate the officer that just had passed. "I think that someone is me." Sedona worked hard to keep her voice calm.

Vaughn moved back in toward Sedona and casually shielded her by leaning in and resting her hand on the wall behind Sedona's head. "Peter, Lorraine. Do you copy?"

"Here," Lorraine answered.

"What's your position?"

"We're approaching the loading area for DHL. Why?"

"The package may be opened by security. Can you investigate ASAP?"

"On it."

"We can't stay here like this. It's too open," Vaughn said.

Sedona surveyed the area. She spotted a unisex handicapped bathroom a short distance away. "There," she pointed.

After assuring themselves that no one was watching, they entered the private bathroom and locked the door.

"Are you okay?" Vaughn asked.

"I'm fine. Sorry about the kiss. It was the first thing I could think of that would hide me from view."

"You're sorry about the kiss?" Vaughn asked.

"Do you want me to be?" Sedona's heart beat hard against her ribs. She wasn't sure whether that was the potential danger of their situation or anticipation of Vaughn's answer.

"Vaughn?" It was Peter.

Sedona closed her eyes and willed her breath to return to normal.

"Here."

"We have serious trouble."

"We're listening."

"The place is on high alert. They're looking for an American—a dangerous terrorist." He paused. "Sedona Ramos."

Sedona's knees buckled and she leaned against the wall.

"Jesus," Vaughn said. "Okay. Let's think this through."

"We could lie low here in the UK until things calm down," Justine said. "By the way, Sabastien and I are sitting on the cargo plane."

"I don't think that's a good answer," Lorraine said. "They're not going to stop looking. She's classified as an imminent threat."

"Damn!"

"How the fuck—"

"Let's worry about the 'how' later," Vaughn broke in. "Right now, we need a plan." When she looked at Sedona, there was sympathy in her eyes.

"I know what to do," Sedona said, holding Vaughn's gaze.

"Hold on. Sedona has an idea."

Sedona moved closer to Vaughn so she could be heard over the coms. They were close enough that Sedona could feel Vaughn's breath on her neck. "Cuff me."

Vaughn rocked back on her heels. "I'm sorry. What?"

"Cuff me. Your cover is law enforcement. Cuff me and take me prisoner. You've apprehended the dangerous terrorist and you're escorting her to Kuwait to one of the CIA's super-secret interrogation facilities. You can't question me properly in the US because of those pesky, inconvenient, due-process laws."

"That'll never fly—" Vaughn started to say.

"It could work," Peter said.

"We'd need to switch to a commercial flight," Justine said. "Sabastien is here with me. He's booting up his laptop to look right now."

"We'd never be flying on a British Airways commercial flight," Vaughn countered.

"You want to get me to Kuwait right away, before any human rights group has a chance to make the torture of an American terror suspect an issue."

"It's a huge risk," Vaughn argued. "We'd be better off making a run for it to the cargo plane."

Sedona could read the worry in Vaughn's aura. She put a hand on her arm. "We'd never make it undetected. A commercial flight is the best chance we have. Once we get to Kuwait, your friend will be waiting with the helicopter, right?"

"Yes."

"Then if we can get to Kuwait safely, we should be fine."

"Sedona's right," Lorraine said. "With the place swarming the way it is, there's no way we can get her onto that cargo plane without someone stopping her."

"There is a British Airways flight leaving for Kuwait in a little more than an hour," Sabastien said. "If you give me the word, I can have us all confirmed on the flight under the aliases we used in Miami. If you want, I can even back time it so it appears we were scheduled for the flight months in advance and we checked in yesterday."

"It's our only chance, Vaughn," Sedona pleaded.

Vaughn chewed her lip. "Okay, Sabastien. Do it. But don't confirm Sedona or me. If you do, it'll raise too many questions."

"You're right," Lorraine said. "If the alert just went out while we were in the air, where did Vaughn apprehend her? How could she have known that she would need a seat on that flight?"

"That's a problem," Justine said.

"Not necessarily," Peter said. "It's not unheard of for US marshals to give no prior notification. It doesn't endear them to the airlines or the flight crew, but sometimes that's the way it goes. You'd better hope that no one was booked in the last row, though. If so, they're going to get bumped off the flight and they're not going to be happy about it."

"Sabastien? Can you see if we'd be bumping anybody to get on the flight?" Sedona asked.

"Of course," Sabastien said. A few seconds, later he said, "You are all clear. The flight is only about seventy-eight percent full. All is well."

"Okay, I guess we've got a plan," Vaughn agreed.

"We've got another issue to consider," Peter said. "If we're going to pull this off, we'd need someone already undercover as a Kuwaiti to meet and escort the prisoner when we arrive."

"You mean someone who's with the Company?" Vaughn asked.

"I can take care of that," Justine offered. "I'll make the call right now. In the meantime, can I make a suggestion?"

"What is it?" Vaughn asked.

"I can't believe the president is aware of Sedona's designation. He would've stopped it. We have to get word to him."

"There's nothing he can do about it without tipping our hand. If he cancels the alert, it either means he knows something—"

"Which would tip off whoever's behind this." Lorraine finished Peter's sentence.

"Or else somehow the word gets out and he looks soft on terrorism. Either way," Peter said, "he can't help us."

"Maybe he can," Vaughn said. "What if all he did was facilitate us getting on that plane? We're going to need some kind of documentation anyway."

Sedona nodded in appreciation. "Vaughn's right. What if the president made a call to Ten Downing Street and asked permission to put me on that plane as a favor—you know, one terrorist-fighting ally to another?"

Lorraine picked up the thread. "He wouldn't have to reveal anything about our actual purpose. He wouldn't really have to give anything away at all."

Vaughn nodded. "Okay."

"Vaughn?" Justine asked. "Where the heck are you, anyway?"

"A private bathroom, why?"

Justine laughed. "The echo is atrocious."

"Sorry. We had to improvise."

"Okay. Don't move," Peter said. "I'll call Kate right now and have her talk to the president."

"Um. That won't be necessary," Sedona said sheepishly.

"Because…?"

"We can call him directly." Sedona shrugged when Vaughn's eyes widened.

"You have a secure line to the president," she said.

"Yeah." Sedona smiled. "Hey, I earned it."

"I don't think it's a good idea for you to make the call," Lorraine said.

"Puts him in a horrible position," Peter elaborated.

"I agree," Sedona said. "That's why I'm handing my burn phone to Vaughn." She took the phone out of her pocket and slapped it into Vaughn's palm. "Try speed dial number one." She winked.

❧❧

"This is the president," the sleepy voice said.

Vaughn stood up a little straighter. "Mr. President, sir. I'm sorry to wake you."

"Who is this?"

"Vaughn Elliot, sir. I'm here with a friend of yours, and she assures me that you personally gave her this number and permission to use it."

"What is it?" Now the president sounded fully awake. "What's happened?"

"Sir, I don't know if you're aware, but I've captured the newest imminent terrorist threat."

"I'm sorry. I'm not following. Who would that be?"

"Sedona Ramos, sir."

"What?" The president's voice was so loud Vaughn had to hold the phone away from her ear. "I didn't authorize that."

"I'm sure you didn't, sir."

"Is she okay?"

Vaughn smiled at the protectiveness in his voice. "For now, sir, but we've got a bit of a situation, and we could really use your help."

"Tell me."

"I don't want to say too much, sir, but as I just indicated, I have apprehended this dangerous terrorist, and I really need to get her to Kuwait ASAP. I know it wouldn't be usual protocol to put such a…dangerous…individual on a commercial plane, but in this case I think it's vital to get her to Kuwait so we can see what she knows."

"I see."

"We're in a bit of bind, sir, and this is our best hope to be able to deal with her ourselves."

"What do you need from me?"

"A call to Ten Downing Street that would smooth the way for me, Deputy US Marshal Cynthia Frederickson, to transport the prisoner on the British Airways flight departing in forty-four minutes from Heathrow would be most helpful. Also, I'll need someone to meet us at the gate with an authenticated note from Interpol confirming the arrangements so I can hand that to the head of security."

"Consider it done. Do you have the prisoner in a secure location right now?"

"For the moment, sir, but time really is of the essence."

"Understood. Give me five minutes and I'll call you back."

"Are those too tight?" Vaughn asked. She hated that she'd had to put leg irons, a belly chain and handcuffs on Sedona. She surreptitiously stroked the side of Sedona's arm beneath the coat draped over Sedona's handcuffs.

"No. I'm fine."

"Are you scared?"

Sedona smiled. "Only a little. I mean it's not like everyone is looking at me suspiciously or anything." Sedona indicated the line of gawkers with a tilt of her head.

Vaughn had received the all-clear from the president to take the flight, with the additional instruction that she would be permitted to board Sedona first, before any of the regular passengers. This way, they could go directly to the back of the plane, where the prisoner would be watched closely and where she wouldn't be a danger to anyone else.

Vaughn helped Sedona navigate the jetway, led her to the last row, and helped her sit. Because of the nature of Sedona's status, they had the row all to themselves. "Are you comfortable enough?"

"Why wouldn't I be?"

Sedona batted her eyelashes playfully at Vaughn. Vaughn wished in the worst way that she could lean over and kiss her. She marveled at how calm, cool, and collected Sedona appeared. It made Vaughn feel even more fiercely protective of her than she already did. In light of her recent ruminations on the flight to London from Miami, Vaughn didn't want to think about what that meant.

She and Sedona observed the passengers as they boarded. Justine and Sabastien got onboard early in the process. Their seats were in the middle of the plane. Peter and Lorraine, looking for all-the-world like newlyweds, boarded nearly last. They sat in first class.

"Do you see anybody that gives you pause?"

Sedona seemed to be surprised by the question.

"What? Was that the wrong thing to ask?" Vaughn asked.

"I'm just a little surprised that you want my opinion."

"Why wouldn't I? You're keenly aware and observant. You picked up on the trouble even before I did back there. If it hadn't been for you, we might've been blown and…" Vaughn couldn't finish the sentence. The thought of Sedona being taken prisoner and hauled off to some jail was not something she wanted to consider.

Sedona closed her eyes and asked the angels for guidance. When she opened her eyes again, Vaughn was staring at her. "I think we're okay."

"What were you just doing?"

"What do you mean?"

"You closed your eyes and your lips were moving."

"They were?" Sedona asked. She shifted slightly in her seat.

Vaughn narrowed her eyes. "That made you nervous."

"What?"

"That I noticed."

"You've lost your mind."

Vaughn smiled and shook her head. "I don't think so, but I'll let you keep your secrets—for now."

Sedona yawned. "It's been kind of a long haul. Mind if I take a nap?"

Vaughn recognized the evasion, but she decided to let it pass. She understood better than most not wanting to lay herself bare. "Go for it." She touched Sedona's hand, mostly because she couldn't stop herself. "Are you going to be able to sleep like this?"

With a sweeping gesture, Vaughn indicated the shackles and the Kevlar vest made necessary by Sedona's wanted-terrorist status. "There's nothing you can do about it without giving us away, can you?"

Vaughn frowned at Sedona's practicality. "I suppose not."

"Then don't worry about it." Sedona leaned back and closed her eyes. "There is one thing you can do for me," she said, after a moment.

"Name it."

"Since I can't snuggle against you, could you put a pillow against the window for me?"

Vaughn's stomach flipped as she realized that there wasn't anything she'd rather do than put her arm around Sedona and hold her while she slept. "Sure," she croaked.

CHAPTER FOURTEEN

E verything is going according to plan." Daniel Hart stood looking over the Capitol rotunda. Next to him, Emily Kincaid shifted uncomfortably.

"Have they caught her yet?"

"No, but it's only a matter of time."

"Are you sure that this will work? Declaring her an enemy combatant, I mean."

Hart bristled. "It's genius. Not only does it save us from having to expend our own resources, but it ensures that she has no credibility even if she manages to tell someone in power what she knows."

"What does Astin think?"

"Who cares what that sniveling jackass thinks," Hart snapped. "His days are numbered." Next to him, he felt her recoil.

"What are you talking about?"

"Grayson has no intention of leaving such a delicate and important operation in the hands of his incompetent nephew."

"Astin has been in charge for years," she huffed. "His uncle has complete confidence in him."

Hart turned around and put his back to the railing so that he was facing her. "Wake up and smell the coffee, Emily. I have no idea what it is you see in that two-bit wanna-be. Do you even realize he's been tapping your phones for months?"

"What?"

Hart's smile was self-satisfied. "That's right. Your hero has been tapping your phones and listening in on your conversations to get intel on your progress on the oil pipeline. He figures he'll have a leg up lobbying the members of your caucus because he'll already know what their positions are and he can concentrate on the most vulnerable members. It gives him extra time to get dirt on them and use it against them to procure their votes."

"Astin would never—"

"Jesus! You're hopeless." Hart pushed off the railing. "Listen, Emily. I like you. I really do. My advice to you is get your head out of your ass before you end up just like Astin."

She opened her mouth to say something, then closed it, then opened it again. "Where is Quinn?"

"He's back on-site, overseeing the production end of things."

"How close is he?"

"Close."

"Good."

"How close are we to pushing the pipeline through?" Hart asked.

"Close. I'm still counting heads, but I should be able to move it out of committee at tomorrow's meeting. Once that happens, we'll get it on the floor calendar so it'll be in perfect position to be fast-tracked when the shit hits the fan."

"Excellent." Hart nodded. "Grayson will be pleased." He started to walk away.

"Daniel, wait."

He turned around. "Yeah?"

"Will you keep me posted on the status of the search?"

"Of course. Let me know when the committee votes the bill out." He walked away, whistling.

❦

Kate stood when the president strode into the library of the White House's private residence.

"Have a seat, Kate." He unbuttoned his suit coat, scrubbed his hands over his face, and selected the winged-back chair opposite her.

"If you don't mind my saying so, sir, you look tired." She didn't add that he also looked years older than he had when he was sworn into office. She had noticed the same changes in President Hyland when she worked for him. There was no question that the office aged its inhabitants.

"Yeah, well, it goes with the job, I think."

"Yes, it does."

"My wife thinks I should consider coloring my hair." He laughed. "Somehow, I don't think I'm quite ready for that step."

"I hear that once you start, you'll never stop."

"Exactly," the president agreed. "Anyway, as you might imagine, I didn't ask you here to discuss my hair." He leaned forward and clasped his hands together. "I heard from Vaughn in the middle of the night."

"Oh?" Kate's heart stuttered. She fully expected that Vaughn would have contacted her rather than going directly to the president. She could only imagine that something had gone really wrong.

"It seems Ms. Ramos has been designated an imminent terror threat."

"Sir?" Kate swallowed hard. "Is she okay? Is the team—"

"As far as I know, they are on a plane to Kuwait and they are fine."

Kate wanted to know more, but she sensed that the president had something else on his mind. "That's not why I'm here, is it?"

"I'm sure you have questions, and I'll answer them, but first, I want to discuss the bigger picture."

"Sir?"

"Someone has made our friend public enemy number one…without my knowledge and without my having read any paperwork on it."

"How is that possible, sir? Wouldn't you have to sign off on something that major or at least be informed?" Kate's mind raced. She stood, started to pace and then remembered where she was. She returned to her seat. "I know it's been a while since I worked here, and 9/11 changed everything, but still…"

"Normally, I would agree with you. I would be kept in the loop, especially since they're accusing her of treason and collusion with al-Qaeda in Iraq."

"What?" Kate jumped up again. She couldn't help it. She had to pace. "Don't they have to have a basis for such a designation?"

"Of course." The president's voice was calm, almost matter-of-fact.

Kate turned back around and headed back to her chair. "They trumped something up."

"Yes."

"How?"

"I don't know yet. That's part of why I wanted to talk to you. I want to be very careful about my next steps."

Kate sat back down. "What are the options?"

"Ultimately, the designation must have come from the Homeland Security Secretary Daniel Hart—apart from me, he's the only one who could have approved it."

Kate nodded. In her day, there hadn't been a Department of Homeland Security, so the protocol was new to her. "Wouldn't there have to be documentation to back that up?"

"Absolutely. That's where it gets interesting."

Kate thought she knew where the president was going. "You're trying to figure out whether Secretary Hart knew what he was doing or whether he was an unwitting dupe."

"That's part of it, yes." Now it was the president's turn to pace. "If Daniel didn't know what he was doing and went on someone else's recommendation, I want to know who that someone was."

"And if he did know…" Kate let the implication hang in the air.

"I hope that's not true, but I have to consider the very real possibility that he was a party to it." The president sat back down. "That's where it gets tricky. I have to decide whether to tip my hand and let him know I'm aware of the designation or wait and see how this plays out going forward."

Kate pursed her lips in thought. "I can see advantages and disadvantages to both scenarios. If you didn't hear about the designation from Secretary Hart, how else might you have found out? Is there another avenue, another reasonable explanation for how you would have come by the information, sir?"

"Good question. It is unlikely, unless there had been something about it on the news, in which case it would have appeared in my briefing."

"I haven't seen anything on the news about it, sir."

"That's because the general public hasn't been made aware of it yet."

"So, if you call Secretary Hart on the carpet and he is complicit, he's going to wonder how you found out about this."

"And if that's the case, we'd be getting one fish, but not the whole school, if you catch my drift."

150

"I do, sir. But maybe there's another way."

"I'm listening."

"You have Sabastien on your side. We could have him poke around in the Homeland Security computer systems to find whatever documentation was provided for the terrorist designation."

The president's eyes lit up. "That's brilliant. We could, indeed. That way, we would know what fiction was created."

"Which would give us a better idea where it might have originated, and whether or not Secretary Hart had anything to do with it."

"Indeed." The president nodded to himself. "I like it. Of course, that presumes that the team arrives safely at their destination and that Sabastien has the proper equipment with him to complete the task."

"True. There's only one way to find out, sir."

The president sighed. "Yes, but we have to wait for them to contact us, since we don't know precisely what their situation is."

"Are they scheduled to call you again, sir?"

"Not specifically, but let's hope they do."

Kate didn't want to take up any more of the president's time, but she needed to know. "Sir? Now can you fill me in on the team's status and their plan?"

When the president finished explaining to her about the hair-raising situation at Heathrow, the desperate race to get the Interpol documentation into Vaughn's hands in time for the flight, and the cover story, Kate thought her head would explode. She blinked. "So what happens when they get to Kuwait?"

"I don't know. Vaughn was very circumspect. I imagine she was trying to limit my exposure."

"I sure hope they have a plan," Kate said.

"Me too, Kate. Me too."

By virtue of her threat status, Sedona and Vaughn would be the last to get off the aircraft. As a result, Sedona watched as Justine and Sabastien exited the plane without a single backward glance. For some reason, this added to her feeling of isolation. Already, she was rattled by Vaughn's complete mastery of the tough deputy US marshal persona. The woman Sedona was coming to know was nowhere in sight, and Sedona was surprised to find that she missed her.

When everyone else was gone, Vaughn motioned for Sedona to get up. She tried to stand, but fell back into the seat. The shackles and Kevlar vest made every motion difficult and awkward.

Vaughn grabbed her roughly by the elbow and yanked her to her feet. Sedona winced but said nothing. She reminded herself that this was not real—it was a necessary deception—an illusion that would end as soon as they were away from prying eyes.

Vaughn jerked Sedona sideways and into the aisle as the flight attendants stood as far back as possible. Sedona could see the fear in their eyes, just as she'd seen the fear in the eyes of the other passengers as they boarded the plane. It was hard to reconcile the person these folks feared with the gentle soul Sedona knew herself to be. She would have to worry about her soul later. Right now, she had a part to play.

Then Vaughn placed a black cloth hood over her head and Sedona swallowed a cry. The instant darkness was disorienting and the hood was stifling. Vaughn had mentioned that this might be necessary, since it was standard protocol, but Sedona was not prepared for just how real the hood made her status feel, nor for what having her third eye covered would do to rob her of her psychic perception.

She stumbled forward, her ankles chafing against the heavy leg irons. She felt Vaughn helping to hold her upright with a hand secured in her belly chain. When they reached the front of the plane, Vaughn yanked the chain to help her pivot toward the exit.

Slowly, carefully, Sedona made her way down the stairs leading to the tarmac. She could feel Vaughn directly behind her. At the bottom of the stairs, Vaughn clamped a hand on her shoulder and urged her forward.

"Keep walking," Vaughn whispered in her ear. "There's a vehicle in front of us. When we reach it, there'll be a Kuwaiti officer who will shove you into the car. Don't worry. He's one of us. I'll be right behind you. Oh, and don't forget to duck so you don't hit your head on the doorframe."

Vaughn's mouth was close enough to her ear that Sedona could feel her breath. Irrationally, she wished she could turn around and see her eyes. Her eyes would tell Sedona everything she needed to know. But that wasn't possible. So she marched forward toward the waiting vehicle, wondering if Vaughn felt the same disconnect that she did.

≈◈≈

Vaughn said nothing on the short drive to the hangar. She could feel Sedona's trembling leg next to her.

The car squealed into the darkness of the bay and the driver cut the engine. In perfect Arabic, the Kuwaiti officer dismissed the driver. When it was clear they were alone, the man turned to face Vaughn and Sedona in the backseat. "Welcome to Kuwait." His American English held a hint of a Mid-Western twang.

"Good to be here, I think," Vaughn answered. She yanked the hood off Sedona's head.

Sedona blinked as her eyes adjusted to the light.

"I'm Charlie, a friend of Justine's. When she told me you needed assistance, she wasn't kidding." Charlie whistled. "Nice accessories, by the way." He indicated Sedona's shackles. "I hear that's the latest in jewelry fashion."

Sedona mustered a wan smile.

"How are we going to get the rest of the team in here?" Vaughn asked.

"I've got it covered. I'm going to go collect them from baggage claim. I'll bring them here. Your helicopter is parked directly behind this hangar. There are no eyes back there, so no one will see you board." He winked. "Well, I'd better get things underway. Will you two be all right on your own for a bit?"

"Don't worry about us," Vaughn said casually.

"Right-o. See you in a few." Charlie jumped out of the car and exited the hangar through a side door, leaving Vaughn and Sedona completely alone.

To her surprise, when Vaughn turned to face Sedona, she saw tears in her eyes. A lump formed in Vaughn's throat. "Hey," she said gently. She pulled Sedona to her and held her close. "There's nothing to worry about, babe. I've got you. I'm right here, and I'm

153

not going to let anything happen to you." She felt Sedona take a shaky breath against her shoulder. She pulled back so she could see Sedona's face. "Let's get you out of these, okay?"

Sedona nodded, and Vaughn noted that she hadn't said a single word in hours. Although she didn't have much to go on, she thought that was out of character.

Vaughn reached into a pocket and found the keys to unlock the restraints. She started by releasing Sedona's hands, then she removed the belly chain, and finally the leg irons.

Sedona rubbed her wrists. "Thanks." She said it so quietly, Vaughn had to strain to hear it.

"Don't mention it." Vaughn gave Sedona a reassuring smile, hoping it would lift her spirits. It occurred to Vaughn that these might be the only quiet minutes they would have alone for a very long time.

She knew she should say something, but she wasn't sure what. The trip had taken a toll on Sedona, she could see that, but it also affected her. The last thing she'd wanted to do was to be detached and cold, but that was required in order to pull off the ruse.

"You called me 'babe,'" Sedona said.

"What?" Vaughn was so deep in thought, she wasn't sure she heard Sedona correctly.

"Just now. You called me babe."

"I did?" Vaughn didn't remember it.

"You did. You said, 'There's nothing to worry about, babe.'"

"Oh." Vaughn searched for something else to say.

"I bet you say that to all the girls." Sedona winked and Vaughn recognized a hint of the real Sedona returning. A wave of relief rushed through her.

"Only the pretty ones. Especially ones that look hot in shackles."

"Good to know. I mean it's not everyone who can pull off the shackle look."

"Very true. Many have tried and failed before you." Vaughn couldn't resist any longer. She reached over and brushed a lock of hair from Sedona's forehead and closed the short distance between them. Tentatively, she brushed her lips across Sedona's. "I'm so sorry for all of that," she whispered. "I wish none of it was necessary."

"I know," Sedona answered. Her mouth was tantalizingly close.

Vaughn leaned forward and claimed Sedona's lips. The kiss was slow and tender, sweet and gentle. She felt her heart thud hard against her ribcage. She couldn't remember the last time she'd wanted to offer comfort with a kiss.

"The others will be here in a minute," Sedona said against her mouth.

"I know." Vaughn's eyes still remained closed. She wanted to savor the moment, to make it last just a little longer.

"This might be hard to explain."

Vaughn sighed. "Yeah." She leaned back and struggled to control the urge to pull Sedona with her.

"If you don't mind, I think I'll get out and stretch." Sedona opened the door and slid out of the car.

Vaughn followed suit. She watched as Sedona undid the straps and removed the Kevlar vest. When she raised her arms upward and stood on her toes to stretch, Sedona's breasts pushed against the thin fabric of her shirt, straining against the material.

More than anything she could remember in a long time, Vaughn wanted to feel those breasts in her mouth. She swallowed hard and looked away. She still had no idea what this thing—this pull—toward Sedona was, but whatever it was, this was neither the time nor the place for it.

"Do you have anything yet?" Orlando Niger asked. He hefted a dumbbell in each hand and watched himself do bicep curls in the mirror.

"Not yet," Daniel Hart said, "but it's only a matter of time. Be patient. The alert only went out eight hours ago." He undertook another set of abdominal crunches on the therapy ball.

"I know, but I'll feel a lot happier when I know she's out of the picture."

"Me too." Hart strained to do one last repetition. "But I know from experience that in cases like these, it can take hours or it can take weeks."

155

Niger dropped one of the dumbbells onto the mat with a thud. "Shit, Daniel. Weeks? We don't have weeks."

"Relax. It isn't going to take that long. We've pointed the proper authorities in the general vicinity where we believe she's headed. It won't be long now."

Niger picked up the dumbbell again and changed to tricep exercises. "And you're sure we got away with it?"

Hart balanced on the ball. "Hell. You're more nervous than a girl on a prom date. I have the ultimate authority to declare someone a terrorist threat. I do not require presidential approval— the designation is solely at my discretion. We're perfectly in the clear. In a day or two, everything will be back on track. Now stop your worrying. I've got it all under control."

CHAPTER FIFTEEN

P eter hugged Sedona close. "Are you okay?" He pulled back, still holding her within the circle of his arms as he held her gaze. His eyes held genuine concern.

"I've had better days," Sedona admitted, "but I'm much improved from an hour ago."

Peter laughed. "I've never been put in shackles, personally, but I've used them on others. They're not the most comfortable things."

"That's the understatement of the year."

"If you two are done," Vaughn said, "we've got some work to do here."

The six of them were sitting around a conference table in an office inside the hangar. Their duffle bags were scattered on the floor, along with two crates.

"What's in the boxes?" Justine asked.

"I took the liberty of procuring us some firepower and some uniforms," Vaughn answered. "Have a look if you want." She unhinged the latch of the first box and pulled back the lid. Inside were six standard-issue Army MP uniforms, accessories, and a cache of weapons—Army-issue M4 rifles, Glocks, Sig Sauers, a couple of .38 Specials, night vision goggles, long-range scopes, silencers, Kevlar vests, and enough ammunition of various kinds to supply all of them. Underneath the top layer were several Steyr rifles—the assassin's ultimate tool.

"Geez, Vaughn, you'd think you were expecting trouble." Lorraine hefted one of the Sig Sauers in her right hand. "How did you get all of this here?"

"Through the same buddy that's punching our ticket to the middle of the Persian Gulf."

"He's obviously a man of many talents," Justine said.

"You might remember him," Vaughn said. "His name is Sparky. He was part of that first op in Cairo."

After a second, Justine's mouth formed an *O*.

"Is that a good 'O' or a bad 'O'?" Sedona asked.

"My recollection of him is that he was a bit arrogant and took some unnecessary risks, but he got the job done and got us out of there safely," Justine said.

"Indeed I did," a burly, bushy-haired man said from the doorway to the office.

"Speak of the devil," Vaughn said, rising to greet him with a chuck on the shoulder.

Sedona watched the exchange with interest, trying to glean hints to Vaughn's past through her associations and interactions. This man seemed to hold real affection for Vaughn.

"What's this I hear about you changing the terms of the deal, Elliott?"

"What do you mean?"

"I just heard from my cargo pilot on my way over here that you never took the DHL flight, yet here you are, at the same time I was expecting you. How's that possible?"

Sedona stiffened. She wondered how well Vaughn knew this guy and whether or not he could be trusted to be read into the mission.

"Actually," Vaughn said, "we simply hitched a different ride. Change of plans." She waved it away as if it was nothing.

Sparky stared hard at Vaughn for several seconds and then shrugged. "Whatever you say."

"What are you doing here if you knew we missed the DHL flight?"

"Call it a hunch. You ready to go?"

"We have a few things to clear up here first. Can you give us about half an hour?"

"Ten-four. When you're ready, I'll be out back."

"What about the hardware? Did you get what I asked for?"

"Check the other crate." He winked and walked out.

Vaughn unlatched the hinges on the second, larger box. Inside, neatly packed, were two small reconnaissance drones along with controllers. The larger drone measured roughly three feet by five feet. The smaller one was the size of a bee.

Peter, who was looking over her shoulder, whistled. "You do have interesting connections."

"They're handy." Vaughn closed the case and addressed the group. "This may be the last opportunity we have to connect to the outside world for a little while, and it's our last chance to have a strategy discussion while we're not in any danger." She made eye contact with everyone in the group. "There are things we need to discuss."

"Like how Sedona became the world's most wanted terrorist," Justine said.

"Like that," Vaughn agreed.

"And what to do about it," Lorraine said.

"And what it means for us as we go forward," Peter said. "Do we change our plans or stick with the program?"

"If I may," Sedona broke in, "I imagine we're not the only ones wondering these things." She stood up and leaned on the back of her chair. "While we've been busy crisscrossing the globe, the president no doubt has been wondering why he wasn't aware of my changed status. Perhaps we ought to check in and see what he knows now."

"Good thinking," Peter said.

Sedona realized everyone was looking at her. "Um, who wants to make the call, since I can't?" She looked at Vaughn.

"I got this," Vaughn said, retrieving Sedona's burn phone from the pocket where she'd put it when she "arrested" Sedona.

They all crowded around the fifteen-inch laptop screen as Sabastien, at the president's order, worked his magic. Within minutes, he was inside the interface of the Department of Homeland Security. Another few keystrokes and he was reading Secretary Daniel Hart's e-mails.

"You know that's frightening, right?" Sedona remarked.

"What?" Sabastien continued to press keys without looking up.

"The ease with which you hack into what are supposedly the most secure computer systems in the world."

"Oh, that." Sabastien lifted one hand and waved away the comment. "Child's play."

"Until you get caught." Vaughn slapped him on the back. To Sedona she said, "That's how Sabastien came to be my go-to guy—he got in the middle of the wrong op."

"So you made him your own personal hacker slave?" Lorraine asked.

"She did," Sabastien agreed. "Hand me the portable printer out of that bag, will you?" He inclined his head toward the duffle bag at Peter's feet. "I assume you will want a hard copy of the documents to review."

"Yes," Vaughn answered. She was standing over Sabastien's shoulder, reading. "Huh."

"What is it?" Justine asked.

"The request for the designation came from the director of the NSA. It seems Sedona is in league with al-Qaeda in Iraq."

"Oh." Sedona's knees buckled for the second time that day and she reached out and put a hand on the table to steady herself. It shouldn't have surprised her, but somehow it did. All those years she spent working diligently, putting her life on the line for her country and in the blink of an eye, all of it was negated.

"Hey," Lorraine said. "Are you all right?"

Sedona nodded. It was easier than trying to find her voice.

Justine came up on her other side and put an arm around her waist. "We're going to get this done and your name is going to be cleared. You're going to be exonerated. Don't worry."

Sedona willed herself not to cry. It was easier to be running for her life than to see her professional career—everything she worked for—wiped away by insidious lies.

As the pages rolled off the printer and Vaughn began to read, her face clouded over with anger. "The sons of bitches." She slapped her hand on the table.

"What?" Peter asked.

"They didn't just make the accusation—they created the evidence. From what I can see here, they created a bunch of fictitious conversations between Sedona and a few of the better-known extremists she's been tracking. They made it look like

Sedona was headed to Baghdad to hand over mission-sensitive information that could jeopardize national security."

Unable to stay upright any longer, Sedona slumped into a chair and buried her head in her hands. The enormity of her plight—the flight from those who were trying to kill her, leaving everything she knew behind, the swirl of unfamiliar emotions she felt around Vaughn, her designation as a dangerous traitor—all of it was too much.

She felt comforting hands on her back and each shoulder. Without looking, she knew it was Justine to her left, Lorraine to her right, and Peter behind her. The warmth and genuine concern she sensed from them touched her heart. Here were absolute strangers who were willing to put their lives on the line for their country with her. More than that, they believed her and stood with her, defending her honor and her integrity.

"Stop feeling sorry for yourself, kiddo. You need to pull yourself together. This isn't like you. Stand up and fight for your reputation. Real tough girls don't cry."

Sedona smiled at the sound of Dom's voice in her head. She almost answered him out loud but caught herself. She cleared her throat and straightened up, drying her eyes on her sleeves. That was when she caught sight of Vaughn. She was looking at her with naked compassion and empathy. Sedona blinked. Up until that point, Vaughn had been hard to read. Right now, there was no mistaking the expression in her eyes. The intensity of it nearly took Sedona's breath away. It was a softness she hadn't imagined Vaughn possessed.

"Sorry, folks. I was just having myself a moment. I promise you, that's not typical for me. I'm tougher than that."

"Anyone would be having bunches of moments in your place," Justine said, kindly. "You're among friends here. There's no shame in being human."

Sedona blew out a big breath. She couldn't afford to feel overwhelmed now. These people, her new friends, were counting on her. Her knowledge of Tuwaitha was invaluable. There would be time to fall apart later. She pushed back and rose out of the chair.

"Okay." She squared her shoulders. "The current director of the NSA doesn't have the knowledge of the inner workings of the agency to pull this off, so I have trouble believing he's the one behind this. He's a political appointment—he keeps the wheels well greased, but he's never been out of the office apart from trips to Capitol Hill and the White House."

She took the pages from Vaughn and scanned them, working hard to stay dispassionate. "Whoever concocted this understands the way field agents work. This person isn't a lightweight—there's too much attention to detail here. Not only that, but this person has knowledge of Arabic."

She skimmed the text of the supposed conversations she'd had for the past two years with several of the top-level al-Qaeda in Iraq terrorists. "No. Somebody knew exactly what needed to be said to get me designated as an imminent threat."

"Okay, then," Vaughn said. "That means we're looking for whatever computer originated the document, right? If it wasn't the director, it had to come from somewhere."

"On it," Sabastien said, without missing a beat.

Sedona marveled at his skill. She considered herself a pretty fair geek, but Sabastien gave the word a whole new meaning. From her vantage point, she watched him enter different parameters—dates, clearance levels, and search terms. He cross-referenced keywords and walked through seemingly impenetrable firewalls with ease.

Fifteen minutes later, he shoved back from the laptop and grinned. "I have him in my crosssights."

"You mean crosshairs, genius," Vaughn said. She peeked at the screen. "What am I looking at?"

Sedona came up alongside. "Wow. Great work, Sabastien." She kissed him on the cheek and chuckled when he blushed.

"Ahem. Wanna share?" Vaughn asked.

Sedona pointed to the screen. "What Sabastien was able to do was to find the computer where the keystrokes originated. Then he cross-referenced that against the employee ID that was signed in to that computer at the time. Then he confirmed the match by hacking into the e-mail account attached to the employee ID to confirm that the person who sent the e-mail was the same person who created the document."

"And the winner is?" Peter asked.

162

"NSA Deputy Director Orlando Niger," Sedona said. It didn't make sense. None of it did. Was he the one responsible for sending the goon squad after her the night she discovered the Tuwaitha file? Was the file meant for him? What, if anything, did he have to do with Tuwaitha?

"What do we know about him?" Lorraine asked.

"Give me a second, and I will give you the slim."

"The skinny," Vaughn said, shaking her head.

"Right," Sabastien said, cracking his knuckles and getting back to work. "Whatever you say."

"Do you know the guy?" Peter asked Sedona.

Mentally, she catalogued the times she'd been in the presence of the NSA management team. "I think I might have met him once or twice, but I'm coming up blank on anything memorable."

"Twice-decorated Gulf War veteran, eighteen-year employee of the NSA. Worked his way up the ranks from crypto-analyst," Vaughn said. She read from whatever it was Sabastien had pulled up on the screen.

"Married with three kids. Named deputy director in 2008 and managed to hold onto the position despite the change in administration. Apparently well regarded in intelligence circles. No major blots on his record. He's described in reviews as a good tactician. He remained active in the national guard for a number of years after the war..."

"Is there any connection between him and Tuwaitha?" Peter asked.

"I am looking." Sabastien continued to pound the keys and click the mouse. "I do not see anything obvious."

"When he served in the Gulf War, was he stationed anywhere near there?" Lorraine asked.

"It looks like he was mostly in Kuwait during Desert Storm, although his company was at the barracks in Dhahran, Saudi Arabia on February 25, 1991, when that Iraqi scud missile hit. That was the source of one of Niger's medals," Vaughn said, continuing to read over Sabastien's shoulder.

"In other words," Sedona said, "he wasn't anywhere near Tuwaitha at any time during his deployment."

"So it would appear," Vaughn agreed.

"Then why would he care about the place? What's it to him?" Justine asked.

"I have no idea," Vaughn said. "But we can't continue to stay here and wonder about it." She consulted her watch. "We need to ship out if we're going to hit our mark."

"We need to call the president back and tell him what we've got," Peter said.

❦

Wayne Grayson was doing pushups in his cell when Fox News came on. He listened with half an ear as the anchors droned on about Congressional gridlock and the economy.

"Incompetent idiots can't find their asses with both hands," he muttered.

"This just in, Fox News has learned exclusively that authorities are looking for a home-grown terrorist with ties to al-Qaeda in Iraq."

Grayson jumped up and turned up the volume.

"This woman, Sedona Ramos, is who authorities are seeking. She is fluent in Arabic and Homeland Security Secretary Daniel Hart has declared her an imminent threat to national security."

Grayson stared at Ramos's picture. She was a good-looking woman. Memorable. That ought to make her easy to find. He smiled wolfishly. "Good work, Daniel."

❦

Daniel Hart stood at attention in front of the desk of the president of the United States.

"Daniel, Daniel, Daniel," the president said. He shook his head and skimmed the open file on his desk before looking up. "Do you know why you're here?"

"I imagine it has to do with the report you requested on Sedona Ramos, sir."

"What I'd like to know, Daniel, is why I had to find out about this on the news." The president's voice was deathly calm. He leaned back and steepled his fingers. He hadn't planned to call Hart to task yet, but perhaps he could use this to his advantage.

164

After his last conversation with Vaughn, the president decided he wanted to do a little more digging—to see if there was any connection between Deputy Director Orlando Niger and Hart before he acted. The Fox News story changed that.

"I'm sorry about that, sir. It was an oversight. The reporter caught me off guard. She already had the story—said she was going to run with it regardless whether I confirmed it or not. I thought it best to make sure the information that got out there was accurate."

The president's eyes flashed. He lunged forward and placed his palms flat on the desk. Accuracy had little to do with any of this, and the implication made him angry on Sedona's behalf. But Hart didn't know that, and the president needed to keep it that way. So he channeled his anger in a different direction. "You had information on a major terrorist, an employee at the NSA with top-secret clearance, and you didn't think it warranted an immediate report to me?"

"I'm sorry, sir. Obviously, that was a bit of bad judgment on my part. I didn't want to bother you with it until we had more information."

"Such as?"

"I believe, sir, we know where the Ramos woman is headed, but I wanted better intelligence before I shared that. I didn't want to take up your time with speculation."

"I see. And just where is it you think she's going?"

Hart shifted from foot to foot, and the president smiled inwardly. He wanted this man to be uncomfortable. It's why he hadn't invited him to sit down, and why he had left him waiting in the Oval Office for over an hour before he made an entrance.

"We have reason to believe she's on her way to meet up with some of the top leaders of al-Qaeda in Iraq."

The president acted surprised. "Really? What makes you think so?"

"She hasn't shown up for work in more than a week, sir, and a search of her work computer turned up some disturbing correspondence between her and some of the people she's been monitoring for the past few years."

"Yes, I see some transcripts of those conversations here." The president pointed to the file. He waited a beat and then pinned

Hart with a piercing look. "How is it that you came to find this evidence?"

"Sir?"

"Well, if you have transcripts, that would seem to indicate that this woman was under suspicion for a period of time."

Hart's right eye twitched. "Um, that's my understanding of the situation, sir."

"Explain."

Hart lifted his chin and ran a finger under his starched shirt collar.

This ought to be good, the president thought.

"Anytime you have employees spending a long period of time in a position where there is interaction of any kind with terrorists, it's important to ensure that they aren't becoming sympathetic to the people they're watching."

"Wait. I'm confused. Was the Ramos woman interacting with these people or just transcribing their conversations?"

Hart cleared his throat and the president enjoyed watching him squirm. *I'd be squirming too, if I was lying to the president and making stuff up out of whole cloth.*

"S-she was supposedly transcribing their conversations, sir, but apparently someone in the chain of command over there at the NSA became suspicious and decided to keep a closer eye on her."

"I see." The president nodded. "Any idea who that somebody was?"

"Sir?"

"If someone over there was sharp enough to pick up on what might be the biggest terror threat in our country right now, I'd like to know who that was."

"I… My understanding, sir, was that it was…" Hart's eyes darted around. "The truth is, I'm not really sure, sir. Can I get back to you on that?"

"You do that, Daniel." The president stood. "And from now on, if anything ever comes up like this again, I want to know about it right away."

"Yes, sir."

The president waited until Hart had almost reached the door. "Oh, and Daniel?"

"Yes, sir?"

166

"I want to know everything you've got on this Ramos woman."
He pretended to think. "In fact, since she's such a high threat, I
want hourly updates on our progress in tracking her down."

"Yes, sir," Hart said, his Adam's apple bobbing.

"You may go now," the president said. He turned away to hide
his smirk.

CHAPTER SIXTEEN

Vaughn checked her rifle yet again. Next to her, she noted Sedona doing the same with her Glock. They hadn't had another minute alone since exited the car on the tarmac in Kuwait.

She wanted desperately to have just another few seconds—long enough to hold Sedona and reassure her that everything was going to be all right—to tell her that she would protect her. The knowledge of that frightened Vaughn almost more than the drop they were about to make into the middle of the Persian Gulf.

"Are you going to be okay?" Vaughn settled for squeezing Sedona's arm. She had to yell to be heard over the helicopter's rotors.

"You're not making me use a parachute, so I should be fine." Sedona smiled. "How about you?"

"I'm fine."

"Sabastien isn't." Sedona nodded in his direction. "He looks like he might wet his pants."

Vaughn laughed. Sedona was right. Sabastien sat with his legs balled up into his chest. His eyes were wild. Vaughn got up and moved over to him.

"What's up, champ?"

"Tell me again how this works." He scratched at the camouflage makeup on his face.

"Okay." Vaughn looked at her watch. "In about eight minutes, we're going to reach our drop point."

"How do you know? We're in the middle of a very large body of water."

Vaughn patted him on the leg. "You're the one that estimated speed and distance, genius, remember?"

"I do. What if I was wrong?"

"When's the last time that happened about a math problem?"

"Never," Sabastien said, lifting his chin.

"Exactly. So, as I was saying... Seven minutes from now when we reach our drop point, the pilot will lower us down to within ten feet of the water."

"How deep is the water?"

"Deep enough. I'll jump first, then Peter and Lorraine will lower the pontoon boat and the supplies. Then Justine will jump, followed by Sedona, followed by Lorraine, followed by you." She squeezed his knee. "Peter will jump last."

"And you are sure this is safe?"

"Can you swim?"

"Of course."

"Then you have nothing to worry about."

"What about alligators?"

"What?" Vaughn threw her head back and laughed.

"Do not make fun of me, Elliott. I am a computer geek, not a warrior. I know nothing of these kinds of things."

"I know, genius." Vaughn got serious for a second. "If I didn't think we needed you to be on scene, you wouldn't be here. You'd be resting comfortably in your Swiss villa or wherever it is you hang out. But we do need you. You're the guy with all the cool toys. You're the guy who can direct us around corners, guide us around patrols, tell us what we're looking at. And, you're the guy who can get us the pictures we need as proof of what's going on here and feed them back to the president."

"What you are saying is that I am important to you."

"Yep."

"Then really, Elliott, you ought to be nicer to me." Sabastien grinned.

"Remember, I'm still your ride home. Don't get too cocky."

"Sixty seconds to target," the pilot relayed into Vaughn's headset.

"Roger that." She looked around at the group. "Show time in T-minus fifty seconds, gang. Everybody set?"

When everyone had given her the thumbs up, Vaughn moved toward the door and slid it open. She felt the chill of the night air on her face and watched as the helicopter lowered into position. The water below churned with the wind from the rotor blades. Just before she jumped, Vaughn snuck one more peek at Sedona. She had her eyes closed as if in prayer, and Vaughn found herself wanting, yet again, to know what it was that went on in Sedona's brain. She was quite possibly the most intriguing woman Vaughn had ever known.

"You're out," the pilot said in her ear. Vaughn sat on the edge of the opening, braced her hands against the metal, and pushed off.

The water was cold and Vaughn shook her head to clear her vision as she rose back to the surface. She gave the thumbs up to Peter, who was leaning out over the edge. He disappeared back inside.

Several seconds later, he and Lorraine appeared on either side of the pontoon boat and began lowering it with the help of a winch. When it hit the water, Vaughn swam to it and released the rope, signaling with her hand that they should retract it.

By the time Vaughn scrambled into the boat and dropped the anchor, Peter and Lorraine were lowering the first of the supplies. Vaughn unhooked them and arranged them. She, Peter, and Lorraine repeated this process until all of the supplies were onboard the boat.

Within minutes, Justine, Sedona, Lorraine, Sabastien, and Peter were all onboard. Vaughn waved the helicopter off and watched as it headed back to Kuwait. She started the boat's motor as Peter scanned the horizon with a night scope.

"Looks like we're clear," Peter said.

"Good." Vaughn tapped Sabastien. "Okay, genius, get our bearing and tell me where to go." She motioned to Lorraine to pull up the anchor.

"Next stop, our friendly Red Cross vessel."

৵৵

"How's the salad?" the president asked Kate. He and his wife were entertaining Kate and Jay with a late dinner in the family dining room.

"Excellent, sir."

"Jay," the president's wife said, "I want you to know I've read all your books. I'm a major fan."

Jay's face lit up. "Oh, wow. You are? That's such a huge compliment coming from you. Thank you, ma'am."

"That is a heck of an endorsement," the president said. "My wife is the pickiest reader I've ever met."

Kate beamed at her wife with pride. "It's so nice of you to invite us to dinner. Thank you."

"I've been spending so much time with you, Kate, my wife was getting nervous." The president patted his wife's hand.

"Nonsense," she said to Kate. "When I heard who your wife was, I just had to have you both to dinner. Sorry it was such short notice."

"That's not a problem, ma'am. Mr. President, surely you weren't name dropping?" Kate asked.

The president shrugged. "Whatever works, I say."

"Mr. President," Jay said. "I know I have you to thank for our little island vacation last week."

"Mmm. Sorry it got cut short," the president replied, his face clouding over. "Speaking of which, we do have a bit of business to discuss."

"Yes, sir," Kate said.

"Can't it wait until after dinner, dear?"

"Actually, I was thinking four brains would be better than two." The president turned to his wife, who, in addition to being a wonderful First Lady, also possessed a keenly sharp analytical mind. "You remember the flash drive you found in the breast pocket of my suit coat a couple of weeks ago?"

The First Lady tapped her lips thoughtfully. "Oh! Yes, I do."

The president recounted the tale of Sedona's discovery and all that had happened since, up until his meeting with Daniel Hart.

"Wow. That's quite a story," the president's wife said.

"Poor Vaughn. It was such a beautiful house. No wonder we had to leave the island so quickly," Jay said. She shook her head in wonder.

"It doesn't end there." The president waited for the staff to clear the salads and serve the main course. "I called our friend Daniel Hart on the carpet this evening."

172

"I thought we decided to hold off on that, sir," Kate said.

"I imagine you're not a fan of Fox News, are you?"

"Frankly, sir, I'd rather have my teeth pulled without Novocain than watch that drivel."

The president laughed. "Tell me how you really feel."

"Did we miss something, sir?"

"Fox News ran an exclusive story on the six o'clock news tonight about a very dangerous homegrown terror suspect."

"Sedona," Kate whispered.

"Complete with a picture," the president confirmed. "Of course, I was briefed immediately by my communications staff."

"Not by Secretary Hart, dear?"

"Apparently, he didn't think the matter warranted my attention."

"What?"

The president held up a hand to ward off his wife's impending tirade. "He said he was waiting to fill me in until he had more information."

"Bullshit. Pardon my English," the First Lady said.

"So where are we now, Mr. President?" Kate asked.

"I let him sweat for a while. I wanted to know whether or not he would tell me where the report came from."

"Did he?"

"No. He hemmed and hawed and said he would get back to me about that."

"Do you think he knows this Deputy Director Niger, sir?" Jay asked.

"I'm not sure." The president sighed. "I wish Sabastien was here to do a little digging. I get the feeling that Hart knows a lot more than he's saying. But, since the report originated with Niger and not Hart, I have no way of knowing whether or not he shares any culpability."

"Or whether he's just a dupe," the First Lady said.

"Exactly."

Jay dabbed her mouth with a napkin and put it on the table. "Sir? I know I'm not a computer geek, but if you'll pardon my saying so, I think what you could use right now is a really good reporter."

"How so?" the president asked.

"You want to know whether there's any connection between Hart and Niger."

The president nodded.

"You don't need a computer geek for that, although I'm sure he could find you the answer."

Kate translated. "Sir, what Jay is saying is, she can help you get to the bottom of this."

"Oh?"

"I don't know if you're aware, but before her career as a novelist, my wife was a top reporter at *Time* magazine."

Jay blushed.

"You know, I think I did know that, but I'd totally forgotten about it."

"If you want someone who can dig and do in-depth research, Jay's your answer, sir."

"I'm sold," the First Lady said.

"Okay," the president agreed. "How long do you think it will take you?"

"I guess it depends what kind of resources I'll have to work with," Jay answered.

"Whatever you need."

"Is there a way to get Deputy Director Niger's employment records, sir? There are a lot of things I can discover just looking around the web, but the NSA is the most secretive agency we have. Although Sabastien no doubt could get you that information, hacking into secure databases isn't in my repertoire."

"As a matter of fact, Sabastien sent me a report on Niger just before they left Kuwait. Vaughn wanted to be sure I had the incriminating evidence in case..." The president stopped short of saying what none of them wanted to consider.

"Well," Jay said hoarsely, "that'll make my job a lot easier."

⊰∙⊱

"Do we have her yet?" Orlando Niger asked. Today he and Daniel Hart were jogging in the chill Washington, D.C. morning air.

"Not yet. I told you, it's just a matter of time. I'm guessing by tonight or tomorrow I'll have a report of her demise on my desk and the president can take credit for another win in the war on terror."

"You looked good on Fox last night, by the way, Daniel. Very important. That reporter's a good-looking piece of ass too."

"Hell-fire in bed, but a pain-in-the-ass. Too high maintenance."

"You're screwing her?" Niger whistled. "Nice."

"Like I said, a good fuck, but she's always wanting me to give her scoops."

"You saying she's not worth it?" They turned the corner toward the Washington Monument.

"Nah. I'll keep banging her until we've got what we need on this story, then I'll dump her ass."

"That's a shame. She's smoking."

"You can have her when I'm done with her."

"No thanks." Niger picked up the pace as they neared their usual stopping point. "I don't take sloppy seconds." They sprinted across the imaginary finish line and both bent over, gasping for air.

When they recovered, Hart started walking. Niger caught up to him after a second.

"Listen, Orlando. There's something we need to talk about."

"Okay."

"The president called me on the carpet last night after the story ran."

Niger's head jerked up. "And?"

"And he was pissed that he was out of the loop."

"What'd you tell him?"

"I told him it was an oversight—that I was waiting to report to him until I had more solid intelligence on her whereabouts."

"Did he buy it?"

"I don't know. He asked a lot of questions."

"What kind of questions?"

"He wanted to know where I got the information. He wanted a name at the NSA. He wanted the person who was suspicious enough of Ramos to have her watched."

Niger pulled them up short by grabbing Hart's elbow. "What the hell did you say?"

"Relax." Hart yanked his arm away. "I told him I'd have to get back to him on that."

"He bought it?"

"For now."

"What are we going to do?"

"We need a story." Hart started walking again in the direction of his car. "I need a name—someone that would've authorized surveillance on Ramos."

"Shit, Daniel."

"Make it up."

"What if he follows up?"

"He's not going to. You think the president has time to fuck around with stuff like that?"

"I think we need to be very careful about this."

"If I give him your name, you look like a hero for identifying a dangerous terrorist."

"I don't want my fingerprints on this."

"If the president asks your boss, your boss is going to tell him you were the one who brought it to his attention."

"Yeah, but somebody had to bring it to my attention. There's no way the deputy director is aware of some agent's activities on that level."

"Well, give me somebody!" Hart thundered. "You want to keep your little hands clean, give me someone else."

Niger furrowed his brow in thought. "Jesus… Jesus."

"I don't think the president will buy that this was Jesus's doing," Hart deadpanned.

"Very funny. It's not your ass on the line."

"Oh no? Who has to give the president hourly updates on the situation?"

"Hourly?" Niger squeaked.

"Welcome to my world."

Niger bit his lip in concentration. "Okay… Okay. How about if we tell him it was the Internal Affairs Department that ordered the investigation? They brought it to the attention of the Inspector General, and he told me about it."

"How did Internal Affairs know to look at Ramos?"

"Anonymous tip."

"Seriously? You think that'll fly?"

"It *does* happen. It really *is* possible that no one would know the original source."

Hart considered. "Okay. I'll try to keep your name out of it. I'll go straight for the Internal Affairs angle and try to shift the subject off that as quickly as possible."

"When do you have to see the president again?"

"Whenever he says so." Hart pressed the button on his key fob to unlock his car. "See you at the gym tomorrow?"

"Do you think that's such a good idea?" Niger asked. "Us being seen together?"

"Relax. As far as anybody knows, we're just a couple of old friends working out together. We've got nothing to worry about."

Jay's hair was sticking up at odd angles. She was deeply engrossed in something on her computer screen and pieces of paper were strewn all over the desk.

Kate came over and kissed her on the forehead. "How's it going?"

"It's going."

"Are you hungry?"

Jay looked up at Kate. "When have you ever known me not to be hungry?"

"Good point." Kate sat on the edge of the desk and held out a spoon.

"What's this?"

"I thought you could use a little brain food." From behind her back, Kate produced a carton of hand-packed ice cream.

"Cookie-dough ice cream? You brought me ice cream?"

"I did."

Jay grabbed the spoon. She pushed herself up out of the chair and kissed Kate on the cheek. "I think I love you."

"That's a good thing," Kate said. "Otherwise, why would you have married me?"

"So I could have someone who could retrieve items off the top shelf, of course."

"You are in so much trouble, Jamison Parker."

"Tell me about it." Jay took a huge spoonful of ice cream. "So, what do you have?"

Jay swallowed and took another generous spoonful. "There's nothing while Niger is at the NSA, but did you know Hart and Niger knew each other twenty years ago?"

"What?"

Jay pointed to the screen and a picture of an army unit in battle fatigues. "See this guy here?" She pointed at a figure in the middle row. "That's Niger." She moved her finger to the upper right corner of the picture. "That's his company commander—Daniel Hart."

"No kidding."

"No kidding."

Kate kissed Jay hard on the lips. "I think I love you too."

"Good to know," Jay said, and stole another, longer kiss. "Good to know."

CHAPTER SEVENTEEN

Two hundred yards to the starboard side, Sedona could see the outline of a large ship. She tapped Peter on the shoulder and pointed. "Is that our ride?"

Peter handed her the night scope. "See for yourself."

Sedona adjusted the sight and focused in on the ship's markings. "Looks like our ship just came in," she said. The Red Cross flag was clearly visible through the scope. They'd been on the water for nearly three hours, moving slowly so as not to attract unwanted attention with the engine noise.

"Okay," Vaughn said. "Let's get a little closer before we give the signal." She maneuvered the boat towards the ship's wake. "Justine?"

"Yeah?"

"What was the pre-arranged signal? You do have one, right?"

"No. I thought we'd just waltz right up to the ship and ask permission to board." Her voice dripped with sarcasm. "Yes, Vaughn, I worked out a series of signals with the security chief."

"How are we doing on time?" Lorraine asked.

Justine consulted her dive watch. "We're within the half hour window I gave him."

"So far, so good," Peter said. He tapped Sedona's leg and she raised an eyebrow in question. "How does it feel to you?" he mouthed.

Sedona smiled. It felt odd, and yet somehow natural, that he would ask her to use her abilities to suss out the situation. She closed her eyes and took a deep, cleansing breath. *Archangels, angels, ascended masters, guides, I need crystal clear guidance*

179

and information here. Is meeting up with this Red Cross ship safe for us? Will we be okay?

"You are fine but limit your exposure."

Sedona nodded in acknowledgment. When she opened her eyes again, Peter was smiling at her. She wasn't sure, but she thought his eyes were twinkling. She gave him a thumbs-up.

That's when she noticed that Vaughn was watching her too. She swallowed hard. Vaughn had already questioned her once about her behavior on the plane when she hadn't realized her lips moved as she talked to the angels. Now this. She hoped Vaughn would be too preoccupied with the impending rendezvous to think much about it. Somehow, though, she imagined that Vaughn had a long memory. Just her luck.

∽∾

"Welcome," the chief of security said as he gave Sedona a hand as she stepped into the hull of the ship.

Vaughn followed immediately behind. She wanted to say she was professional enough not to stare at Sedona's ass directly in front of her, but she would've been lying. When her eyes finally tracked upward, she saw the way the chief of security looked at Sedona's face and she had an irrational urge to cold-cock the man.

"Hi," she said, stepping between the two of them. "Thanks for helping us out."

"Thank my boss—he's the one that set this up." He gestured toward the passageway. "You're welcome to get cleaned up in the crew's quarters. Everyone's asleep, but there are a few extra bunks if you want to catch some shuteye."

"Thanks—" Vaughn started to say. Sedona gripped her forearm and squeezed. Out of the corner of her eye, she saw Sedona's barely perceptible shake of the head. Puzzled, Vaughn nonetheless altered her intended answer. "If you just have a head somewhere down here, that'll be good. We'll get cleaned up there and stay out of everybody's way."

Sedona gave an equally imperceptible nod. The rest of the team simply went about arranging their gear so that they would have a makeshift place to sit.

"As you wish," the chief of security said. "Are you sure you wouldn't rather get more comfortable in actual berths?"

"No, thanks. We're fine," Vaughn answered.

"In that case, there's a head over here." He led the way between rows of wooden crates to a narrow door with a unisex bathroom sign.

"Excellent. Thanks."

"If you're sure you don't need anything else..."

"No, we're good, thanks."

"Very well."

"When we arrive in Baghdad," Vaughn said, "we'll wait for your signal that all is clear, then we'll disembark."

"Fine. See you a little later, then."

When he was gone, Vaughn turned to Sedona. "Want to tell me what that was all about?"

Sedona shrugged. "Call it a hunch. I just think we really need to limit our exposure. After all, I'm a wanted fugitive, and we don't know who we can trust."

Vaughn frowned. The explanation was logical and sound, but somehow, she felt there was more Sedona wasn't telling her. She stowed her own gear and settled in for the ride up the Persian Gulf and through the mouth of the Tigris River to Baghdad.

Wayne Grayson scowled at his nephew through the scarred Plexiglas and picked up the phone to talk to him. "I know what Daniel's been up to—I can see his efforts are paying off by watching the news. I know what Quinn is up to because I've got sources in here that keep me up to date. I know Kincaid got the pipeline through her committee and in position for a floor vote, because I read it in the newspaper." Grayson cradled the phone between his ear and his shoulder and examined his fingernails. "The question, Astin, is what the hell have you been doing while everyone else is doing something relevant?"

Astin stared at a point over his uncle's head. "I got us actionable information that the Ramos woman would be on a flight from JFK to Istanbul via Frankfurt this morning."

"But she wasn't on that flight, now was she?" Grayson kept his voice quiet. In his experience, this outwardly calm demeanor made him more feared than any blustering could do.

Astin adjusted his tie. "No, sir. B-but that doesn't mean she's not still going to Istanbul."

"How many men did we waste cooling their heels at JFK watching for Ramos?"

"It wasn't a waste." Astin pouted. "It was good intel and it was worth the expenditure of manpower."

A vein throbbed in Grayson's forehead. He sat forward in his chair and grabbed the phone from between his neck and shoulder with his handcuffed hand. "Really? And you're qualified to judge that because…?"

"What do you mean?" Astin leaned back to create more space between them.

"What qualifies you to make strategic decisions, Astin?"

"I'm in charge—"

"No, Astin." Grayson leaned closer still and fixed his nephew with a withering look. "I'm in charge." He poked himself in the chest with his thumb. "I've let you play in the sandbox, hoping that you would grow into the role and bring honor to this family."

Astin's face reddened. "I am a successful businessman in my own right. I run a huge oil company. People cower before me!"

"No, Astin. You're a pissant little nobody. I let you make crappy business decisions as head of one of my smallest, most inconsequential companies because I knew it didn't matter if you fucked things up there. And people cower because you're a sadistic son-of-a-bitch—a completely irresponsible loose cannon."

Astin stared, slack-jawed.

"You're done." Grayson sat back and stretched his legs out.

"W-what do you mean, done?"

"I mean you're relieved of any 'command' responsibilities beyond your little oil company. Do you understand what I'm telling you?"

When Astin simply sat there, unmoving, Grayson stood up and leaned on the table on his side of the partition. "I'm making Hart my second-in-command. You'll keep your precious place as one of 'The Four.'" The last he said derisively. "But if I find out you've interfered in any way, I'll make sure you'll be peeing through a straw for the rest of your life. Now do you understand what I'm telling you?"

Astin nodded dumbly and Grayson started to put the phone down. Then he thought better of it. "Oh, and Astin? If anything happens to Steven Ochs or his pitiful cat—"

"Who?"

"The computer geek that told you about the JFK flight. If so much as a hair on his head is out of place, or if so much as a whisker is missing from his cat, your pecker won't be the only thing you have to worry about."

"Well, Daniel? What's the situation with our imminent terrorist threat? Do you have her in custody yet?" The president put Hart on speakerphone so that Kate and Jay, who were sitting on a sofa in the president's office in the residence, could listen in.

"No, sir, but it's just a matter of time. Another day or two and we should have her. Our dragnet is closing in."

"Really?" The president made a face indicating incredulity for Kate and Jay's benefit.

"Absolutely, sir."

"How do you know that?"

"Um, as I indicated yesterday, Mr. President, we have strong reason to believe that Ramos is heading to Baghdad. I've got people scouring for her at every border crossing and every major transportation outlet. There's no way she can slip past us."

"I see. Good work, Daniel."

"Thank you, sir."

"How are you coming on the answer you were going to get me?"

"Sir? I'm not sure what you're referring to."

"When you were in my office last night, I asked you who, specifically, at the NSA was responsible for catching on to the Ramos woman and having her put under surveillance. I'm assuming you have an answer for me now."

"Oh, that, sir. Actually, the answer to that question is that I don't know."

"You didn't investigate the matter, after I specifically asked you to get me more information?"

"No. I-it isn't that, sir."

"What is it, then?"

"Well, sir. The tip was given anonymously to the NSA's Internal Affairs Department. They took it from there."

"I see." The president looked at Kate and Jay and held his hands palm up. He mouthed, "Anything more you want to know?"

Both women shook their heads.

"All right, Daniel. Keep me posted." The president disconnected the call. "Well," he said to Kate and Jay, "what do you think?"

Kate answered first. "Although we're pretty sure he's lying through his teeth about not knowing specifically where the report originated, we can't prove yet that he definitively knew it was Niger."

Jay picked up the thought. "What if Niger submitted the tip anonymously?"

"Why would he?" the president asked. "He's in a position of authority. All he would have to do is assign someone to monitor Sedona's activities and it would be done. He wouldn't need Internal Affairs for that."

"True," Kate said. "But we still don't have a smoking gun."

"You could double-check his story, sir," Jay said. "You could ask the director of the NSA for a copy of the internal affairs report."

"My guess is one doesn't exist," Kate said.

"I'm sure you're right," the president agreed. "Have you ever met my director for the NSA?"

"No, sir," both women said.

"Let's just say I seriously doubt he has his finger on the day-to-day workings of his agency." The president folded his arms. "As a result, the first thing he'd do when I made a request like that is have Niger take care of it for him. Then the director would put his name on it and send it to me. In which case, we're no closer to knowing the truth than we were before."

"Not necessarily, sir," Jay said. "If there really isn't any internal affairs report and you request to see one, Niger likely would panic and try to manufacture one, in order to distance himself from the situation."

"Hmm. Very true," the president said. He was impressed with Jay's analytical thinking. "But we'd still need someone like Sabastien to hack into the system and determine where any report I get originated."

"Yeah," Kate agreed. "But at least it would keep Niger scrambling and strike some fear into his heart. If he is working with Hart, perhaps they might try to meet or have a discussion. If we had surveillance in place, that could give us good information."

"The only problem is that we don't know if there's someone absolutely clean we can get to do the surveillance," the president said.

Kate and Jay looked at each other. "Maybe we do, sir," Jay said.

Kate nodded. "Peter has a consulting partner—his name is Max Kingston. I've known him almost as long as I've known Peter. When I was the spokesperson for the New York State prison system, Max was in charge of the agency's Corrections Emergency Response Team. I know Peter trusts him with his life."

"Heck, honey," Jay said, "Max saved your life or helped to."

The president weighed the possibilities. "It could work. At the very least, we'd have more information than we have now. The only downside I can see is that if I ask for the internal affairs report, Hart is going to know I'm suspicious."

"Respectfully, sir, I disagree," Jay said. "Hart is going to know that you're thorough, and you're very serious about this imminent terror threat. If he believes you are keen to stay on top of it, he might interpret that to mean capturing Sedona is going to be your number one priority."

"I bet he'd like that," Kate said.

"I bet he would." The president picked up the phone and asked the White House operator to get him the director of the NSA. When he was done relaying his request for the internal affairs file, he turned back to his guests. "So, when can your man Max get here?"

"I'll call him right now, sir," Kate said. "If he's in town, and I believe he is, he can be on the job within the hour."

"Excellent," the president said. "Now there's only one problem."

"What's that, sir?"

"We know that every allied law enforcement agency around the world is looking for Sedona, including the remaining US forces in Iraq. How on earth are they going to get where they're going without being intercepted?"

✧✧

The team gathered up their gear. The ship had docked some forty minutes ago and they were just waiting for the all-clear from the security chief. Sedona stuffed the jacket she was using as a pillow into her duffle and scrutinized her Army Combat Uniform to make sure everything was regulation, right down to ensuring that the trousers did not extend farther than the third eyelet of the boots. Then she donned the thirty-pound Improved Outer Tactical Vest and secured it. She would wait to don the reflective sunglasses and strap on the Advanced Combat Helmet with a mount for the night vision scope until they were outside.

She could feel Vaughn's eyes on her, but she chose to ignore her. The strategy worked fine until Vaughn spoke in her ear.

"Now that we're here, would you care to explain why it was necessary for us to sleep on a metal floor instead of in more comfortable berths?"

Sedona resisted the urge to look at Vaughn directly. Instead, she picked up a military-issue M4 rifle and eyeballed the sight on it. "I told you, I wanted to limit our exposure. The fewer people who know we're here and get a look at us, the better."

"And the sleeping crew would have been problematic because…?"

Finally, Sedona shifted to face Vaughn. "Do you really believe that not one of those crewmembers would hear the commotion we would've made? Did you want to take a chance like that? For what? So your delicate bottom could be more comfortable for a few hours? Honestly, Vaughn, I didn't think you were that kind of girl." Sedona hoped that derision would deter Vaughn from pushing the point any farther.

"Hardly," Vaughn scoffed. "I can't help thinking there's something else going on in that head of yours. I just don't know what it is yet."

"When you figure it out, send me an e-mail," Sedona said, hoping her tone signaled the end of the discussion. "In the meantime, how about if we discuss the route we're going to take to get to our ground transportation. I know my guys are in range. Once I make the call, they'll head to our usual meeting point. We just have to figure out how to get from here to there on foot without arousing any suspicions."

"Okay, gang," Vaughn said, reluctantly abandoning her line of questioning. "Huddle up." She waited until everyone was close. "Our cover story is that we're a squad from the 411th. Note the patch on your left shoulder right below the Military Police insignia. For now, we're going to have to show only the weapons a soldier would carry. So, use the Sigs, since they're the closest things we've got to a Beretta-92F, and put those in the serpa holster. Use the M4 as the long rifle. Put that in the tactical sling and your clips in the ammo pouches on your vest. Tuck everything else away."

"Obviously, we're not taking these crates with us," Lorraine pointed to the boxes with all their additional accessories, food, weapons, ammunition, and the two drones. "So what are we doing with all of that?"

"Divide it up. We're taking it on our backs," Vaughn said.

"What?" Sabastien's eyes were wide. "Already this clothing weighs more than I do. I will never be able to walk."

"This will be good training for you. You ought to get out from behind a desk every once in a while." Vaughn cuffed him affectionately on the side of his head.

"I'll take some of your stuff," Sedona offered Sabastien. "Give me those." She pointed to the ammunition clips.

Vaughn tsked. "I can't believe you're going to let a girl carry your load."

"She volunteered." Sabastien grinned.

"In return," Sedona winked at him, "you have to figure out our walking route to get to the café where we're meeting up with Ahmed and Umar."

"It is a deal," Sabastien said.

"I'll carry the drones," Peter said. "By the way, Sabastien, don't necessarily pick the shortest route. We need to protect Sedona at all costs. I'm sure every soldier on patrol and every civilian private security contractor knows who she is by now." He gave Sedona a sympathetic look.

Sedona's stomach did a nervous flip. It wasn't that she'd forgotten about her outlaw status, it was that she had consciously willed herself not to think about it. "I'll be wearing a helmet and reflective sunglasses."

"Even so," Vaughn said, "Peter's right. Aren't you the one who was arguing for less exposure?" Vaughn smirked. "Find us the least traveled route, genius. But try to make it so it doesn't take us too far out of our way. We have a date with some very bad people at a nice little outpost called Tuwaitha."

CHAPTER EIGHTEEN

I told you this would happen!" Orlando Niger's body vibrated with anger. He didn't care that the fear showed in his eyes. He was damned afraid. "The president wants to see the fucking internal affairs report. What the fuck am I supposed to do now?" He poked Daniel Hart in the chest. "You got me into this. You get me out."

"Relax." Hart swatted away Niger's hand. "Manufacture the damn report. This isn't rocket science."

"What if they trace it back to me?"

"You said yourself, the NSA is hacker-proof. It's why we had the satellite images sent to you in the first place."

"Yeah. You can see how that turned out," Niger sneered.

"That was a fluke."

"A fluke that brought the president of the United States down on our heads."

"Listen, soldier. Now is not the time for retreat. You're a decorated veteran. I never saw you afraid in battle. What the hell is going on with you?"

"This is different," Niger muttered. He signed up to go to war on behalf of his country. This—this was something else entirely. The cause was not his. Hell, he didn't even know what the endgame was. When he asked, he was told it was a need-to-know basis, and he didn't need to know. Had he not owed his life to Hart…

"Get it done," Hart said, leaving no more room for discussion. "Send it to me before you send it to that idiot boss of yours so I can make sure it's what we need." He slapped Niger on the back a little harder than necessary and walked away.

Niger stared after him, wondering just what the hell he'd signed up for and wishing more than anything that he hadn't done it.

❦❧

The president stood with his arms folded across his chest, his eyes riveted to the big television set as the meeting between Orlando Niger and Daniel Hart unfolded on the screen. His expression was grim. "This is good work, Mr. Kingston."

"Max, sir."

"Max, then."

"Kate, Jay? Looks like we've got our smoking gun."

"I'd say so, Mr. President," Kate said, "but I can't help feeling there's something more than what we're seeing here."

"She's right," Jay agreed. "Max, back it up to the beginning, will you?" When the camera caught Niger full on, Jay said, "Pause it right there." She turned to the president. "Note his expression, sir. He's really afraid."

"So it would appear."

"Sir," Kate jumped in, "Orlando Niger is a twice-decorated war veteran. Yet here, he looks like he's quaking in his shoes."

"Let's hear his next sentence, Max," Jay said.

Max pushed "play" once again, and they watched Niger and listened to his words.

"Stop." Kate motioned to Max. "Mr. President, you heard him. 'You got me into this. You get me out.' That makes it sound as if Hart is not holding the end of the leash, doesn't it?"

"Not to mention the fact that he pokes Hart in the chest. Niger clearly is afraid, but it isn't of Hart," Jay added.

"What are you suggesting, ladies?" The president watched the silent communication between Kate and Jay with interest. They certainly made a great team.

"Let it play out a little longer, sir," Kate said. "If you bring Hart and Niger in right now and there are other players out there, we might lose the opportunity to grab them. If they fade into the woodwork and we haven't identified them, then they're still a threat."

The president nodded. "More importantly, we still don't know what's going on at Tuwaitha. Until we know that, the only thing we have them on is lying to me, falsifying a report, and wrongly accusing an innocent woman of treason. Frankly, that isn't much in the scheme of things."

"Sir, if I might make a suggestion?"

"Sure, Jay."

"Let Max here continue to monitor Secretary Hart. It seems clear that he is more heavily involved than Deputy Director Niger, just based on their conversation."

"So it would seem."

"Who knows? Maybe he'll lead us to someone else."

"Do it." The president ordered Max. He uncrossed his arms and walked over to his desk to pick up his iPad. "According to my calendar, I leave for nuclear proliferation talks with the Russians in ten days." He looked at his guests. "I'd sure like to have this thing wrapped up by then."

"Sir, we know the team was in Kuwait yesterday," Kate said. "By now, I'd imagine they have arrived at or are close to their destination. With any luck, you'll have some answers within a day or two."

"I certainly hope you're right, Kate. Still, with Sedona's status as a wanted fugitive, I imagine things are less than simple or straightforward. I really wish there was more I could do."

Vaughn, Sedona, Lorraine, Justine, and Sabastien crouched within earshot just inside the ship's cargo hold, watching as Peter approached a checkpoint set up at the end of the gangway.

"Hey," Peter said casually. "What's going on?"

"Haven't you heard, man?"

"Heard what?"

"We're on high alert. Seems we've got ourselves an American terrorist on her way to meet with the jihadists."

"No shit. Really?"

"You didn't know about this? You been living under a rock or what? We all got briefed on this yesterday."

"Just back from leave," Peter said. "I hitched a last-minute ride back on this Red Cross ship."

"Must be nice."

"Yeah, it was." Peter glanced over the man's shoulder at the official NSA picture of Sedona. "This who we're looking for?"

"Yeah. Too bad. She's hot."

"Yeah, she sure is," Peter agreed. "So what's the deal? What do we care about a Red Cross ship?"

"You were on it—this ship came from Kuwait. Our orders are to inspect every incoming foreign or neutral vessel or transportation site from any of the border countries."

"That's a lot of manpower hours."

"Tell me about it. I've been here for over ten hours already."

"Wanna take a break?" Peter asked.

"I don't get relieved for another hour," the soldier said.

"Well, if you just want to take a piss or get off your feet for ten minutes, I'll take over here."

The soldier seemed to hesitate.

"The ship's empty, right? Everybody already got off? I didn't see anybody behind me."

"I did look at the manifest," the soldier said. "The count as they got off matched my roster and I questioned some of the crew randomly. None of them said they saw anybody matching her description."

"See." Peter smiled at him. "I can handle watching an empty ship for a few minutes while you take a blow. Go for it."

"Yeah?" The soldier smiled.

"You bet," Peter said.

"Cool. See you in ten, man." The soldier started to take off. "And thanks."

"No biggie," Peter said, waving him away. When the soldier was completely out of sight and the coast was clear, Peter gave the pre-arranged signal. Lorraine, Sabastien, Vaughn, Sedona, and Justine emerged from the shadows. All donned their helmets and dark, reflective sunglasses.

"Nicely done," Vaughn said.

"Yeah, well, I strongly suggest you guys get moving. I'll catch up to you at the rendezvous point."

"I don't like the idea of you staying behind without any backup," Sedona said.

Peter looked at her affectionately. "I'll be fine. You, on the other hand, need to disappear." He made a shooing motion.

"I agree," Vaughn said. "We've got to get you away from here."

"How are you going to know which way to go?" Sedona asked Peter.

"I can guide him over the coms," Sabastien offered. "Because he is not you, he can take a more direct route. It is even possible that he will arrive before we do."

"See? I'm in great hands." Peter took the GPS tracker Sabastien handed him so he could keep a fix on his location. "By the way," Peter said as the rest of the group headed off, "In the picture they're using of you, your hair is long. I like the new hairdo better."

Sedona looked back and smiled. "Me too."

Vaughn led the way with Lorraine walking alongside Sedona and Justine and Sabastien trailing behind. For all intents and purposes, the group looked like a squad on patrol. Given what they'd already encountered, this would allow them to blend with their environment.

In the twelve blocks they'd traveled since leaving the ship, they avoided four American patrols and two more checkpoints. The checkpoints, according to what they could pick up from their vantage points in the shadows of alleys and side streets, were set up specifically to hunt for Sedona, and the patrols were on high alert.

For nearly a block, the only sound was the crunching of their boots on the dirt and gravel. Sedona kept herself on high alert. She prayed to Archangel Michael to surround the group with purple light for protection. She asked Archangels Metatron, Zadkiel, and Jeramiel to keep her ear chakras and her third eye clear and open so that she could hear and see Divine guidance with crystal clarity. She surrounded all of them with a cadre of guardian angels to act as sentries on their journey. When she could think of nothing else to do or ask for to keep them safe, she prayed for Peter's safety.

"Hey."

Sedona jumped when Vaughn appeared by her side. Lorraine was now taking point. "You're not nervous, are you?" Vaughn chuckled.

"No. I was just lost in thought."

"I bet you were. Me too, as a matter of fact."

"Oh?"

"Yep." Vaughn lowered her voice so only Sedona could hear her. "I was thinking about what happened back there at the checkpoint. You know, where the soldier said he randomly asked crew members if any of them recognized you?"

Sedona swallowed hard. She could see where this was going, and she wasn't entirely sure how to get around it this time. Vaughn seemed determined to unmask Sedona's psychic abilities.

When Sedona said nothing, Vaughn pushed on. "So, it turns out you were right about limiting our exposure to the crew. If we had ventured into their quarters, it is quite possible that one or more of them could've gotten a look at you or at least wondered what we all were doing there."

"That was just sound strategy."

"Maybe…or maybe you knew something you weren't sharing."

"How would I know something like that?" Sedona kept her voice light and hoped that Vaughn would let it go.

"Honestly? I don't know. But I am wondering. When something happens once, I chalk it up to chance. Twice? Coincidence. But that's the third or fourth time you've suggested or known something and it's turned out to be accurate. I can't chalk that up to coincidence."

"You're trained to be suspicious of everything."

"I'm also trained to watch for synchronicities, cause and effect, and patterns."

"But mostly, you're trained to be suspicious." Sedona wagged a finger at Vaughn. "Over-active imagination as a child? Or just plain old adult paranoia?"

"Shh," Lorraine said. She motioned for the group to stop and move back against the wall of the nearest building. "Patrol at twelve o'clock, headed directly this way—thirty feet at most. What do you want to do?" She asked Vaughn.

Sedona looked around. There was no escape. *Archangel Michael, what would you have us do?*

194

"I will shield you. Walk as a unit and act as if you have just checked this street."

"Keep walking," Sedona said to the group. "Lorraine, greet them as they go by. I'll walk behind Vaughn, since she's the tallest, and stay closest to the wall to avoid a head-on look. Justine, walk to my right and just slightly in front of me so your shoulder shields me from view. If they say anything, we just did a sweep of this street and can save them the trouble."

Vaughn looked at her oddly. The rest of the group looked at Vaughn. The patrol was less than twenty feet away. Vaughn narrowed her eyes at Sedona one more time, but Sedona steadily held her gaze.

"Do what she says."

Fifteen feet. Ten feet. Sedona concentrated on her breath. *Archangel Michael, please take away any fear I might have about being discovered.* Five feet.

"Hey," said the lead soldier of the approaching unit. "What are you doing here? This is our sector."

"Is it?" Lorraine asked. "I must've heard the staff sergeant wrong." She shrugged. "Anyway, we just swept this street, so we can save you the trouble. It's clear."

"Thanks, but we have to head that way as part of the grid search for that American terror suspect."

Sedona's heart jumped. She could feel similar reactions all around her in the group. She fought to maintain her composure.

The soldier continued, "The instructions were pretty clear. I can't understand how your staff sergeant could've screwed that up."

Again, Lorraine shrugged. "Bad sense of direction, I guess. I'll radio in and find out where we're supposed to be. You guys be safe out here."

"Same to you. Hope you figure out where the heck you're supposed to be."

"Yeah. Me too." Lorraine waved them away as the group continued forward.

When they were a safe distance away, Sedona closed her eyes and blew out an explosive breath. Her legs felt like rubber.

"How did you know that would work?" Vaughn asked.

Sedona sighed. She wondered what it would take to get Vaughn to let the subject go. "I didn't. We just got lucky."

"Again," Vaughn pointed out. "Boy, we sure are lucky these days."

"Yep. We sure are."

෴

Max Kingston sat in a plain white van on Constitution Avenue and turned up the volume on the ear bud he was using to monitor Department of Homeland Security Secretary Daniel Hart. It was simple to gain access to Hart's phone when he put it on the sink in the men's room at the Capitol and simpler still to use it as a receiver to pick up all of his conversations. The man was almost never without that phone. It certainly made Max's job easy.

So far, Max was having trouble piecing together anything that made sense about his movements. He made a round of visits to Capitol Hill to meet with various congressmen and senators on a variety of topics. Then he sat down for coffee with a high-priced defense attorney best known for representing white-collar criminals. At the moment, he was having lunch at an exclusive club for the rich and powerful.

None of it seemed particularly interesting or important to Max, but he took pictures of every person with whom Hart came in contact just the same. Maybe Kate and Jay could find a pattern in it.

Max did notice that the pretty senator whom Hart met in the Capitol rotunda was the same woman he was having lunch with now. Max wondered if they were having an affair. He didn't have audio on the Capitol conversation because it took place before Hart went to the men's room. And there was so much ambient noise in the club it was hard to get a clear fix on a conversation.

When Hart came out with the woman, they were engaged in what appeared to be a heated conversation with another man.

"It's settled, Astin. End of conversation."

"You're making a big mistake, Daniel."

"The mistake was ever giving you as much leeway as we did."

"You can't talk to me like that."

"The hell I can't."

196

"Stop it," the senator said, literally stepping between them. Max thought she looked weary. "We're not getting anywhere fighting amongst ourselves. What's done is done. We'll just have to see how this plays out."

"Since when did you grow a set of balls?" the man called Astin asked the senator.

As he watched through the long camera lens, Max could see the redness creep up the woman's neck. "I don't know who you are anymore," she said to the man. Now Max clearly could see that she was sad as she turned her collar up and walked away.

Hart walked in the opposite direction towards his waiting car.

The third man simply stood on the steps looking morose.

ক্ষ্ণ

"I do hope the news is good, Stanley," Wayne Grayson said to his lawyer. "I grow weary of the incompetence of those I've tasked with important jobs."

"At the moment, there is not much to tell, sir. Hart is warming up to his role as *de facto* head—"

"Don't call him that," Grayson snapped. "I am the head of this organization. There is no other. Hart is simply a caretaker."

"Yes, sir." The lawyer pulled on the French cuffs of his expensive shirt. "In that case, let me say that the search for the very dangerous American terrorist goes on. The thinking continues to be that she either is headed for Iraq or she is already there. Senator Kincaid is poised to act on the pipeline legislation as soon as you give the word."

"Good."

"Hart tells me the president has become very interested in our terrorist."

"Oh?" Grayson sat up a little straighter. "Explain."

"It seems he is very anxious to know everything about this woman's background at the NSA, how she came under suspicion, and exactly what she was up to. He's requested the full internal affairs report."

"What internal affairs report?"

"The one Hart told the president existed when he asked what led the NSA to suspect her of nefarious activities."

"He told the president what?" The vein stood out in Grayson's forehead and his face was nearly purple.

"Apparently, the president called Hart on the carpet for not informing him directly of the Ramos woman's terrorist designation. He demanded hourly updates from here on out and the name of the person who was savvy enough to suspect her of being a jihadist. Hart told him the tip came from an anonymous source directly to Internal Affairs, and that Internal Affairs then conducted an investigation. Now the president wants to see that report."

"Of all the asinine…" Grayson pointed a bony finger at his lawyer. "We can't get sidetracked now. What is Hart doing about it?"

"He's having his man dummy up an internal affairs report to give the president."

Grayson stroked his chin. "It might work. But it's a hell of a chance."

"If the president is as interested as he seems to be in this Ramos woman, it might work to your advantage, sir. After all, he might order more resources to search for her and take her out."

"That's one possibility," Grayson said. "Let's just hope you're right."

Still, he didn't like that there were so many variables in play at once. Too many balls were up in the air and he could only hope that all of them were caught safely.

CHAPTER NINETEEN

The café where Sedona arranged to meet Ahmed and Umar was within sight. If they could make it another two hundred yards, they finally could get off the street and she could stop feeling so completely exposed. In the three miles they walked, they saw close to a dozen patrols and narrowly escaped detection three times.

"That's the place, up ahead on the right."

"Okay," Vaughn said. She surveyed their surroundings. The street was teeming with people. Merchants hawked their wares and beat up jalopies crawled along at a snail's pace, dodging the pedestrians.

"I don't know what's worse," Lorraine commented, "the naked exposure of the deserted streets or the number of potential threats in a crowd like this."

"I'll take the empty streets any day," Justine replied. Like the others, her head swiveled from side to side watching for anyone who might be dangerous.

"I wish Peter was here," Sabastien said. "I do not like being the only male."

"Are you saying you don't trust us girls to protect you?" Sedona asked.

"No, no. It is not that. I have seen Vaughn Elliott in action. I am in good hands. It's just—"

"Umar!" Sedona called. He was standing out on the curb, obviously waiting for her. She took a step forward, her hand raised in greeting. As she did, she heard the sound of hundreds of angels' wings beating loudly in her ears. They sounded agitated. She had less than a fraction of a second to wonder why before a searing pain slammed her in the chest, knocking her off her feet. She blinked once, twice. The world spun in slow motion. She felt the weight of Vaughn's body as she landed on top of her, covering her like a blanket. Vaughn was gesturing, saying something. Sedona tried but failed to make out the words. Then everything went silent.

༄༅

Vaughn saw the muzzle flash as Sedona stepped forward. She pinpointed the location—just behind the very frightened looking man pointing in Sedona's direction. Although her head told her to take out the shooter, her heart had her lunging for Sedona, to get her out of harm's way. Out of the corner of her eye, she watched the shooter's head snap back. She registered the fact that the shot came from a different vantage point. Then she saw Peter running toward the frightened man, whose shirt and face were covered with blood.

Sedona's eyes rolled back in her head and Vaughn's heart stuttered. "No. Damn it, you are not going to die on me here." Her voice shook with emotion. She put her hand over Sedona's chest. When she pulled it away, it was free of blood. "Thank you, God. Thank you."

She turned her head. Lorraine was to her right, covering her with an M4. "Get Peter. We have to get out of here. Now!"

Justine kneeled to Vaughn's left. "Let me have a look."

"I think her vest caught it," Vaughn said. "We're sitting ducks out here. We have to go."

Justine gestured toward the street with her head. "I think Peter's commandeering our ride." A vehicle came screeching to a halt next to them a second later.

"Help me load her," Vaughn said to Justine. "Lorraine, cover us."

"Got it." Lorraine's weapon was in the ready position, her finger poised over the trigger.

Vaughn grabbed Sedona's unconscious form under the arms while Justine took her ankles. Together they lifted her into the back of a Hummer. "Everybody in," she yelled. "Sabastien?"

"Here," he squeaked.

"Justine, Lorraine, Peter?"

"Everyone's accounted for," Peter said.

"Step on it." Vaughn said, as Lorraine closed her and Sedona in. Vaughn was lying on her side, her hand stroking Sedona's cheek. "Hang in there, baby," she whispered in her ear, although she knew Sedona couldn't hear her.

"Let me evaluate her," Justine said, climbing over the seat and into the back with Vaughn.

Vaughn closed her eyes. She didn't want to let go. She felt Justine's hand cover hers and squeeze.

"I promise, I'll take good care of her, Vaughn. Please, let me have a look. We need to be sure she isn't hit anywhere else."

Vaughn nodded. She leaned over one last time, her lips hovering over Sedona's. "I'm right here. Don't you get any funny ideas..."

Vaughn yielded her place to Justine and, as she did so, she noticed the two extra passengers. One of them was the frightened man from in front of the café—the man who pointed out Sedona to the shooter. She vaulted over the seat and grabbed him by the throat. His eyes bulged out of his head. "Who the fuck are you?" She shook him.

"Easy," Lorraine said, tapping her arm. "Looks like he wasn't a willing participant." She tilted her head in the direction of the other Iraqi. "This is Sedona's friend Ahmed. The man you're choking is his cousin, Umar."

Vaughn looked from one of them to the other. Ahmed was crying. In very broken English, he asked, "Is will Sedona go good?" He rocked back and forth in his seat.

Vaughn struggled against the urge to squeeze the life out of Umar. He was making gurgling noises in his throat. Just a little more pressure...

"Vaughn!" Lorraine commanded. "That won't change anything."

A tear leaked out of Vaughn's eye and trickled down her cheek. She loosened her grip and let her hand drop into her lap.

From the driver's seat, Peter said, "The shooter was American. Private contractor from what I could tell. Military-trained, though."

"I want to know—" Vaughn paused to get the shakiness out of her voice. "I want to know why these two are here. He"—she

201

indicated Umar—"sold her out." Vaughn glanced over the seat to see what Justine was doing. She could see that Justine had removed Sedona's vest and her shirt was open. Vaughn's breath caught. She turned back around.

Peter addressed Ahmed and Umar in Arabic. "Explain yourselves. Because right now, I'm the only thing standing between you and that woman who wants to kill you."

"We meant Sedona no harm," Ahmed said. The words tumbled out over each other. "She is our friend. These men—they are very bad. They overheard us rejoicing about seeing our good friend Sedona again. They pointed guns at us and threatened us with death if we did not talk. They wanted to know what we knew about Sedona. When they found out that we were meeting her, they took Umar hostage and forced him to identify her."

"What are they saying?" Vaughn asked.

Peter relayed the conversation.

"Are they telling the truth?"

Ahmed and Umar nodded vigorously in unison.

"You understand English?"

"A little."

"What did those men tell you about why they were looking for Sedona?"

"Money," Ahmed said. "B-Boun…" He let his hand fall in a helpless gesture.

"Bounty?" Lorraine supplied.

Ahmed nodded. He looked miserable.

"They put a price on her head?" Vaughn asked. The anger flashed red-hot in her.

Umar reached into his pocket. As he did so, Vaughn pointed her pistol in his face. He screamed, his fingers frozen halfway out of his pants.

Vaughn reached in for him and pulled out a piece of paper. She lowered her weapon and scanned the writing.

"What is it?" Lorraine asked.

"It's more or less a 'Wanted Dead or Dead' poster."

"What?" Peter asked.

Vaughn read the document a second time. "It's an order, written in English, to kill her on sight." The bile rose in her throat.

202

"Why would they not want to take her alive? Arrest her?" Sabastien asked.

"Because," Peter said, "they don't want her to talk."

Vaughn's head spun. She thought she would be sick.

⋘⋙

Sedona's head throbbed. Tentatively, she opened one eye. Vaughn's concerned face swam into view. Sedona tried to sit up, but Vaughn restrained her with a gentle hand on her chest. "W-wha—?"

"It's okay. You're going to be okay," Vaughn said, hovering over her.

Sedona could have sworn she saw a tear on Vaughn's cheek. She opened the other eye. "Are you"—Sedona coughed and searing pain shot through her chest—"crying?"

Vaughn put a comforting hand on her shoulder, as Sedona caught her breath. "I don't know what you're talking about," Vaughn rubbed her cheek against her sleeve.

"I saw that. W-what hap...happened? W-where am I?"

"You got shot in the heart," Vaughn said, laughing and crying at the same time. "Fortunately for you, the sniper picked the one place you're apparently invulnerable."

As if, Sedona thought, groggily. "If y-you're talking to me"— she coughed again and Vaughn stroked her cheek—"then I must not be dead."

"You're tough to kill." Vaughn reached behind Sedona for something. When she settled back down, she had Sedona's Improved Outer Tactical Vest in her hand. There was a bullet lodged in the left chest area.

"Oh." Sedona tried to process that someone shot her in the heart. Were it not for that vest, she would be dead right now. She lifted her hand and let her fingers run over her heart. The area was painfully tender and even the slight pressure made her gasp.

"Justine left some pain meds for you. Let me get you some water."

"No." Sedona shook her head, but the motion made her dizzy. "W-why does my head hurt so much?"

"Your head hit the road. You've got a pretty good concussion. Your chest is bruised. That's why it's so painful. Even though the vest caught the bullet, you still felt the impact of the round." Vaughn's voice caught and she turned away.

"I th-thought you were a t-tough girl," Sedona teased. She reached out for Vaughn's hand and intertwined their fingers. "B-by the w-way, w-where are we?"

"Your friend Ahmed's home." Vaughn said it with distaste. "It wouldn't have been my first choice, but we had to get you somewhere safe and out of sight so you could rest and we could regroup."

"Oh," Sedona mumbled as she drifted off.

⤚⤙

The president slapped the spiral-bound briefing book Homeland Security Secretary Daniel Hart sent him on the table in front of him. "Disgusting piece of fiction." He slid the book across the table to Kate.

She read as Jay looked over her shoulder. "I give him points for inventiveness."

"And embellishment," Jay added.

"I'd really like to have him marched out of his office in handcuffs right now in front of his entire staff."

"As satisfying as that might be in the short-term, sir…"

"I know." The president sighed. "We're better served waiting until we have more information and a handle on the scope of this thing."

Before the president could say another word, a phone buzzed from inside his pants pocket. He pulled it out quickly and glanced at the caller ID. He held up a finger to Kate and Jay to signal that they should wait.

"This is the president."

"Sir, this is Vaughn Elliott."

"Yes, Vaughn. I'm going to put you on speaker. I've got Kate Kyle and Jay Parker here with me. They've been very helpful on this end." The president put the phone on the desk and hit the speaker button. "Go ahead, Vaughn."

"Sir, we've run into some complications."

"We're listening."

"Without going into too much detail, sir, we've come under extraordinary scrutiny. There are patrols everywhere, all tasked with finding the terror suspect."

"I'm not surprised," the president said. He leaned over the phone. "Homeland Security Secretary Hart has been very thorough and quite...inventive. It seems he and NSA Deputy Director Orlando Niger are old army buddies. We believe they are in this together, although it looks as though there might be more players."

"Understood, sir. But the patrols are not our biggest problem. Sedo—um, someone got shot on our way to our final destination, sir."

The president heard the catch in Vaughn's voice. It mirrored the sinking feeling he had in his gut. Across from him, he saw Kate and Jay grasp hands. Their faces were ashen. He imagined his was too. "Is she—"

"Lucky to be alive, sir. Military vest caught the bullet to the heart. She's got a concussion and a badly bruised chest, but otherwise is okay."

"Thank God."

"The shooter was a professional—an American private contractor, sir."

"What's his status?"

"Gone. Peter took him out right before he got the round off that would've been for Sedon—the target's forehead. But, sir? The biggest problem is what was on his person. He had documentation indicating that the objective was not to take any prisoners."

The president blinked. "Are you saying—"

"Dead only, sir. The order was kill on sight without question. A bounty was attached."

The president slumped down in the nearest chair. "Oh, my God."

"They're trying to make sure she can't talk," Kate said.

"Yes," Vaughn confirmed.

"With the terrorist designation, they can't guarantee that," Jay said, indignantly. "If a legitimate military unit arrested her, they wouldn't kill her unless she posed an imminent threat. They would take her into custody. What would Hart do about that?"

"We've been wondering the same thing," Vaughn said. "And that brings me to the reason I'm calling."

"Go ahead."

"We think having her arrested might give us our best chance."

"What did you say?" the president asked.

"You don't really mean that," Kate said.

"Not precisely," Vaughn said. "But if Secretary Hart thought she'd been arrested…"

Jay jumped up. "It's brilliant!" She clapped her hands together. "Sir, if you tell Secretary Hart that you've been informed personally of Sedona's arrest, he'll go wild trying to get to her before she can talk."

"Okay," the president said.

"If you publicly announce her arrest, sir, it boxes Hart into a corner," Kate said. "He'd have to call off the terrorist alert."

"Or I could do it myself," the president said. "That would take the official heat off your team, Vaughn."

"It certainly would help, sir. Then we'd just have to worry about the private contractors that are no doubt guarding our target. It would mean that our chances of reaching our destination would be much improved."

"It also would give you more incriminating evidence on Secretary Hart if he starts to lose his cool," Jay pointed out.

The president shook his head. "He can always hide behind the explanation that he wants to personally oversee this very dangerous suspect's treatment."

"Still, it would have him chasing his tail for a while, sir," Kate said.

"If you really did arrest a suspect like that, where would you send her, sir? If you can say," Jay asked.

"Most likely a US airbase in Kuwait," the president said. "But I don't want Hart leaving the country, in case we have to take him into custody."

"You could always give him an assignment that required him to stay in town, sir," Jay suggested. "That might frustrate him even more."

"Remind me never to piss you off, Jay," the president said, laughing.

"Vaughn?" Kate asked.

"Yeah?"

"I assume you're in a safe place?"

"For now," Vaughn said. "But I don't want to push our luck for too long."

"I hear you. How soon do you anticipate your team will be ready to move forward?"

"Probably within twenty-four hours."

"So I need to move quickly on the arrest announcement," the president said.

"That would be very helpful, sir," Vaughn agreed. "The sooner, the better."

The president looked at his watch. "I still have time to call a hasty news conference for this afternoon and have it hit all the major news outlets for the evening news and for the morning papers."

"The fact that it's a rush would lend credence to the idea that this is a breaking development," Kate said. "That's good. Very good."

"The timing would work out well for us, sir, since that means by morning we should be clear to move out."

"I'll do it within the hour," the president said. "A shame I won't have time to consult with Secretary Hart before the news conference, don't you think?"

"Yes, sir," Jay said.

"Is there anything else you need on this end, Vaughn?" the president asked.

"Not right now, sir. Peter has made contact with a...more local expert on raw uranium. We didn't want to risk bringing in an American expert without knowing how far this thing goes."

"Understood. Which reminds me, tell Peter we have his partner Max running surveillance on Hart right now."

"Anything interesting, sir?" Vaughn asked.

"A meeting with Niger in which they discussed fabricating the internal affairs report that led to the terrorist designation. Otherwise, just a series of meetings on Capitol Hill, which goes with his position, and a meeting with a high-priced defense attorney named Stanley Davidson."

"Maybe he's anticipating needing Davidson's services," Vaughn cracked.

"Maybe," the president agreed. "Anyway, we'll continue to watch him and see what develops on this side of the world."

"Once we get in, Sabastien will be able to send you real-time images, sir, along with on-the-spot analysis from the uranium expert."

"Excellent."

"Vaughn?"

"Yes, Jay?"

"Is she going to be all right?"

"For now." There was some noise in the background. "If there's nothing else, sir, I really need to get going."

"Right," the president said. He checked his watch again. "Just as well. I have a news conference to call."

"Thank you for your assistance, sir."

"Thank you, Vaughn. I appreciate everything you and your team are doing out there. Stay safe."

"That's one of the goals, sir. Bye."

"Godspeed, Vaughn." The line disconnected. The president put the phone back in his pocket.

CHAPTER TWENTY

L adies and gentlemen of the press," the president began. He was standing behind the lectern in the White House pressroom. All the major networks and cable news stations were carrying his remarks live. "Thank you for coming on such short notice. I'm going to make a brief statement here. I will not be taking questions."

The president waited for the whir of the cameras to abate and the members of the broadcast media who had been doing live reports to settle down.

"At approximately ten fifteen p.m., Iraqi time, that's less than an hour ago, at my personal direction, an elite Special Operations Task Force, hand-picked by me, took into custody an American citizen and wanted terrorist. As you know, for the past week, our forces and our allies around the world have been on high alert, looking for Sedona Ramos, who is believed to be an imminent threat to our national security.

"Ms. Ramos was arrested without incident inside a private residence in Baghdad, where it is believed she had arranged to meet with leaders of al-Qaeda in Iraq. I am assured that the meeting never took place." The president paused for effect and made eye contact with several of the better-known journalists in the room.

"It is not our practice to comment on the details of such operations for obvious reasons, and I will not do so now. I am very proud of my team. These highly skilled warriors put themselves in harm's way for the good of our nation and our people, and we owe them a debt of gratitude. We are all safer for their heroic efforts. Thank you."

As the president stepped away from the podium and waved, he could hear the shouted questions.

"Where is Ramos now, sir?"

"Mr. President, what did she know?"

"Were there any leaders of al-Qaeda in Iraq present? Were any of them taken prisoner?"

The president waved one more time and disappeared out the door. He gave a perfunctory nod to his press secretary and the other members of his staff standing nearby, all of whom wanted his attention, and headed directly for the private residence, where Kate and Jay were waiting.

When he arrived, he removed his suit jacket and loosened his tie. "What did you think?"

"It was masterful, sir," Kate said. Her smile was wide. "You stuck remarkably close to the truth in many places, and that will be important for later on, when you're ready to reveal the actual story."

"I have no doubt that, wherever he is right now, Secretary Hart is going apoplectic," Jay said.

"I hope you're right, Jay," the president said. "I sincerely hope you're right."

⤜⤛

"I didn't know a fucking thing about it!" Daniel Hart boomed into the phone. "How is that possible? I want to know why I wasn't read into the mission and I want to know now."

The volume was so loud that Max Kingston had to hold the listening device away from his ear. This was Hart's third call since the president finished speaking. First, he called the secretary of defense and then it was the chairman of the Joint Chiefs of Staff.

"You're the director of the fucking CIA, what do you mean you weren't consulted?"

Max used a joystick to adjust the angle of Hart's hacked webcam so he could watch Hart imploding.

"If you're lying to me, so help me God..." He slammed the receiver down and made a lewd gesture with his finger. "Shit!" He picked up what appeared to be a stress ball and threw it across the room.

210

"Mr. Secretary?"

The executive assistant's voice sounded distorted to Max, filtered as it was through Hart's office intercom.

Hart hit the intercom key. "What?"

"I have NSA Deputy Director Niger on line two for you, sir."

"Tell him to go fuck himself," Hart muttered to himself, before depressing the intercom key again. "Tell him I'm busy."

"I did, sir. He's very insistent. Frankly, sir, he sounds a bit frazzled."

Hart looked for something else to throw. This time, he counted to three before pushing the intercom button. "Put him through."

"I don't have time for you," Hart said. Without waiting for Niger to ask, he added, "And no, I don't know anything. Don't call me again. I'll get in touch with you. Not the other way around."

Again, Hart slammed down the receiver.

"Agnes?" Hart bellowed into the intercom. "Get me an appointment with the president. Right now. I don't care what it takes. I need to see him."

Wayne Grayson finished watching the president's news conference in the tiny recreation room at the end of his cellblock. His hands twisted together so tightly they tingled from lack of circulation. When the broadcast was over, he found the nearest guard. "I want to make a phone call."

"It's after hours for calls."

"Don't give me that bullshit. It's a power play and you know it. It's no skin off your nose to give me five minutes of phone time."

The guard folded his arms over his chest.

Grayson played his ace. "How's your mother feeling? Is that new hip working out for her? What a shame she had to wait so long. It's a crime how much they charge the uninsured." He tutted. "Sure glad I could help out with that."

The guard frowned. "Five minutes."

"Thanks." Grayson smirked. "I'll be talking to my lawyer, so attorney-client privilege applies."

The guard shook his head. "Sure it does."

211

Grayson went to the phone bank and dialed the collect call to Stanley Davidson.

"Davidson."

"Stanley. I was very disappointed with the president's press conference just now." When Davidson didn't reply, Grayson said, "Are you there, Stanley?"

"I'm here. I'm sure you were, Mr. Grayson."

"What are we doing about that?"

"I'm sorry?"

"I said," Grayson raised his voice, "what are we doing about it?"

"I don't know what you want me to say here."

"I want you to say that Hart knows where the fuck this woman is and that he's taking steps to make sure she can't talk."

"I haven't talked to Daniel, sir."

"Take care of it, Stanley. Now. Remember what I said—no loose ends."

"I'll make a phone call."

Grayson disconnected the call and shuffled back to his cell.

A Steyr rifle in her hands, Vaughn stood in the doorway of Ahmed's home looking out at the pitch black, silent village. She scanned up and down the street, looking for and expecting trouble. Justine came up alongside her.

"Are you okay?"

"Why wouldn't I be?" Vaughn's eyes never left the street.

Justine touched her arm. "She's going to be fine, you know. Her chest will be bruised and sore for a week or two and she'll probably still have a headache for the next twenty-four hours, but other than that, she's a lucky girl."

Vaughn spared a quick glance at her friend. "Thanks for taking care of her."

"Of course."

They stood for a moment in companionable silence.

"Is everyone else asleep?" Vaughn asked.

"I'm not," Peter said, as he joined them. "You okay?" he asked Vaughn.

212

"Why the hell is everyone so concerned about me?" Vaughn snapped. "I'm fine. Why wouldn't I be?" She saw the look that passed between Justine and Peter. Was she really that transparent? She sighed in exasperation. "Peter, where are we with our nuclear scientist? Is he going to be here in the morning?"

"He's flying in from Istanbul. Ahmed is going to pick him up at the airport. He should be able to join us by the afternoon."

Vaughn spared Peter a look. "Do we really trust Ahmed after what happened?"

"Do we really have a choice? We can't spare one of us and we still need to keep a low profile. Even without the official attention, we all know there's a private goon squad out there gunning for us—and especially for Sedona. I don't know about you"—Peter's voice cracked and he took a second to compose himself—"but I can't stand the thought of them taking her out. Watching her fall like that—"

"Don't," Vaughn said. She held out a shaky hand. "Just don't." She felt the tears swim in her eyes and she willed them away. "Fine. The scientist will get here when he does." She pivoted and walked into the house. Over her shoulder she said, "It's one of your turns to stand watch."

She was tired, and she didn't want to think, she didn't want to feel. She just wanted... She just wanted to be with Sedona, to hold her, to feel her breath against her cheek. She was tired of fighting it and more tired of trying to pretend she wasn't completely smitten, especially since nobody seemed to be fooled, including her.

She moved quietly through the house to the private room where Sedona was convalescing. She stripped down to her t-shirt and panties. For a long moment, she stood there, watching Sedona sleep. She was so beautiful and serene. Suddenly, in her mind's eye, Vaughn saw an image of the bullet slamming into Sedona, her body jerking backward, and the look of surprise on her face.

Vaughn let out an involuntary cry and Sedona shifted restlessly. She moaned in pain from the movement. Vaughn immediately knelt down beside her.

Although Sedona didn't appear to have awakened, her calm expression morphed into a mask of discomfort. Vaughn hesitated only for a second before lying down next to her and gently pulling Sedona into her arms. "You're okay, sweetheart. I've got you."

As their heartbeats settled into one rhythm, Vaughn took a deep breath. It should have felt wrong, she reasoned. She should be feeling guilty. After all, it was only six months ago that Sage walked out. Surely she shouldn't be over Sage already.

But it didn't feel wrong lying here with Sedona. In fact, it felt so very, very right. It wasn't that Vaughn hadn't cared for Sage, she did. In her own way, she loved her. But it never felt like this. This was... Vaughn didn't know what it was. But it was by far the most she'd felt for anyone since Sara.

The familiar stab of pain pierced Vaughn's heart. Automatically, she put her free hand to the scar she bore—a constant reminder of the explosion that ripped her world apart.

Unconsciously, Sedona snuggled against Vaughn. Her hand drifted to Vaughn's scar and Vaughn opened her eyes. Sedona's breathing remained slow and steady. How could she know, even in her sleep, what it was Vaughn needed? The comforting touch soothed Vaughn, and within seconds, she was asleep.

She could feel the panic rising in Vaughn's chest. A bright flash turned night into day and the physical injury made her writhe in agony. But it was Vaughn's emotional devastation that ripped at Sedona's heart.

Sedona gasped and levitated off the mattress and a jolt of real pain bloomed in her chest as she came awake. She swallowed a groan. Sweat stained her t-shirt.

She turned her head and a thousand gongs banged against her skull. When her vision cleared, there was Vaughn, peacefully asleep, her arm wrapped tightly around Sedona's shoulder.

Sedona's eyes tracked to where her fingers rested lightly on Vaughn's scar. She remembered what Justine told her on the plane about Sara.

Oh, Vaughn. I'm so sorry! Angels? Why did you show me that? Why did you have me relive Vaughn's experience? I know you never do anything without a purpose, so I ask you to help me see with crystal clarity the reasons you shared that memory with me. This I ask you with your blessings. Amen.

As exhaustion claimed her one more time, Sedona mouthed the words, "Archangel Raphael, please use your green healing light to repair any physical damage from Vaughn's injury. Archangel Azrael, please, heal Vaughn's heart, for she carries within her so much pain, so much suffering."

Sedona caressed the scar one more time before moving her hand to Vaughn's abdomen. Her eyes drooped and she let herself drift off to sleep once again.

When next she woke, Vaughn was dressed, sitting by the side of the mattress, and staring at her. "What? Am I drooling or something?"

Vaughn laughed. "No. I didn't want to wake you, but we really should get going, if you're up to it."

Sedona blinked. Her head still throbbed. Carefully, slowly, she lifted it off the pillow. As she did so, Vaughn slipped in behind her and cradled her.

"How do you feel?"

Sedona closed her eyes. *Very safe and cared for.* She opened her eyes again. Out loud, she said, "It's not ideal, but a couple of ibuprofen ought to make it doable."

"What about your chest?"

Sedona took a deep breath. "It feels like Thor took his hammer to my chest, but I can breathe. Let me stand up and I'll have a better idea how useful I'm going to be."

Vaughn dropped her arms to her side and scrambled out of the way. Sedona felt an instant of hurt radiate from Vaughn's heart. She captured Vaughn's hand and squeezed. "Thank you."

"For what?"

"For being my protector. For taking such wonderful care of me. For risking your life for me." Sedona moved in and kissed Vaughn on the lips. It wasn't a kiss of welcome but a gesture of gratitude. When she pulled back, Vaughn's eyes still were closed and Sedona's throat tightened. Was Vaughn falling in love with her? Unable to process the thought, Sedona set it aside. They had a job to do.

Slowly, carefully, she stood. "Standing still works." She hoped her smile would be contagious.

"That's something."

Justine knocked on the wall just outside the room. "How's the patient?"

Sedona noted that Vaughn took two steps back.

"We're evaluating that right now," Sedona said.

"Would you care for a professional opinion?"

"Of course."

"You don't need me for this. I'll go and see how everyone else is doing." Vaughn walked out without a backward glance.

Sedona wanted to go after her—to say… What, exactly?

"Don't worry," Justine said. She nodded in the direction Vaughn went. "She hasn't quite figured it all out yet, but she will."

"What do you mean?"

Justine stilled her hands where they were palpating Sedona's bruised left chest. Their faces were less than a foot apart. "You're a very perceptive woman. Please don't tell me you haven't figured out that Vaughn is falling in love with you."

Sedona blinked. She wasn't expecting Justine to parrot back her own thoughts so plainly.

"Sorry. That was out of line. None of my business." Justine resumed her exam. "Does this hurt?"

Sedona flinched.

"I'll take that for a yes." Justine moved her hands slightly to the right. "How about this?"

Sedona recoiled.

"I'll take that for a big yes."

Sedona noted Justine's frown. When she looked down, she realized that Justine was testing the area directly over her heart. Her stomach flipped. "He was a pretty good shot, huh?"

Justine's eyes misted. "You could say that."

"What happened to him?"

"Peter took him out."

"Oh."

"He was using Ahmed and Umar, threatening them with a gun if they didn't identify you for him."

"How did he know they knew me?"

"Apparently, your friends were celebrating your return in the café before we arrived and this guy overheard them."

216

Sedona closed her eyes. "Sedona's not exactly a common name. I should have thought to tell them not to say anything out loud about what they were doing. That was my fault."

"Nobody blames you."

"Where are they? Ahmed and Umar?"

"They're outside waiting for us."

"I should talk to them."

"You should know that Vaughn scared the daylights out of them. She wasn't as sure as Peter was that they were innocent dupes."

"She has a suspicious mind."

"With good reason."

"Of course." Sedona buttoned her Army uniform shirt. "But in this case, I know these men. They are good friends. They might be naïve, but they would never intentionally allow harm to come to me."

"So they said."

Sedona sighed. "I better go see them. They're probably completely freaked out."

"That would be an understatement. I think Vaughn's out there threatening their lives if they don't come through this afternoon."

"What happens this afternoon?"

"We need them to go to the airport in Baghdad and pick up the raw uranium expert we're flying in from Turkey."

"In that case, I better hustle."

"The president wouldn't see me." Daniel Hart sat at a coffee shop in Alexandria, Virginia with Stanley Davidson. The place was crawling with college kids.

"That's not Mr. Grayson's problem."

"I know that." Hart shredded a napkin. "I can't get anyone to tell me anything."

"I strongly urge you to figure out a way to discover where they're holding the prisoner. Mr. Grayson has made it abundantly clear that there are to be no loose ends."

"I can't have her killed if I don't know where she is!" Hart whispered harshly. "The closest I can come right now is to assume

217

they took her to a military base in Kuwait. That would be standard protocol."

"So why aren't you directing a search of such facilities?" Davidson asked.

"It isn't that simple." Hart picked up another napkin to shred. "Do you have any idea how many possibilities there are?"

"No, but I suggest you figure it out. Mr. Grayson is quite adamant on this point."

"No kidding. You think I want her blabbing? I'm in a more compromising situation than anybody on this one."

"Then I suggest you leave that poor napkin alone and get to work."

CHAPTER TWENTY-ONE

The perimeter around the Tuwaitha complex was heavily guarded. Vaughn counted at least two dozen patrols of private paramilitary units encircling the main facility. She imagined there were at least an equal number of squads inside the gates. Peter was lying next to her behind the berm they'd chosen as their reconnaissance point. A short distance away, the rest of the team was in the SUV they'd borrowed from Umar.

"Lots of attention for a place that's abandoned, don't you think?" Vaughn asked.

"I do. Interesting firepower too." He was looking through a long-range scope. "MP-5 submachine guns."

"Yeah, I saw that. You'd think they were expecting trouble." Vaughn inserted her ear bud. "Sabastien? Can you hear me?"

"Yes."

"Everything okay back there?"

"We found a place off the road I think will work. It is close enough to pick up the smallest drone's signal, about five hundred meters."

"Will you be able to get a satellite uplink from there?"

"Yes."

"Roger. Lorraine?"

"Here."

"Are you comfortable with the sight lines?"

"It's not ideal, but we can make it work."

"Okay. I think we've seen what we need to see for now. Let's get going. See you in a minute."

When they were all in the vehicle and on their way back to Ahmed's home, Vaughn addressed the group. "Now that we've had a look around, we know what we're up against, at least on the outside. Tonight we'll come back and launch the larger drone so we can have a look inside the complex."

"I have reviewed all of the laptop's programming," Sabastien said. "I ran a small test while you and Peter were out there. I bet you did not even know I had you under drone surveillance."

"I hope you got my good side," Peter said.

"The images were very clear and crisp and the recording technology worked just fine."

"Good." Vaughn turned to Sedona, who was slumped in the back, just in case they passed any traffic. "You okay back there?"

"Fine, thanks."

"How are you feeling?"

Sedona rolled her eyes. "You don't need to worry about me. I'm ready."

"Right." Vaughn cleared her throat. "You're going to be watching over Sabastien's shoulder and mine too, looking at the video feed live so that you can direct me as I fly the drone through the place. You're the only one who knows the layout. We've got infrared, heat-seeking capability, so we should be able to get a good idea how many people they've got working in there, plus, we can run facial recognition on anybody we find interesting. While I'm directing the drone on one computer, Sabastien will be editing the video on the second laptop in live time and taking care of the facial recognition searches."

"Okay."

"Peter and Lorraine, you've got lookout duty outside the vehicle."

"What about me?" Justine asked.

"You're going to babysit our nuclear scientist. We don't know anything about this guy, except that he came recommended by a third party. I'm not crazy about bringing anybody else into the op, but we need to know exactly what it is they're doing inside. Assuming none of us is an expert in yellowcake or nuclear weapons, we have no choice but to trust an outsider."

"What is it you want from him? Surely you're not sending him in there."

"No. We're going to use the smaller drone to get shots of the manufacturing operation, since it seems likely they're building some kind of bomb. We need this guy to tell us what we're looking at and what it's designed to do."

"Does he know where we're taking him?" Justine asked.

"He was told only that our destination was a nuclear facility outside Baghdad," Peter said. "My sources say he's an expert in the field in this part of the world."

"I wonder why he's not working on this project, then?" Sedona asked.

"I don't know. I guess we'll have to ask him that. Here he is now."

They pulled up to Ahmed's home and piled out. Ahmed and Umar were sitting outside with the latest arrival. He was a slight man, with stooped shoulders and large glasses.

"Welcome," Vaughn said. "Thanks for being here. You speak English?"

"Impeccably, I should hope," the scientist replied. "I studied at Oxford and Harvard."

"I'm Vaughn. This woman," Vaughn pulled Justine forward, "is Justine. Anything you need, she'll be your go-to person."

"Very well."

"We should all get some rest," Vaughn said. "It's going to be a long night."

∽∾

"Are you guys okay?" Sedona asked Ahmed and Umar in Arabic. The three of them sat on the floor in the front room of Ahmed's home.

Ahmed spoke first. "We are so, so sorry for what happened to you yesterday, my friend. We would never harm you."

"I know that," Sedona said. "You didn't know you weren't supposed to talk about my arrival. I should have told you."

"Why do so many people want to hurt you?" Umar asked softly. "I do not understand."

Sedona gave him a smile filled with irony. "I don't really understand myself. I wish I did."

"We will protect you." Ahmed sat up straighter.

Sedona shook her head sadly. "No, my friends. I can take care of myself. I'm sorry to have brought you into this." She looked at

Umar. "I'm sorry for what happened at the café and afterwards. You must have been so scared."

Umar ducked his head. Sedona could see that his eyelashes shimmered with tears. "I failed you."

"No. No, you didn't. How could you have known?"

"Your friend, she hates us."

"Vaughn?" Sedona said. "No, she was just worried about me. She's not that bad, really."

Ahmed smiled wisely. "No, I think she hates us. Like so many Americans, she thinks we are all terrorists and anti-American."

"I don't believe that," Sedona said. She had seen into Vaughn's heart—there was no prejudice there. "It's her job to be suspicious of everyone."

"She does it well," Umar said, rubbing the sore place on his throat.

"Yes," Sedona admitted, "she does."

∽৯৯৵

Tuwaitha was buzzing with activity, despite the fact that it was nighttime. Every building was lit up. So far, they'd seen evidence of nearly one hundred people moving about.

"There's a passageway between those two buildings," Sedona told Vaughn as she watched the drone's progress through the shadows. "See that little crease there?" She pointed on the screen.

"Where does it lead?"

"To the manufacturing plant or at least to what used to be the manufacturing plant."

Vaughn manipulated the joystick to the right, sliding into the space Sedona indicated. "Which of these buildings gets us to pay dirt?"

"They both held pieces of the operation, but I'd say you're most interested in the building on the left." Sedona massaged her temples. Her head pounded so hard she wondered how she could hear her own thoughts. More importantly, she feared that she would not hear the angels talking to her if she needed them.

The drone hovered outside a window. Vaughn zoomed in.

"Over there." Sedona indicated an area to the left of center. "See if you can get a better shot of that."

Vaughn cursed. "I can't get a fix on it with this. I'm going to have to switch to the smaller drone." Carefully, she turned the drone around and directed it back to their location.

"Sabastien, while I'm trading these out, send the video we just took to the president. In the message, tell him we're going in for a better look."

"Okay." Sabastien handed Sedona a thin, round, cylindrical tube. "If you would please put this on the roof."

"What is it?" Justine asked.

"It is a laser uplink. It will allow me to establish a secure link with a satellite from which to transmit the video."

"But I thought they caught us the last time we tried to use a satellite."

"That was different. In that case, we were taking pictures of their facility. In this case, we are pointed in the opposite direction."

"Okay. All set." Sedona said, lowering herself back in through the open window.

"Behold the magic," Sabastien said. It took less than thirty seconds for him to hook up with the satellite, and not much longer than that to transmit a rush packet with all of the video contained within.

"Where does it go now?" Justine asked.

"The secure communications center in the White House. A hand-picked Navy Captain will receive it and walk it directly to the president so he can view it on an iPhone."

"How do you know that?" Sedona asked.

"I set up the system myself," Sabastien said, puffing out his chest with pride.

"Okay, genius. Launch number two is away." Vaughn positioned herself in front of her laptop and Sedona leaned over her shoulder from the back seat.

As the drone approached the compound, they watched on screen as one of the guards walked back through the gate. "Zoom in on him," Sedona said. "Get his face."

"Why?" Vaughn asked.

"Because he did the same thing exactly half an hour ago. He's on a specific schedule. I think it might be worthwhile to see where he's going."

Vaughn shrugged but followed the man's progress as he walked through the compound into a building. She directed the drone through the open door and stayed with the guard as he traveled down a corridor and ducked his head into an office.

"What do you think he's doing?" Justine asked.

"Reporting to the watch commander," Vaughn and Sedona said simultaneously.

"He must be like a major—they probably want a minimal amount of activity traveling in and out, so they put one guy in charge of shuttling between the troops on the outside and the commander in charge on the inside," Vaughn elaborated.

Sedona closed her eyes and tried to tune in to her intuition. The massive headache and the pain in her chest were making it difficult. *Angels, please, find a way to give me the information I need so that I know it with crystal clarity.*

"Are you okay?" Justine asked close to her ear.

"Yes." She reached over Vaughn's shoulder and pointed to the man coming out of the office. "He's the one you want to follow. Stay with him."

It seemed for a moment as if Vaughn would object, but she closed her mouth and maneuvered the joystick carefully to the left so that the drone followed directly behind and above the man they presumed to be the watch commander. He opened a door at the other end of the hallway and the drone followed him through the opening and into a wide-open area.

"Where are we?" Vaughn asked.

"The heart of the operation," Sedona said. "Gotcha." She pumped a fist. "Stay with him, I have a feeling he's going to lead us to someone we really want to meet."

Vaughn shook her head, but complied.

"What?"

"I've stopped questioning your mysterious ways…for now. I may not understand how or why you come up with your information—"

"I—"

"Before you say anything like, 'It's just a hunch,' I'm telling you I acknowledge that, somehow, you seem to know things and your choices always seem to work out."

"Well, except for walking into a bullet," Sedona muttered.

Vaughn coughed. "I could've gone all night without you reminding me of that."

"Me too, actually," Sedona said. "There!" She jabbed the laptop screen with her finger. "Get that guy's picture."

Vaughn zoomed in and captured the man's face. "Sabastien?"

"I am in it."

"On it," Vaughn corrected.

Sabastien's fingers flew over the keyboard as he typed in commands. He used the mouse to outline the man's face and clicked to finalize the selection. Within seconds, millions of faces cascaded down the screen. Less than ten seconds after that, the computer beeped.

"What is it?" Sedona asked.

"We have a match."

Sedona shifted to look over Sabastien's shoulder. "Oh, my."

"I'm listening," Vaughn said.

"He's Randolph Quinn. According to his bio, he's one of the most wanted men on the planet. For at least a decade, he was the top bomb maker for the IRA. He disappeared from sight after the Brits and the IRA reached a cease-fire. No one's seen him since."

"We have," Vaughn said grimly. "Sabastien, send that to the president right away."

"Vaughn, you'd better call and tell him. Whoever hired him means business," Sedona said.

"What makes you think he's a hired gun and not the guy in charge?"

"Men like Quinn take orders. They do other people's bidding. They like to control things, but they don't like to take responsibility."

"Sedona's right," Justine said. Next to her in the back seat, the scientist choked and coughed. "Are you okay?" she asked him.

He nodded and held up a hand. "I think I just need a minute of fresh air." He coughed again. "If I could just step outside for a second?"

"Justine, go with him. And keep it quiet out there."

The scientist opened the door and stumbled outside. Justine followed behind him.

When they were gone, Sedona said, "Vaughn, I need you to trust me on this. Think about it—this guy is Irish. Everyone else

225

we've encountered has been American. Someone hired him or cut him in because of his particular skill set. There's no way he's calling the shots over one of the president's cabinet members. Hart would never allow it. We just have to figure out how all this is connected and why."

Vaughn capitulated. "Put the president on speaker. I need to keep flying this thing. We still need to see exactly what he's building so our scientist can tell us what we're dealing with." Vaughn motioned to Sedona to dial the number and put the phone on the seat next to her.

"Hello."

"Mr. President? Vaughn Elliott, sir."

"I just received your images."

"So you can see a little bit of the scope of this thing."

"Yes."

Sedona thought the president sounded grim.

"Sir? There's more."

"I'm listening."

"We ran the facial recognition software and identified the man we believe is in charge of the operation over here."

"And?"

"He's Randolph Quinn, sir. Interpol has been searching for him for years. He was the IRA's top bomb-making expert. He's Irish."

"Damn."

Sedona wanted to join the conversation, but she knew that until everything was fully resolved, she needed to keep her distance from the president.

"I'm attempting to ascertain right now what it is they're manufacturing over here, whoever 'they' are. Sedo—uh, we believe that while he might be in charge over here, someone else is pulling the strings."

"That's probably true. Max Kingston is still tracking Daniel Hart. He's due to report back to me later today. Perhaps we'll know more then."

"Yes, sir." Several seconds of silence ensued. "Sir?"

"Yes?"

"If Quinn is here and this turns out to be bad…"

"I see where you're going." There was a pause on the other end of the line. "Phone in again if you can. If not, I authorize you to take all necessary steps to eliminate the threat. I just wish we knew what the endgame was."

"I will, if at all possible, sir, try to capture Quinn alive so we can get the answer to that."

"You and your team be careful, Vaughn."

"Yes, sir." Vaughn hit the off key. "Where to?" she asked Sedona as she continued to control the drone.

"Head to your right, to that well-lit area over toward the corner. See all those people in Hazmat suits?" Sedona pointed to an area on the screen.

"Here?"

"A little farther to the right... Okay, look around there."

Vaughn turned the drone in several directions, making sure to get several angles. "Where's our scientist?"

"Justine?" Sedona hailed her over the coms.

"Coming."

Several moments later, the car door opened and Justine and the scientist slid back onto the seat.

"See this?" Vaughn asked. She indicated the video currently being shot by the drone. "What are we looking at?"

The scientist scooted forward, closer to Sedona and she felt her heart rate, or more precisely, his energy signature, rapidly speed up. "Th-that appears to be some raw uranium and a processing operation."

"What are they doing with it?" Vaughn asked. "What's this over here?" She pointed to another area.

Sedona's back contracted sharply, as if she was being stabbed. She sucked in a sharp breath.

"It would appear to me that they are creating some sort of explosive device."

"What kind?"

He was sweating profusely and the pain in Sedona's chest and back intensified. *Archangel Michael, what do I need to know?*

"Th-the uranium already in the drums is encased in layers of cement, as you can see," the scientist said. "When combined with enough Semtex or some other explosive, the result would be what you refer to as a 'dirty bomb.' In this case, perhaps several dirty bombs."

"How powerful?"

"From what I can see here, they could take out a significant number of people."

"People? Not buildings?" Vaughn asked.

"No. Not buildings."

"How far along in the process are they?"

"They appear to be nearly finished," the scientist said quietly.

"Vaughn!" Sedona gripped Vaughn's shoulder.

"What?" Vaughn didn't turn around.

"We have a more immediate problem."

"What is it?"

"Him." Sedona lunged at the scientist and wrestled him face down into the seat.

"What the hell?" Vaughn asked.

"Justine? Was he ever out of your sight out there?" Sedona rose up and kneeled on the man's back, pushing his face into the seat.

"H-he said he had to relieve himself. Why?"

"Search his pockets for a phone."

"We searched him before we left—"

"Do it," Vaughn said.

"I don't—" the scientist started to say.

"Quiet," Sedona said.

Justine patted down his pockets.

"Look in his socks," Sedona said.

Justine did as Sedona suggested. From his right sock, she pulled out a small flip phone. "I'll be a…"

"Check the last phone number on his call list," Sedona said. "Sabastien? Find out who it belongs to."

Justine read off the number.

"It belongs to an attorney in Washington," Sabastien said. "Stanley Davidson. It says here he is a defense attorney."

CHAPTER TWENTY-TWO

Y ou needed a defense attorney? Out here?" Vaughn stood over the trembling scientist. He was handcuffed and seated outside the car with his back against the back passenger-side wheel well.

Vaughn slapped him hard across the face. "I'm going to ask you again, because we're a little short on time here. Why were you calling this man?"

When he didn't answer, Vaughn raised her hand again to strike him.

"Don't." Sedona stepped in. Her face looked ashen and her hand shook.

Vaughn looked from her to the scientist and back again. She grabbed a fistful of the scientist's shirt. "Tell me what I want to know."

Sedona moved between them and squatted in front of the scientist. "Listen, we can help you." Her voice was soft and sympathetic. Vaughn vibrated with anger and adrenaline.

"Vaughn. I know," Sedona said. She glanced up at her, her eyes pleading. "I'll get you what you need right now, but beating the crap out of this man isn't the way to go. He's scared out of his mind." She looked back down at the trembling man. "You are, aren't you? I know they're blackmailing you, but I promise you, if you help us, we can help you."

The man sobbed.

"What do they have over you?"

"M-my family."

"Your wife and two daughters, right?" Sedona asked.

"H-how did you know that?"

Vaughn was asking herself the same thing.

Sedona continued, "We can send a team to rescue them."

"I-I...don't know where they are."

"I do," Sedona said. Vaughn watched as she closed her eyes in concentration, then opened them again. "They are safe, for now. But these people will kill them...and you. They won't think twice about it once you've outlived your usefulness to them, which I suspect you just did."

Vaughn wondered if Sedona was bluffing. If so, she was doing a masterful job.

"Please. I know you didn't do this willingly. You can help us stop them. But we have to act right now. Do you understand?"

The scientist nodded.

"Good. Who is Stanley Davidson and what did you just tell him?"

"H-he's a lawyer. I do not know him personally. He contacted me after my family was taken. He told me he worked on behalf of other interests. He said if I did not help them, they would kill Annia and our children. Please. I do not want them to die." Tears streamed down his face.

"We'll do everything we can to prevent that." Sedona said.

Vaughn wanted to jump in—wanted to speed up the questioning—but he was responding to Sedona and she knew that rushing him at this point would be counterproductive.

"What, exactly, did you just tell him?"

"I-I told him that you weren't in custody as they thought. I told him you were here."

Vaughn couldn't stand it any longer. "How did they know you'd be able to find that out?"

"Th-they didn't. When they came to me, they told me that I might be approached by a woman named Sedona Ramos. She was going to want me to verify what was going on at Tuwaitha."

"When was that?" Vaughn asked.

"A week ago. They said that if I was approached, I was to agree to do the work and then report back to them everything I found out." He looked at Sedona. "But then they called me back two days ago and told me the instructions had changed. I wouldn't be approached by Sedona Ramos, because she was in jail. I should still maybe expect to be contacted by others wanting me to do exactly what you asked me to do."

"So when you called her by name," he glanced at Justine, "I knew I had to report that they were misinformed."

"That's why you needed to get out of the car."

"Yes." He hung his head.

"What did this Stanley Davidson say when you spoke to him? Did you reach him, specifically?"

"Yes. He told me I had done well and ordered me to report any further developments. He seemed in a big hurry to get off the phone."

"You didn't give him any of the particulars about our exact location or numbers or any of our plans?" Vaughn asked.

"No. I did not want to help them. You see? I gave them only what was necessary to keep my girls alive." He began to cry again.

Sedona gave his arm an encouraging pat. "You didn't mention that we sent information to the president?"

"No."

Sedona nodded. "He's telling the truth."

"And you know that because...?" Vaughn asked.

"You didn't tell this man that we identified Randolph Quinn or that we were using drones to get information?"

"No."

Sedona nodded again.

"I only told him that he was mistaken about your whereabouts. Nothing more. I swear."

"Okay. I believe you."

"Sedona? Can I talk to you a minute?" Vaughn dragged Sedona a short distance away and removed both of their ear buds to prevent being overheard. "What the hell was that?"

"What?"

Vaughn ran her fingers through her hair agitatedly. "We don't have time for this. How did you know those things?" She watched a series of emotions flit across Sedona's face.

"I don't know that you can handle the truth."

"Try me."

"Okay." Sedona took a deep breath and squared her feet. "I'm spiritually gifted."

"Say that again?"

Sedona sighed and shook her head. "I'm clairvoyant, clairaudient, clairsentient, claircognizant. Psychic. I talk to angels. There. Now you know." She started to walk away.

Vaughn blinked several times, trying to process what she heard. "You're telling me you read people's minds? That's how you knew all those 'hunches' were right?"

"I listen to the information the angels give me. Sometimes it comes in the form of intuition, sometimes they speak to me, sometimes I see it, sometimes I know it. If you want, we can talk about this later. Right now, it seems to me we have more important things to worry about." Sedona inserted her ear bud and walked back to where Justine was standing guard over the scientist.

Vaughn replaced her ear bud, as well, and joined them. She wasn't done processing, but Sedona was right—there were more pressing matters to attend to. "Peter, Lorraine? Do you read me?"

"Loud and clear," Peter said.

"Ditto," Lorraine answered.

"What's our situation?"

"No change. All's humming along."

"Okay. I assume you've been listening to what's been happening here."

"Yes," Peter and Lorraine said in unison.

"We need to wrap this up," Lorraine said. "They know we're here now. It won't be long before they come looking."

"I agree," Justine said.

"*Oui*, please," Sabastien said from the front passenger seat of the SUV.

"I can't yet," Vaughn said.

"What?" Justine asked.

"We need to finish this," Sedona supplied. "We have to take out the facility. Whatever it is they have planned, we can't allow it to go forward. Now that my presence is known, they'll connect the dots and figure out that the president is on to them. They're going to be desperate. That either means they push up their timetable for implementation or they turn tail and run, disappearing into the woodwork."

"Either way," Vaughn jumped in, "there's some really dangerous shit in there and one very dangerous man. We need to finish what we came here to do."

"What do you propose?" Peter asked.

"I'm going to go in there and take out the bombs. Hopefully, I'll be able to grab Quinn in the process and we can wring more information out of him."

"You can't go in there by yourself," Sedona said.

"I have to. There's no way to get more than one of us in. You saw the routine. There's one weak spot. It's the major who travels between the units outside and the watch commander inside. That's the way in."

"I don't like it," Justine said. "What would you do once you got in there?"

"She could set off an explosive charge and detonate the yellowcake." The scientist said it sheepishly.

"One more time?" Vaughn looked down at him.

"If you had a small container, two pounds of Semtex or C-4, four or five D batteries, blasting caps, and a cell phone to use as a remote control initiator, you could set a directional charge aimed at those drums."

"Exactly what would happen?" Vaughn asked.

"The resulting explosion would contaminate the yellowcake and render it useless."

"What kind of casualties are we talking about?" Sedona asked.

The scientist considered his answer. "Anyone in the immediate vicinity would be killed quite quickly. Anyone else anywhere in the facility would die of contamination, likely within a couple of days or perhaps a little longer. The area most likely would be deadly toxic for at least one hundred years."

"Oh my God." Sedona slumped against the side of the SUV. "There are a lot of people in there."

Vaughn's heart constricted. "I know."

"What are our other options?" Peter asked.

"I'm not sure I see any," Vaughn said.

"There's an alarm switch. There has to be in any facility where there's a risk of contamination or leakage," Sedona said. "What if you tripped the alarm after you set the charge and before you detonated it? It would give people a chance to get out of there in time."

"Yes, but where would they go? They'd still be on the grounds. It would just mean a slower, more painful death for them," Vaughn argued.

"That facility is built with very thick walls. All such places are," the scientist pointed out. "The blast you'd be setting would be in the most fortified part of the grounds. If those people could get even a few hundred yards off the grounds, they could be fine."

"Vaughn." Sedona's eyes pleaded with her. "Please."

Vaughn tried not to get lost in those eyes. She tried to ignore her own heart, which balked at causing so much death and destruction. But how many more lives would be saved by eliminating the threat?

"If I may, there is one more possibility," Sabastien said.

"Let's have it."

"While you all have been debating the fate of mankind, I have been hacking into the facility's control interface."

"Do you mean to tell me that they defended against someone taking a photograph via satellite but not against someone hacking into their servers?" Sedona asked.

"So it would appear. It is a common fault of arrogant people," Sabastien said. "Here is what I propose. I already am poised to trip the alarm you referenced and several more for good measure. That would send people scurrying like little bunnies."

"Mice," Vaughn corrected automatically.

"As you wish."

"But what about setting the bomb?" Lorraine asked.

"Mr. Bomb man, you couldn't hear the discussion through our communications system, so let me ask you something. If we had a way remotely to trip the alarm, is there also a way remotely to set the explosive?" Vaughn asked.

"Of course. You could load the same bomb I described making onto the larger drone, fly it in as people were running through the door in a panic, and remotely detonate it after you saw that everyone left the premises."

Vaughn leaned down and clapped him on the shoulder. "Why didn't you say so in the first place?" She helped him up. "Okay.

Your job is to make the bomb and get it ready. How quickly can it be done?"

≪⟡⟡≫

"I can't believe you guys wanted to come sit through this with me." Max Kingston parked the white work van around the corner from the building Daniel Hart had just entered.

"I've never been on an honest-to-goodness stakeout before," Jay said. "This'll be fun." She raised her chopsticks in salute and shoveled in a mouthful of pork-fried rice.

"You just wanted an excuse to eat," Kate said.

"Since when do I need an excuse?"

"She has a point," Max said. He navigated his way into the back of the van where surveillance equipment, including video monitors, audio recorders, and various and sundry other bits of technology took up one entire wall. "Let's see if we can figure out who else is in a rush to get here."

"Hart sure took off from his office like his pants were on fire after he got that phone call," Jay said. "So where are we?"

"I googled the address," Kate said. "Looks like it belongs to that lawyer."

"Stanley Davidson?" Max asked.

"Yeah."

"His name sure seems to come up a lot lately," Jay said. She glanced up from her takeout carton in time to see a well-dressed woman sprinting up the stairs. "Isn't that—?"

"Congresswoman Emily Kincaid of Texas, I believe," Max said. "I saw her with Hart at the Capitol the other day. I couldn't hear what they were saying. I thought maybe they were an item."

Jay set the food aside and picked up the laptop she brought with her. She opened a web browser and looked up the Congresswoman's biography. "She's the chairperson of the Senate Energy Committee."

"What would she have to do with Homeland Security?" Kate mused.

"Like I said, I thought maybe they were an item," Max said.

"I'm not buying it," Jay said.

At that moment, another man ran up the steps. "There sure are a lot of folks in a hurry today," Max said, snapping the man's picture. "I also saw him with Hart and Kincaid the other day."

"Which means that unless they're having a kinky threesome, there's something else going on here," Kate said. "Any idea who he is, Max?"

"I only caught his first name last time, but I remembered it because it was unusual. It was Astin."

"Like the car?" Jay asked.

"I think so," Max said.

"Not exactly a common name. Let's google it and see if anything pops."

Kate laughed. "I don't know how you did it all those years."

"Did what?" Jay asked.

"Managed to do investigative reporting without the aid of a search engine."

"Beats me." Jay stuck her tongue out at Kate.

"All right, Stanley, what was so urgent?"

"That would be the Astin guy," Max said. "I recognize his whiny voice."

"Astin's right, Stanley. I was in the middle of a very important meeting with the Majority Leader. What couldn't wait?" Senator Kincaid asked.

"We have big, big trouble," Hart said. His voice was trembling.

"How big?" Kincaid asked.

"Catastrophic big," Hart answered.

"You're probably just being hysterical." Astin sounded bored. "Don't be overly dramatic."

"Listen, you idiot—"

"Gentlemen, and lady, I'm afraid Daniel is correct."

"That's Davidson," Max supplied.

"We have a dire situation on our hands."

"Out with it, Stanley," Astin whined.

"It seems Sedona Ramos is not in custody in Kuwait or anywhere else."

Jay stopped eating. Kate sat up straighter. "Turn it up, Max."

Max turned up the volume.

236

"That's right," Davidson said. "I received a very disturbing call from a source a little while ago informing me that Ramos is, in fact, sitting outside the grounds of Tuwaitha even as we speak."

"That's not possible," Kincaid said. "The president went on national television to announce her capture."

"Either he was badly misinformed or he knows a lot more than we gave him credit for," Astin said.

"It's the latter," Hart said. He sounded miserable. "I knew something was funny when he kept pushing me to reveal my source for the terrorist designation. I don't know how he knows, but he does."

"You can't be sure of that. Maybe somebody in the field gave him bad information," Kincaid said.

"What does Quinn say?" Hart asked. "Did you talk to him, Stanley?"

"I tried to raise him over there, but he must be out on the production floor. Fucking cell phone reception is horrible in that place. The walls are too damn thick."

"We have to talk to Mr. Grayson," Kincaid said. "We have to put a stop to this."

"Who did she just say?" Kate asked. She stood up in the van and hit her head on the ceiling. "Ouch!"

"I could have sworn she said Grayson," Jay said.

Max, who was wearing headphones on one ear, nodded.

"There could be more than one, honey," Jay said to Kate.

"I already met with Mr. Grayson. He insists that we move forward. We are too close and there's too much at stake," Davidson said.

"What the hell does he have to lose," Hart complained, "he's already locked up for life."

Kate grabbed Jay's laptop off her lap. "Hey! What are you doing?"

"Looking for connections between all of these characters. If the Commission is still in business, you can bet somehow all of these seemingly disconnected players are tied to one man. Wayne Grayson."

"Start with Davidson, then," Jay suggested.

Kate plugged in the names Wayne Grayson and Stanley Davidson. "There's one," she said, grimly. "It seems Mr. Davidson is trying to get Grayson a pardon."

"As if," Jay said. "So Davidson can meet with Grayson in private because he has attorney-client privilege. Nice."

"I'll remind you that you owe your appointment to this office to Mr. Grayson, Daniel. Is that any way to talk about your benefactor?"

"He doesn't own me. I got held over by this administration on my own merits."

"Surely you don't honestly believe that, do you?" Davidson asked. "Check again to see where the pressure on the president came from to keep you in that post. Then check where the votes came from in the Senate to reconfirm you."

"But Daniel is right," Kincaid said. "This is insanity. We should step back while we still can."

"And how did you become chairperson of the Energy Committee, Emily?"

"Mr. Grayson," she mumbled.

"We won't even talk about all the lovely cash in your campaign war chest that allowed you to beat your opponent in the last election."

"Some things never change," Kate said. "He's got his hooks in everyone."

"What's in it for him?" Max wondered aloud.

"You mean, apart from the ego trip of thinking he runs the world?" Jay asked.

"Well, I can walk away unscathed," Astin said. "He told me, himself, he doesn't want me to have any real role in "The Four.""

"Your uncle had particularly pointed words for you, Astin," Davidson said.

"His uncle?" Jay asked.

"He said, and I quote, 'Tell that nebbish Astin that Calico Petroleum stands to take over the lion's share of the oil production in the western world if he doesn't fuck it up. Tell him I'm watching.' End quote.

"Your uncle intends for you to buy the oil rights to every new contract that comes up as a result of Senator Kincaid's fortuitously timed oil pipeline bill, which, coincidentally, just happens to be ready for a floor vote right now.

"All of the Arab Spring mayhem in the Middle East and North Africa already is threatening oil exports. If you add in the detonation of all these dirty bombs by rival oil-rich nations like Kuwait, Iran, and Iraq, it will choke off the availability of oil imports and drive the price of gas in this country to astronomical heights. Emergency passage of Senator Kincaid's bill would rush construction of the pipeline from Canada to Texas and fast-track oil drilling in the Arctic and other off-shore locations."

"And Calico Petroleum will be there to save the day," Astin gloated.

"Not to mention rake in a ransom," Kincaid said.

"Oh my God," Jay said.

"That's the endgame. We've got to get this to the president," Kate said. "Max, can you upload a file of what you've got so far and give it to me on a flash drive?"

"Sure."

"Jay and I will rush this over to the White House right now. You stay and see if anything else incriminating or illuminating comes up. We've got to stop this."

"How are you going to get to the White House?" Max asked.

"Cab," Jay said, stepping out of the van and putting her hand up to hail one.

CHAPTER TWENTY-THREE

W hat about rounding up Quinn?" Sedona asked. She didn't like the idea of his escaping underneath their noses when there was something they could do about it.

"My guess is, if his handlers have gotten hold of him by now, he'll assume we somehow set off the alarm and he'll stay put," Peter said.

"In which case, he'll be toast in a matter of minutes," Vaughn said.

"If not and he runs out like the rest," Lorraine chimed in, "chances are he won't get far. We can have every military unit still in the country looking for him in a matter of hours."

"Are we ready to go?" Vaughn asked, as the scientist dusted off his hands.

"We are."

"Wait!" Sedona said. "Don't you think we should run it past the president first?"

Peter and Vaughn both shook their heads. "If anything goes wrong, like a massive loss of life, this needs to be on us, not the president of the United States," Peter said.

"If it goes right, he can take all the credit," Vaughn said.

"Not only that, but the longer we sit here, the more likely it is we get discovered. We've already been here too long as it is," Lorraine said.

"Okay," Sedona agreed. "Let's do this."

"Sabastien," Vaughn said. "Do your thing."

With the press of his left mouse button, a cacophony of alarms sounded. "I am pausing five seconds between each different sector to help rump up the fear."

"Ramp up," Sedona corrected.

"Just so." He clicked the mouse again, and more alarms pealed.

Vaughn launched the drone and steered it well over the heads of the crowds that were now streaming out the front gate. They left on foot and by car. The members of the units that had been guarding the facility were among the first to abandon their posts.

Sedona watched Vaughn's laptop screen. These people were genuinely terrified.

"Going through the first checkpoint," Vaughn announced, as she piloted the drone via the joystick.

"I am setting off the last alarm," Sabastien announced. "It is done."

"Sabastien?" Sedona asked. "Can you pilot the other drone?"

"Yes." Sabastien picked up the second joystick and connected it to control the bee-sized drone. "Where would you like to go?"

"I want to see if we can find Randolph Quinn with it," Sedona said.

"Good thinking." Peter squeezed her hand.

"I can do better than that," Sabastien said. "Because we have captured his face with the recognition software, I can set the drone to specifically and automatically search for the match in real-time."

"In other words, it will seek only him?"

"Yes."

"That's so cool." Sedona leaned forward and kissed Sabastien on the cheek, causing him to blush bright red.

"Okay," Vaughn announced, "I'm through into the production area." She turned to the scientist. "Now what?"

The scientist scooted forward in his seat. "That's your target." He pointed at an area roughly thirty feet farther into the room and ten feet to the left of the drone's current position. "When you get there, set it down on that table and detonate it."

"How will we know if everybody's out?" Justine asked.

"We won't know for sure," Peter said. "We'll just have to do our best and give them as much time as we can."

Sedona continued to watch Sabastien's screen as the drone roamed about in a seemingly random pattern. "There!"

Peter, Lorraine, and Justine all shifted to see what she was seeing. "There he is. The son-of-a-bitch is running toward your drone, Vaughn. He must've spotted it."

Vaughn pushed the joystick all the way forward, speeding up the drone's flight.

"Put it down, now," the scientist said.

Sedona announced, "Quinn is about twenty feet away."

"If you wait another few seconds, he will be almost on top of the blast, but not quite," the scientist said.

"In other words, he won't be close enough to stop it, but he will be close enough to be killed instantly."

"Yes."

"Understood."

Sedona didn't know if she could watch. "What will happen when the bomb detonates?"

"Very little, actually. You will not see any destruction of the building. In fact, the only way you will be able to tell from here that it worked will be that the drone will go blank."

"Now, Vaughn!" Lorraine urged.

Vaughn depressed the button. The image on the laptop screen flickered then went completely blank. She sat back and closed her eyes.

Sedona closed her eyes, as well. *Archangel Michael, please escort any lost souls to the light. Please, angels, bring them peace and comfort on their journey. And so it is.*

"I want to talk to my lawyer," Wayne Grayson bellowed.

"That shouldn't be a problem," the Deputy US Marshal said. "He'll be here any minute. Of course, he'll be wearing shackles just like you. Maybe you can play chess against each other for the one hour a day each of you will be allowed out of your solitary confinement cells."

The prisoner van came to a halt and the back door swung open. The marshal hopped out first, then helped Grayson down onto the pavement for the perp walk into the federal courthouse for his arraignment.

Once inside, Grayson squinted as cameras flashed everywhere. He held up his arms as if warding off blows.

Officers of the court escorted him to a seat on a bench in the front row. He looked back as a commotion broke out when the entry doors swung open. The members of the media present along the aisles surged forward to capture the moment as federal marshals ushered in Homeland Security Secretary Daniel Hart, US Senator Emily Kincaid, NSA Deputy Director Orlando Niger, noted defense attorney Stanley Davidson, and Calico Petroleum CEO Astin Trulander. All of them were wearing identical prison jumpsuits and shackles.

Grayson sifted through a mental list of judges on the federal bench who owed him a favor.

Sedona let her gaze travel around. The party was in full swing, the ribs were on the grill, the beer and wine were flowing, and her backyard was fully alive for the first time she could remember since…well, since before Rachel died.

She watched as Peter and Lorraine tried to teach Sabastien to play bocce. He was, of course, hopeless. She could hear Kate and Vaughn trash talking with each other about their racquetball game from that morning, and Jay was entertaining Justine.

"If you plan on eating, I suggest you all come and get it," she announced.

"Mmm. These smell great," Jay said, as she heaped a half rack of ribs, cornbread, corn-on-the-cob and mashed potatoes onto her plate.

Sedona chuckled. How it was possible for one small woman to eat so much food in one sitting was beyond her. "How do you stay so slim?"

"I have no idea," Jay said.

"I keep her pretty busy," Kate said. She came up alongside and wrapped an arm around her wife's shoulder.

Sedona could feel so much love flowing through their soulmate connection. It left a poignant ache in that place in her heart that Rachel used to fill. She struggled to shrug off the melancholy.

They were halfway through eating before any of them brought up the subject that remained on all of their minds.

"I went down to the courthouse to watch them arraign Grayson," Kate said.

"The problem is, what more can they do to him that they haven't already done?" Jay asked.

"They can continue to narrow his world," Lorraine said.

"Severely restrict his access to outside," Peter added.

"You all knew this guy from before?" Sedona asked.

"Unfortunately, yes," Kate answered. "Back in the late 1980s, he ran a shadowy organization called the Commission. They had tentacles everywhere—government, business, entertainment, sports... You name it, they had a connection to it."

"We thought we'd wiped it out with the arrest and convictions of Grayson and some of his colleagues," Jay said.

"Now it seems pretty clear they're still out there finding ways to disrupt the world," Peter said.

Lorraine raised her glass. "I propose a toast. To the end of the Commission."

"Here, here," everyone agreed, as they all clinked glasses.

"I'm sorry the president couldn't make it," Sedona said. "He sent his regrets from the nuclear non-proliferation talks with Russia."

"I'm so glad he was able to publicly clear your name," Justine said.

"If he hadn't, I'm sure Sabastien would've mucked with the file and eliminated any blots on Sedona's record anyway," Lorraine said. She ruffled Sabastien's hair.

"Are you going back to the NSA?" Peter asked.

Sedona toyed with her mashed potatoes. "I don't know yet. I don't think so. I think I'm just going to take a little time and figure out what I want, you know?"

Heads nodded sympathetically around the table.

As everyone helped clear the dishes away, Sedona noted that Vaughn hadn't said two words since they'd sat down. She followed Vaughn as she was emptying the trash.

"You don't have to take out my garbage, you know."

"I know."

"Are you okay?"

"Sure. Why?"

"You're awfully quiet," Sedona said.

"This is how I usually am."

"That's because you spend too much time alone."

"About that," Vaughn said.

"Hey!" Sedona's neighbor Dex yelled from across the street. He ran to greet her with a big hug. He stepped back, still holding her in the circle of his arms. "You look fabulous. I'm so glad you're back. Life was dull without you around."

"Sure it was." Sedona smiled. "By the way, if I haven't said so already, thanks for your help."

"I'm not sure how telling you there was a bunch of really bad men in dark SUVs ransacking your home was helpful, but anytime."

"Dex, I'd like you to meet a friend of mine, Vaughn Elliott. Vaughn, this is my friend Dex." Sedona faltered at the end of the introduction. She could have sworn she saw a look of recognition pass between Vaughn and Dex.

"Nice to meet you," Dex said.

"A pleasure," Vaughn agreed, shaking his hand.

"I've gotta run, sugar," Dex said to Sedona. He kissed her on the cheek. "Ta for now." Halfway across the street he turned back. "Nice to meet you…"

"Vaughn."

"Right. Nice to meet you, Vaughn." He laughed and disappeared into his house.

"What was that about?" Sedona asked Vaughn.

"What was what about?"

"Dex's reaction to you. It was almost as if… Do you know him?"

"Our paths might have crossed somewhere along the line."

"In what capacity?"

"You'll have to ask your buddy about that. Right now, it seems to me you're entertaining guests." Vaughn pulled Sedona toward the backyard, effectively ending the interrogation.

Sedona wanted to pursue the matter. She wanted to know how Vaughn and Dex knew each other. Could Dex be CIA? Sedona thought back to something Dex said when she called him. Hadn't he said, *I can help you, but only if you level with me?* What had he meant by that?

"Just tell me—"

"Thanks for a wonderful party," Lorraine said.

"You're all leaving?" Lorraine and Peter, Kate and Jay, Justine, and Sabastien were gathering up their things.

"I don't know how you're still standing, but we're all still jetlagged."

Peter hugged Sedona close. "Keep in touch."

"I will."

"I hope next time our paths cross, it'll be for something fun," Jay said.

"I'm right there with you," Sedona agreed.

"You take care of yourself," Kate leaned over and gave her a heartfelt squeeze.

"I have enjoyed getting to know you very much," Sabastien said.

"Me too." Sedona leaned forward and gave him a soft kiss on the cheek. "Be sure to drop a line every now and again."

"Don't worry. I will be watching your bottom."

"Your back," Vaughn corrected. She cuffed him on the back of the head.

"Oh, yes. That too," Sabastien said.

Justine pulled him by the hand. "I'm his ride since, as you can see, he's had a little too much to drink."

"Yeah," Sedona agreed, "but he's a cute drunk."

"Did you hear that? She thinks I am cute."

"Come on, Sabastien." Justine waved. "I hope to see you soon."

Just like that, only Sedona and Vaughn remained. It was the first time they'd been completely alone since the car on the tarmac in Kuwait.

"Do you want another beer?" Sedona asked.

"No, I'm good."

They stood awkwardly looking at each other for a few seconds.

"Want to tell me about you and Dex now?"

Vaughn shook her head. "I don't want to spend our time on that."

"Oh?"

Vaughn reached out as if to touch Sedona, but instead let her hand drop to her side. "I wanted to... That is... Can I ask you something?"

"Sure. What is it you want to know?"

"Lots of things, as it turns out," Vaughn said. "But let's start with the psychic thing."

"Ah." Sedona frowned. She'd been wondering when Vaughn was going to bring that up.

"Why do you have that look on your face?"

"Because invariably, when people find out about my abilities, they decide I'm a freak and they get all nervous around me thinking I'm reading their minds all the time."

"Are you?"

"Of course not. My motto is always 'See, don't seek.'"

"What does that mean?"

"It means just because I can know, doesn't mean I should. I don't pay attention unless someone asks me to look into something for them. Otherwise, I know things, see things, hear things, feel things, because the angels want me to know them. If it's for my Divine best good, or someone else's, the angels might give me the piece of information."

"Like what happened in Iraq."

"Yes, like that. In those instances, the information was necessary to keep us safe or to protect the lives of others."

"Okay, I can see that. Nice work, by the way, pinpointing the location of that scientist's family. Because of you, they've got a happy future."

"My turn," Sedona said.

"Okay, that's fair."

"Why were you so willing to blow up your own house, and why is it that you seem so unaffected by it?"

"Unaffected?" Tears sprang to Vaughn's eyes and she looked away.

"I'm sorry. It's just—it didn't feel as if it touched you."

248

"Not true," Vaughn said. "All my life I've been trained to keep my feelings locked up tightly inside. I guess it's just become second nature to me."

"Your profession reinforced your own nature."

"Yes, I guess that's true."

"I can see that. But Vaughn, you're not working now."

"I know." Finally, one of the tears fell.

"Come over here and sit down." Sedona took her by the hand and led her to a patio chair. "You could have avoided it, you know."

"I remember you saying that to me at the time. You were really steamed about it."

"It just seemed to me like you wouldn't entertain any alternatives. Yet I 'knew' that blowing up the house was unnecessary to achieve the goal."

"Was that the psychic thing again?"

"Yes. But I wasn't ready to tell you about that, so I tried using logic."

"That'll teach you," Vaughn laughed.

"Why, Vaughn? Why were you really so hell-bent on destroying a home I know you loved?"

Vaughn looked down at her hands. "When you all descended on my place like locusts, I lost my privacy." She held up a hand to forestall Sedona's comment. "When the goon squad came to town, I knew my peaceful, anonymous existence had been permanently disrupted. It just felt like that time in my life, the time for isolation and ignoring the world, was over. I guess blowing up the house was a symbolic gesture."

"Well, no one can accuse you of not making grand gestures."

Vaughn leaned forward. "My turn again?"

Sedona felt Vaughn's heart rate pick up. She steeled herself. "Sure."

"How is it possible that a magical woman like you isn't married? I-I know we haven't known each other very long," Vaughn rushed ahead, "but I know what I feel for you is more real than anything I've felt in a very, very long time." She wet her lips and took Sedona's hands in hers. "I never thought I'd say this to anyone again, but I'm falling in love with you, Sedona."

"Don't." Sedona stood up, breaking the contact. "You can't, Vaughn."

Vaughn stood, also. "Why not? What are you saying?"

"You don't know anything about me except bits and pieces."

"So tell me." Vaughn's eyes showed the vulnerability in her soul, and it was almost too much for Sedona to bear.

"All right." Sedona turned away. "You asked why I'm not married. There was a woman." Sedona cleared her throat. "Her name was Rachel. She was the most beautiful woman in the world to me."

Vaughn came up behind her and hugged her, but Sedona pushed her hands away. "No. Let me get this out."

"I'm sorry."

"It's okay." Sedona turned back around and gazed at Vaughn kindly. "Rachel and I were like two halves of a whole. She was my sun and my moon and I was her stars. In her eyes, I saw the reflection of my own soul. Her breath was an extension of mine and our hearts beat in perfect synchronicity."

"What happened?" Vaughn asked quietly.

"She got cancer. The doctors thought they'd caught it early enough, but they were wrong." Sedona sobbed. "For all my work with the angels, for all my prayers to Archangel Raphael to heal her, I couldn't save the one person I really wanted to save."

"I'm so, so sorry." Vaughn wiped a tear from her own cheek.

"I know." Sedona smiled sadly. "For a long time I questioned why God and the angels gave me these abilities if I couldn't use them to save Rachel—Rachel, who was such a bright light."

"Did you get an answer?"

"Eventually, I came to understand what I knew all along—that Rachel spent as much time with me as she was meant to spend in this lifetime. I know we've been together many times before and I know we'll be together many times again. Our souls are bound together. We're all made of energy. Energy never dies, it just reconstitutes. Rachel's energy and mine will always seek each other."

"I wish I believed that."

"Your soul mate was Sara."

Vaughn's head snapped up. "How do you know about her?"

"You and the angels told me." At Vaughn's perplexed look, Sedona said, "That night in Ahmed's house when you held me. My hand touched your scar and I relived what happened to you."

Vaughn gasped.

"I couldn't have seen that unless on some level you gave me permission. Nor would the angels have shown me unless there was a reason for it. Now I know what that reason is."

"Oh?"

"The angels want me to bring you and Sara closure."

"What do you mean?"

Sedona closed her eyes and opened them. "You may not realize it, but Sara's with you all the time. I can prove it to you, if you want."

"I don't—"

"Sara is referencing a huge book she dropped on your foot. She's laughing about it. What does that mean?"

Vaughn's jaw hung open. "That's how we met. It was in Art History class. She dropped the textbook on my foot."

"You know there's no way I could know that, Vaughn, unless Sara told me."

"I've never told that story to anybody." Vaughn started to cry and Sedona took her hand.

"Sara doesn't want you to cry. She wants you to stop blaming yourself for what happened. She says she's the one who decided to go without you. She wanted to prove herself."

"She didn't need to prove herself!"

"She can see that now, Vaughn. There are many things we can see on the other side that we can't understand here. She also wants you to come back to the land of the living. She's telling you to open your heart again—really open your heart again."

"That's what I feel like I'm doing with you," Vaughn said.

"I know, and I must say you have touched my heart in ways I no longer thought possible. Maybe someday down the road, if you're still interested and I'm ready… But for right here, right now, we both have too much healing to do on our own. I can't tell you where our lives are going to take us, Vaughn."

"You can. You just choose not to."

That prompted a surprised laugh from Sedona. "Fair enough. I can tell you some things about where your life is going to take you."

"Do I want to know?"

"I don't know, do you? I can tell you this—you are who you have always been. Your life, your purpose, is to protect others. It's what you've always done. It's who you've always been. And so it will be until the end of time. You're not meant to live your days in solitude on some island, tempting as that might be."

"Humph."

"And, might I add, the world is a better place for having you in it." Sedona moved forward into Vaughn's arms and kissed her on the mouth. "Thank you for once again taking up the mantle of the warrior, Vaughn Elliott. The world needs you. Even someone without any psychic abilities can see that."

THE END

Addendum

Sedona's Method
for
Clearing, Grounding, and Protecting Herself

Take in a deep, cleansing breath, then another, and another. On each inhale, imagine yourself breathing in the essence of the Universe—Divine white light and perfect love. With each exhale, imagine yourself eliminating a gray mist that represents any negativity or fear.

Invoke Archangel Michael to cut any cords of fear.

Ask Archangel Michael, Archangel Raguel, Archangel Jophiel, Archangel Haniel, and the Ascended Masters El Morya and Lady Nada to turn on the spiritual vacuum cleaner and vacuum away any lower energies or remnants of shadows that might be in your field.

Imagine the pure waters of a beautiful waterfall washing away any lingering energies. Then call upon Archangel Metatron to use his geometric shapes to clear and open all of your chakras.

Envision a cylinder of clear quartz rising from Mother Earth to surround you and reach all the way to the Masters, sealing in healing and expanding all of your positive energy.

Then imagine a cylinder of Archangel Michael's cobalt blue and ask for the cobalt blue to allow to pass through only that which is for your Divine Highest Good, to block out all else, and to filter out any remaining energies that do not belong to you or are not for your Divine Highest Good.

Summon a cylinder of purple light to rise around the clear quartz and the cobalt blue, sealing in absolute protection and blocking out any and all negatives.

Finally, finish off with a cylinder of rose quartz, ensuring that only light and love can enter your space.

About the Author

An award-winning former broadcast journalist, former press secretary to the New York state senate minority leader, former public information officer for the nation's third largest prison system, and former editor of a national art magazine, Lynn Ames is a nationally recognized speaker and CEO of a public relations firm with a particular expertise in image, crisis communications planning, and crisis management.

Ms. Ames's other works include *The Price of Fame* (Book One in the Kate & Jay trilogy), *The Cost of Commitment* (Book Two in the Kate & Jay trilogy), *The Value of Valor* (winner of the 2007 Arizona Book Award and Book Three in the Kate & Jay trilogy), *One ~ Love* (formerly published as *The Flip Side of Desire*), *Heartsong, Eyes on the Stars* (winner of a 2011 Golden Crown Literary award), *Beyond Instinct* (Book One in the Mission: Classified series), and *Outsiders* (winner of a 2010 Golden Crown Literary award).

More about the author, including contact information, news about sequels and other original upcoming works, pictures of locations mentioned in this novel, links to resources related to issues raised in this book, author interviews, and purchasing assistance can be found at www.lynnames.com. You can also friend Lynn on Facebook and follow her on Twitter.

Other Books in Print by Lynn Ames

The Mission: Classified Series
Beyond Instinct – Book One in the Mission: Classified Series
ISBN: 978-1-936429-02-8
Vaughn Elliott is a member of the State Department's Diplomatic Security Force. Someone high up in the United States government has pulled rank, hand-selecting her to oversee security for a visit by congressional VIPs to the West African nation of Mali. The question is, who picked her for the job and why?

Sage McNally, a career diplomat, is the political officer at the US Embassy in Mali. As control officer for the congressional visit, she is tasked to brief Vaughn regarding the political climate in the region.

The two women are instantly attracted to each other and share a wild night of passion. The next morning, Sage disappears while running, leaving behind signs of a scuffle. Why was Sage taken and by whom? Where is she being held?

Vaughn's attempts to get answers are thwarted at every turn. Even Sage does not know why she's been targeted.

Independently, Sage and Vaughn struggle to make sense of the seemingly senseless. By the time each of them figures it out, it could be too late for Sage.

As the clock ticks inexorably toward the congressional visit, the stakes get even higher, and Vaughn is faced with unspeakable choices. Her decisions will make the difference between life and death. Will she choose duty or her own code of honor?

Stand-Alone Romances

Eyes on the Stars

ISBN: 978-1-936429-00-4

Jessie Keaton and Claudia Sherwood were as different as night and day. But when their nation needed experienced female pilots, their reactions were identical: heed the call. In early 1943, the two women joined the Women Airforce Service Pilots—WASP—and reported to Avenger Field in Sweetwater, Texas, where they promptly fell head-over-heels in love.

The life of a WASP was often perilous by definition. Being two women in love added another layer of complication entirely, leading to ostracism and worse. Like many others, Jessie and Claudia hid their relationship, going on dates with men to avert suspicion. The ruse worked well until one seemingly innocent afternoon ruined everything.

Two lives tragically altered. Two hearts ripped apart. And a second chance more than fifty years in the making.

From the airfields of World War II, to the East Room of the Obama White House, follow the lives of two extraordinary women whose love transcends time and place.

Heartsong

ISBN: 978-0-9840521-3-4

After three years spent mourning the death of her partner in a tragic climbing accident, Danica Warren has re-emerged in the public eye. With a best-selling memoir, a blockbuster movie about her heroic efforts to save three other climbers, and a successful career on the motivational speaking circuit, Danica has convinced herself that her life can be full without love.

When Chase Crosley walks into Danica's field of vision everything changes. Danica is suddenly faced with questions she's never pondered.

Is there really one love that transcends all concepts of space and time? One great love that joins two hearts so that they beat as one? One moment of recognition when twin flames join and burn together?

Will Danica and Chase be able to overcome the barriers standing between them and find forever? And can that love be sustained, even in the face of cruel circumstances and fate?

One ~ Love, (formerly *The Flip Side of Desire*)
ISBN: 978-0-9840521-2-7
Trystan Lightfoot allowed herself to love once in her life; the experience broke her heart and strengthened her resolve never to fall in love again. At forty, however, she still longs for the comfort of a woman's arms. She finds temporary solace in meaningless, albeit adventuresome encounters, burying her pain and her emotions deep inside where no one can reach. No one, that is, until she meets C.J. Winslow.

C.J. Winslow is the model-pretty-but-aging professional tennis star the Women's Tennis Federation is counting on to dispel the image that all great female tennis players are lesbians. And her lesbianism isn't the only secret she's hiding. A traumatic event from her childhood is taking its toll both on and off the court.

Together Trystan and C.J. must find a way beyond their pasts to discover lasting love.

The Kate and Jay Series
The Price of Fame
ISBN: 978-0-9840521-4-1
When local television news anchor Katherine Kyle is thrust into the national spotlight, it sets in motion a chain of events that will change her life forever. Jamison "Jay" Parker is an intensely career-driven Time magazine reporter. The first time she saw Kate, she fell in love. The last time she saw her, Kate was rescuing her. That was five years ago , and she never expected to see her again. Then circumstances and an assignment bring them back together.

Kate and Jay's lives intertwine, leading them on a journey to love and happiness, until fate and fame threaten to tear them apart. What is the price of fame? For Kate, the cost just might be everything. For Jay, it could be the other half of her soul.

The Cost of Commitment
ISBN: 978-0-9840521-5-8
Kate and Jay want nothing more than to focus on their love. But as Kate settles into a new profession, she and Jay are caught in the middle of a deadly scheme and find themselves pawns in a larger game in which the stakes are nothing less than control of the country.

In her novel of corruption, greed, romance, and danger, Lynn Ames takes us on an unforgettable journey of harrowing conspiracy—and establishes herself as a mistress of suspense.

The Cost of Commitment—it could be everything...

The Value of Valor
ISBN: 978-0-9840521-6-5
Katherine Kyle is the press secretary to the president of the United States. Her lover, Jamison Parker, is a respected writer for Time magazine. Separated by unthinkable tragedy, the two must struggle to survive against impossible odds...

A powerful, shadowy organization wants to advance its own global agenda. To succeed, the president must be eliminated. Only one person knows the truth and can put a stop to the scheme.

It will take every ounce of courage and strength Kate possesses to stay alive long enough to expose the plot. Meanwhile, Jay must cheat death and race across continents to be by her lover's side...

This hair-raising thriller will grip you from the start and won't let you go until the ride is over.

The Value of Valor—it's priceless.

Anthology Collections
Outsiders
ISBN: 978-0-979-92545-0
What happens when you take five beloved, powerhouse authors, each with a unique voice and style, give them one word to work with, and put them between the sheets together, no holds barred?

Magic!!

Brisk Press presents Lynn Ames, Georgia Beers, JD Glass, Susan X. Meagher and Susan Smith, all together under the same cover with the aim to satisfy your every literary taste. This incredible combination offers something for everyone—a smorgasbord of fiction unlike anything you'll find anywhere else.

A Native American raised on the Reservation ventures outside the comfort and familiarity of her own world to help a lost soul embrace the gifts that set her apart. * A reluctantly wealthy woman uses all of her resources anonymously to help those who cannot help themselves. * Three individuals, three aspects of the self, combine to create balance and harmony at last for a popular trio of characters. * Two nomadic women from very different walks of life discover common ground—and a lot more—during a blackout in New York City. * A traditional, old school butch must confront her community and her own belief system when she falls for a much younger transman.

Five authors—five novellas. Outsiders—one remarkable book.

All Lynn Ames books are available through www.lynnames.com, from your favorite local bookstore, or through other online venues.

You can purchase other Phoenix Rising Press books online at www.phoenixrisingpress.com or at your local bookstore.

Published by
Phoenix Rising Press
Phoenix, AZ

Visit us on the Web: Phoenix Rising Press

Here at Phoenix Rising Press, our goal is to provide you, the reader, with top quality, entertaining, well-written, well-edited works that leave you wanting more. We give our authors free rein to let their imaginations soar. We believe that nurturing that kind of unbridled creativity and encouraging our authors to write what's in their hearts results in the kinds of books you can't put down.

Whether you crave romances, mysteries, fantasy/science fiction, short stories, thrillers, or something else, when you pick up a Phoenix Rising Press book, you know you've found a good read. So sit back, relax, get comfortable, and enjoy!

Phoenix Rising Press
Phoenix, AZ

Lightning Source UK Ltd.
Milton Keynes UK
UKOW05f1040230913

217738UK00002B/224/P